'A luminous ~~novel~~ ... ~~of~~ ... love . . . Hear~~tbreaking~~, full o~~f~~ ... always been there, not even f~~or~~ ... ~~tr~~ue. I haven't read anything this good in a ~~long time~~ ...'
Rachel Joyce, author of *The Unlikely Pilgrimage of Harold Fry*

'A heartfelt tale of brutal parental love . . . one of the most convincing portraits of a mother–daughter bond that I have read.' *The Times*

'*The Distance Home* is a deeply involving portrait of the American postwar family: its promises and disruptions . . . surrounded by a rich, shimmering, sensuous landscape.'
Jennifer Egan, author of *A Visit from the Goon Squad*

'Evocative, moving and deeply immersive . . . There is an undeniable beauty to this epic portrayal of the complex and intimate nature of human relationships – well worth a read.' *Woman & Home*

'In Paula Saunders' *The Distance Home*, a family's story traces the intricate, often subterranean lines that connect damage to redemption, creation to dissolution, and the everyday to the eternal, just to name several of its moving and startling aspects. It's a true, and rare, accomplishment.' Michael Cunningham, author of *The Hours*

'Paula Saunders has given us a riveting family saga for the ages . . . it kept me turning pages in the wee hours. One of the best books I've read in years – destined to become a classic.'
Mary Karr, author of *The Liars' Club*

'Honest, and true, and more – this soul-searching first novel offers everywhere that most mysterious and essential of artistic achievements: heart.'
Douglas Unger, author of *Leaving the Land* and *Voices from Silence*

'Extraordinary . . . Paula Saunders writes beautiful, evocative prose that engages you in every aspect of this world. *The Distance Home* is heartbreaking and full of compassion while also managing to be exacting, precise and truthful. It accomplishes ~~what great~~ fiction should: we ~~...~~ *Others*

THE
Distance Home

Paula Saunders grew up in South Dakota. She is a graduate of the Syracuse University creative writing program, and was awarded a postgraduate Albert Schweitzer Fellowship in the Humanities at the State University of New York at Albany, under then-Schweitzer Chair, Toni Morrison. She lives in California with her husband. They have two grown daughters.

THE
Distance Home

Paula Saunders

PICADOR

First published 2018 by Random House, an imprint and division of
Penguin Random House LLC, New York

First published in the UK in paperback 2018 by Picador
First published in hardback 2019 by Picador

This paperback edition first published 2020 by Picador
an imprint of Pan Macmillan
The Smithson, 6 Briset Street, London EC1M 5NR
Associated companies throughout the world
www.panmacmillan.com

ISBN 978-1-5098-9534-2

For Elwood, Rosemary, and Mark, in memory;
and for Sara—dear sister, dear friend.

For George, Caitlin, and Alena,
who make this place my home.

It is hard to follow one great vision in this world of darkness and of many changing shadows. Among those shadows, men get lost.

———

But anywhere is the center of the world.

Black Elk, as quoted by
John G. Neihardt in
Black Elk Speaks

Part One

1

The End: A Refrain

"It's you or me next," René said to get a laugh.

Her brother had already passed away, as had her father. Now René and her sister were once again driving the length of the state. Black cattle dotted the yellow hillsides. Out their open windows, long-abandoned homesteads flew by—roofs pitched eerily to one side, windmills cracked in half, groaning. With this one more passing, it was down to just the two of them.

Mostly René had been steely, while Jayne had been unable to stop crying. René was older, but it didn't matter how old they were. Their mother had finally stopped messing the bed and tearing her clothes off in the middle of the night, ending up naked and haywire on the mattress or sprawled, drooling, on the carpet next to it, her translucent body shimmering with sweat. She'd lain unconscious for the final week, cold and luminous as porcelain, as the girls came in to handle her by hip bones and shoulder blades, to turn her this way and that.

They would bury her ashes next to their father's and brother's.

They'd been busy—cleaned and sold her house, divided everything without jealousy or rancor. In so many ways it was all done, and in so many ways it was just beginning.

"You girls will miss her," someone had said at the service. "No one in the world can love you like your mother does."

René had nodded and smiled coolly, dismissing the sentiment as tired and trite, while Jayne reached for a tissue.

"Thank you for coming," René had said. She'd found herself repeating the same line all morning, as if by rote, wondering if it was the right thing to say or if perhaps there was something fundamentally cold and incorrect about her that was causing her to sound standoffish and transparently unfeeling.

2

Eve

Yvonne, called Eve, grew up around the corner and down the long dirt road from Al, two houses from the muddy banks of the Bad River, just where it joined with the Missouri, so there was always the problem of flood and river smell. On wash day she and her mother would change the sheets, moving top sheet to bottom, because it hadn't been too badly used, then bottom sheet to the washtub, through the wringer, and out onto the line, where the wind was kicking up dirt and chicken scat. Despite the sun-burnt yard, the pile of old tractor tires, the chickens underfoot, and the yellow haze that rose around the confluence of the two rivers, Eve never considered herself a country girl. She was just on the wrong side of the Missouri. Across the water, in Pierre, the state capital, were the politicians and doctors, the green lawns with walkways and trimmed hedges. On her side, in old Fort Pierre, were the bars, the yards full of chickens and stray cats, the overgrown lots thick with snakes and broken-down cars, and on the hill as you were coming down into town, a plaque indicating a stop on the Lewis and Clark Expedition.

She knew from the beginning she'd have to have grit, have to make her own way, so she'd come up with a plan to apply to the South Dakota College of Business, to be an executive secretary, a professional girl. Then the uniformed men had arrived at her door, holding their hats like dinner plates, to say that her eldest brother, Buddy, had been killed by a land mine in Germany, on his way home, the war already won. And not two weeks later—as the house was still reeling in grief, her mother still laid up in bed—her baby brother, Tom, the skinny little six-year-old Eve was mostly raising herself, combing his hair for school and yelling for him to get in out of the rain, drowned in the dried-up Bad River, disappearing into a sinkhole so deep that no one was ever able to recover his remains.

And suddenly, at seventeen, Eve was weary. She was tired of watching her little sister, Fanny, flirt with the priests, lifting her skirt at every town dance to show off her raggedy underthings, making an ass of herself, and tired of seeing her mother—a woman who'd never sat down in all her life—stunned and speechless with grief, first unable to rise from her bed, then unwilling to get up from her chair, her once-auburn hair a shock of white, her strong, steady hands taken with uncontrollable tremors, and her father, who after a day or two of stumbling through the house as if blind, simply went back to work, an invisible weight pressing him forward, bending his spine, so that each day seemed to set him a little closer to the earth.

So Eve finalized the year's last edition of the school newspaper, wrote the class remembrances for the yearbook, finished her run as lead in the senior play, graduated valedictorian from Fort Pierre High School, and made up her mind to marry Al from up the street, as he'd been asking her to do. When her folks refused to grant permission for her to marry him ahead of legal age, she bit her tongue and set her wedding for the day of her eighteenth birthday.

Al was tall with glossy black curls, fine cowboy boots, and a smile big enough to make the town girls blush and call him "Pretty Boy." But it wasn't just his looks that spoke to Eve. Al had a dignity, an elegance, a quality of *floating above* that captured her attention and seemed to match her idea of what was right. Plus, he had a red-and-white convertible, a sweet green motorboat on a tow in the driveway, and his folks had the nicest house this side of the Missouri—stately, with fieldstone pillars, fresh white paint, and a wrap-around porch overlooking Deadwood Street, the only paved, tree-lined thoroughfare in town.

He'd been in the service, training as a bombardier in North Carolina, when Germany surrendered and the boys started coming home. And during all his time away, he told Eve, he'd been thinking about her—about how she had the greatest legs in town. So when he got back to Fort Pierre, he came straight to the café where she was working after school. He'd come in during her breaks just to sit with her in a booth and help her refill ketchup bottles and salt shakers, occasionally wrapping his feet around her slim ankles or letting a hand fall under the table to graze her firm, bare calves. He'd even loiter all through the dinner service just to walk her home. They went on picnics, they went on boat rides, they dressed up in their best clothes and went out to the movies, and in no time, they fell in love.

So Eve and Al were married with both a wedding cake and a birthday cake, her old dad walking her down the aisle with his mouth pulled into a crescent-moon frown. Then Eve leaned out the window of Al's new pickup for a photo, tossed her bouquet, and they took off for Chicago. And just a week later, they came back and moved in with Al's parents, occupying the little basement apartment, not taking the least notice of his mother's heavy tread above them.

Still, it wasn't lost on Eve that, whenever they happened to speak, her new mother-in-law, Emma—who'd known her since Eve was a tow-headed tomboy running the streets in her brothers' hand-me-down overalls, climbing trees and throwing stones down by the Bad River—would now feign visible shock at her presence, unfailingly turning her head away and sniffing as though she'd just smelled something vinegary. Most likely Emma was busy wondering how her fine boy could have ended up married to that little street urchin whose father plowed the county roads and filled in pot holes, sweating in the sun all day, whose pack of older brothers were known all over town for their fall-down-drunk escapades, whose rat-haired little sister was out and about at all hours of day and night. It was some innate prescience of this very thing, Eve figured, that had made her sweet old dad, who loved her like the first light of morning, initially say, "No, that ain't gon' be," when she'd asked his permission, then, on her wedding day, turn his mouth down into a semicircle of gloom.

So Eve was eighteen, newly married, and suddenly a "grass widow," alone in her new in-laws' basement apartment as Al struck out to make the only living he knew how, following his father onto the road, into the business of trading cattle.

And while Al was busy learning an occupation he had no interest in and had been hoping all his life to avoid, Eve kept her position at the town café and took a job at the telephone company. She listened in on calls between men and women, married, but not to each other. Holding her cigarette between her lips as she plugged them in, she quickly got to know who was with whom and when and where. At night she served burgers to the same guys who'd met their illicit lovers just hours before and were now treating their families to dinner. Then she served steaks to the after-hours crowd, which most often included her new father-in-law, who, no matter how finely he dressed, clearly headed the list of town drunks.

The night he passed out face-first into the sizzling hunk of beef she'd just set in front of him, she figured he was such an ass for running around with that high school cheerleader from Pierre, courting the girl on her parents' front steps for all the world to see, that she just left him there. Facedown. Served him right.

"What's the difference between a gentleman and a dirty old man?" she started saying to anybody who'd listen. "Money," she'd answer, not laughing.

And all the while Al was on the road.

He finally got his first deal—an order from a buyer over east, an acquaintance of his dad's, for two hundred head of Hereford cattle—and he sought out every cattleman across three states, stopped at every sale barn, found twenty head here, thirty there, selecting what he felt was the best bunch of Herefords in the Midwest. Then he and his dad met the buyer at the feedlot for delivery, and as the two of them held the gate and *hee-ya*ed the livestock into the corral, there passed, mixed in with all the rest, a few cows—"maybe two, maybe three"—with half brown-colored faces. Al beamed at the great-looking cattle now shuffling and running and kicking up dirt, but as they lifted the gate behind the last cow, swinging it across and latching the wood with the wire, his dad gave him a sharp kick to the heel. Standing close, eyes blazing from under the rim of his cattleman's hat, he had just one thing to say: "Don't you *ever* do that to me again."

"Now, you know Herefords, traditionally, have the all-white face," Al explained to Eve that night when he got back home. "But there isn't one iota of difference between a Hereford with an all-white face and a Hereford with a half-brown or even a full-brown face. Not one. And those were some great cattle, Eve. Why, a guy couldn't find any better than those cattle anywhere." Then he quieted and hung his head.

"Seems pretty unfair" was all Eve said, though she had a mind to say more, given that she happened to know for a fact that Al's dad had recently been escorting that little cheerleader to the Pierre Hotel, giving her silk stockings and ungodly, strappy high heels, along with any number of decanters of brandy.

Al nodded.

The sale had gone off all right and the buyer was happy, he told her, but the drive home had been long. Al had set his eyes to the rolling plains and dreamed of running down the steps to Eve, unfolding the check, letting her get a good look at it. In the morning, he said, they could head straight to the bank and open their first account.

In that little basement apartment, Eve and Al got along. They'd go fishing in the Missouri in his little outboard motorboat, or they'd get dressed up—Al in a pressed white nubby short-sleeved shirt and cuffed zoot-cut pants with a thin belt, Eve in the new pedal pushers and sleeveless zipper-back jumper top she'd made for herself from the latest Butterick pattern—and they'd drive to the pasture outside of town and play golf. They'd make a day of it like they were movie stars—put the top down on Al's Rambler, bring a picnic of fried chicken and potato salad.

And after some years had passed, as Eve and Al were in no hurry to give up their license to do as they pleased, finally Leon was born—ten pounds, eleven ounces, and twenty-one inches long—with olive skin and, from somewhere buried deep in the silence of the genetic line, the beautiful high cheekbones and broad nose of the Sioux. And three years later, there was a girl, whom Al had wanted to call Susan until Eve finally put her foot down, insisting on René, with one *e* and the French diacritical *accent aigu* right out of nowhere, as if it had fallen through the starry expanse of the night sky on the vast western prairie and landed on her name. And it was her arrival, complete with her own abrupt and fiery nature, along with Al's full head of thick, black hair—which the nuns in the hospital were so tickled by that they'd combed it into the latest Mamie Eisenhower hairdo, bangs and all, before handing her to Eve—that seemed to fix the trajectories in place and set the course for what was to come.

3

Fault Lines Set in the
Swirling Cosmos

What comes together falls apart. Parties are planned, celebrated, then disperse and dissolve as though they were no more than dreams; seasons come and go like magic tricks, flowers blooming then fading, snowbanks swelling then melting away. How could it be different for families? There's coming together and moving apart, being young and growing old, being here and being gone.

Still, to two young people just starting out, joined by two more just opening their eyes, this truth is hidden by the hopes and dreams that the filling of their hearts tells them are now certainly within their grasp—primarily, that they will be happy. After all, affection, love, is everything. If only things are handled correctly, if only care is taken and attention paid, there will be no falling away. They'll nurture and care for one another, love and protect and abide with each other. What need could there be for a harsh word, a raised voice? Who could be so careless? Who'd make such a mistake? No. They're young and strong and determined. There will be only the glory and joy of coming together and staying, coming together and building, building, building.

They were suddenly a family of four in the little apartment below Al's mother, and with the dirty diapers that now reliably occupied the toilet, needing either rinsing out or soaking, life began to center on the plumbing. Al would come in from the road and, too tired half the time to see what was in front of him, urinate on the diapers, then flush. So the pipes would clog and Emma would be furious and cross with Eve, claiming that Eve was blindly flushing them down, likely along with her sanitary pads. It didn't matter that it only happened when Al was home, or that the plumber only ever pulled diapers from the sewer line; Emma insisted it was Eve— who'd grown up with nothing but an outhouse, "for Lord's sake!"— who was now wreaking havoc on her house.

"Just as I might have predicted!" Emma would stress to Al in a whisper just loud enough for Eve to overhear.

Though Al liked the idea of dodging the blame, he hated to side with his mother, because as far as he could remember, she'd never sided with him. Hadn't it been his mother who'd stood beside his older sister at the front door each morning, the two of them doubled over with laughter as he'd headed out to first grade, their pet goat butting and biting him as he ran as fast as he could through the front yard? By the time he'd got to the other side of the gate, he'd have dropped all his books and pencils and broken down in tears, late for school and too afraid to go back and gather up his things. Wasn't that a hoot! That goat was as tall as he was, and Al was so panicked about having to go out through that yard he could hardly eat breakfast. And hadn't it been his own mother who'd beaten him nearly to death—a beating he remembered well enough to cite decades later, when they all came together to put her ashes in the ground?

"Of course, I did set the neighbor's barn on fire," he'd admitted, and all the elderly aunts and grown cousins gathered at the burial plot had laughed. "Still," he'd said. "I was just a kid." And with that, he'd wandered away from the family circle, to have a cigarette and to stand alone, gazing across the open prairie as if measuring the curve of the far horizon.

So when it came to the plumbing, like with other things behind and ahead of him, Al simply wanted out of it. And not intending to take his mother's side, yet certain he couldn't have possibly done everything Eve was accusing him of, he excused himself, leaving it for the women to figure out on their own.

"Mother, it's your own son who's done it," Eve said the day the pipes finally gave way, leaving muddy puddles in the far corners of the unfinished utility area.

As Al took up his suitcase and started for the door, Emma gasped and stamped her foot at Eve. "He wouldn't!"

"Well, he did," Eve said with all the simplicity and directness of her youth. "This time and last time and the time before that. I'm sorry to say so, but it's just a fact, which you can clearly see, since it doesn't ever happen when he's not here. Not once."

"Well, I never!" Emma hissed. "Never in my life—!"

And as Al's car pulled onto Deadwood Street, headed out of town, aiming for the open highway, Emma turned her back on Eve and stomped up the inside stairs so forcefully that her heels made the wooden stairwell ring out like a church bell.

Their boy, Leon, was so good. He was content and happy to do anything. He'd work in the kitchen with Eve, rolling dough for sugar cookies, cutting out shapes, using his step-up to reach the counter, then dragging it across the floor to get into the sudsy water and help with the dishes. He'd push René back and forth in her stroller to stop her from fussing, and run to give her whatever she needed—a bottle, a toy, a bite of his cracker. He'd let her pinch his ears and pull his hair as he put his smiling face next to hers for a photo.

But from the beginning René was different. She was difficult. She was always wanting something, and she seemed to know just what she wanted, and when, and how, and how much, and what for. Whenever anyone tried to put her down, she'd scream so hard that, in order to get through the day, Eve would have to call in all the relatives to rock her. Aunts rocked her, grandmas rocked her, older cousins rocked her, neighbors rocked her, even her brother rocked her before they all gave up, exhausted, and handed her back to Eve, the only one left, the only one still willing.

"Someone had better hand her a scepter," Eve would say wearily, rocking and rocking, as the range and volume of René's demands annihilated the will of anyone who dared come near.

"That little darling is intelligent, curious, single-minded," Emma would counter whenever she happened to be nearby, favoring René in spite of everything, seeming to purposely set her above the rest of them, above Leon. "I say. Just a shining light."

"Well," Eve would venture, wanting to recalibrate, to set things straight, "she's certainly figured out how to scream bloody murder. I'll grant you that."

Then one day, when all the rocking and patting and cooing in creation was obviously not going to be enough, Eve finally decided that, all evidence to the contrary, René didn't run the world. She was just going to put her in her crib, close the door, and go back to the storybook she'd been trying to read with Leon—the one about the big truck making the new road. So, while Leon waited patiently, Eve jiggled René off to the bedroom.

Even with the door closed, they had to cover their ears. Leon shut his eyes and snuggled into Eve's lap because he was really very sweet-hearted and couldn't stand to hear the wailing.

"M-maybe we should g-g-g-go g-get her," he said, looking up at Eve.

"No. She's okay."

"She's c-c-crying so much."

"Yes. That's all right."

Though Leon was good and patient, though you could take him anywhere and he was never any trouble—he'd sit looking at a book or rolling a toy truck across the floor, turning from time to time to check on his mother—he had a stammer, and Emma was happy to make it clear that she didn't like that. Whenever Al was in earshot, she'd seize the opportunity and say something about it directly, something like "He's a strange one" or "Too bad. Such a shame the boy can't seem to manage."

"Just slow down for him," Eve would plead with Al when they were alone. "Let him take his time. He can do it if you just listen to him."

Sometimes Al would remember to try, but mostly he'd just put on a worried grimace or, worse, look to Eve with pleading eyes, as if *he* were the helpless child. "Why can't he spit out the simplest things? *C-c-c-car*. What's wrong with him?" he'd say, turning his back on the boy, which was plenty enough to make Eve burn.

And whenever Leon stuttered in front of Emma, she'd stop him sharply and bend to throw a pointed finger in his face, saying, "Now, stop that, Leon! Think! Think before you say something!"

And Leon would be quiet and not say a word.

All the while René continued on, getting into every drawer, never listening, always whining and complaining and screaming if she didn't get her way, as Emma smiled and cooed and bent to touch her cheek or give her a bite of something sweet.

So Eve's heart was breaking for her boy, who was so good and so gentle, now wholly abandoned by the grandmother he used to make puzzles and bake cakes with. But she knew better than to start something with her mother-in-law. There was already enough poisoned water in the house to fill up a dry well, and there was no way to explain something like simple kindness, anyway—not to someone who didn't already understand it. She knew that much.

"She's a teacher, for crying out loud," Al would say whenever Eve brought it up to him. "I'm sure she knows the right way to fix it."

"And I'm telling you, she's making it worse!" Eve would fire back.

And suddenly Eve and Al were going at it every time he came home, with things like "Your mother—!" and "Why can't you just—!" and "Are you really such an ignoramus—!" and "How can you possibly think—!" They were born fighters—descendants of people who'd held on for their lives against drought, infestation, disease, and freezing weather—and anyone who heard them agreed that they were likely just getting warmed up.

And like that, the fault lines were established: Emma preferred René; Al preferred René because Emma preferred her and he knew better than to go looking for trouble; and Eve preferred Leon and Jayne, who was born just after Eve and Al finally found a way to move out on their own, and who was also to be numbered among the tender-hearted.

4

Mousetrap

Due to the risky nature of the cattle business, Al wouldn't even consider signing up with some banker for a mortgage, so Eve and Al lived in Emma's basement until they'd saved enough for a little place Al found in Philip, ninety miles west of Fort Pierre. It was a Rainbow Division home, part of a postwar prairie housing project, a dumpy little cracker box with a lopsided, dilapidated school bus stuck in the barren, red muck of the front yard. Inside, all the drains were backed up and the hoarded, moldy accumulations of the previous owner were piled to the tops of the windows, but they could pay cash for it and have enough left to do the work that needed doing.

First, they'd have to tow the bus to the crusher. Then they could haul the stacks of old newspapers across the road and make a bonfire. Once the house was cleared out, they'd dig a trench around the foundation to get into the crawl space and fix the plumbing. Then Al would reshingle the roof. Eve could level out the yard, and Al could truck in rock. They'd lay the front with white granite gravel Al could get cheap from the quarry; then Eve could start her rose garden up along the front of the house while Al dug holes around the back perimeter to set six-foot fence posts in cement, to improve the view across the alley and offer some privacy from the neighbors. When they were done, they'd paint that house a cheery, open yellow, the color of the sun, and Eve would plant bright red geraniums in the window boxes, keeping them watered and clipped back, blooming against the odds.

So Eve and Al moved in and got to work. It was backbreaking, pleasant work. There wasn't anything that didn't need doing, and they worked night and day. Al was home for whole long weeks at a time, out in the blistering sun, happy to be building something he'd be able to call his own. He'd poke his head in the back door, covered in dirt and crud, and ask for a glass of water.

"Sure, honey." Eve would hand it out to him, filled to the brim. "I'll be right out, soon as I get things squared away in here."

And she was good to her word. She'd finish inside, get the new baby, Jayne, down for a nap, then put on her gloves and be out hauling or clearing. They worked side by side, talking, laughing, reviewing the plans.

Though Philip, South Dakota, was home to the golden, arid flatness of the plains—to fields, buttes, ravines all coming to form a single line in the distance; to cold winters, hot summers, and just enough rain for the overdue sun shower to etch out gullies before leaving a rainbow arching overhead; to hard red clay and brown grass, yucca and cactus, rattlers, blue racers, and bull snakes; to thigh-high tumbleweeds blowing across the open fields, even blowing around downtown—little by little they built what could only be called an oasis. It was a lush, blooming slice of paradise, likely easily seen on a photograph from space, if such a thing had existed: a little dot of green.

Eve had always wanted a view from up high, and this little fairy-tale house on the corner, from which she could see to the ends of the earth in nearly three directions, finally seemed like a good beginning. Though she wasn't actually on top of anyone, at least her mother-in-law wasn't stomping over her head. At least here, there would be no one rising above her. It was just what she needed, like a brand-new start.

And after Al was back on the road, having kissed her farewell in their new living room with the picture window, taking off his cowboy hat and bending her backward like something out of the movies, she made friends with the neighbor ladies from down the street, whose husbands were also missing, driving truck or farming some distance away. They'd strike up a game of Wahoo and let the kids run wild for whole long afternoons while they smoked cigarettes and drank tea, holding the babies in their laps, throwing dice and moving marbles, their cries of victory and defeat echoing out the open windows and across the fields, making prairie dogs run for their holes.

On his first day of school at Scotty Philip Elementary, Leon stood by the front door fidgeting and fretting in the scratchy plaid pants and matching wool vest Eve had gone to the trouble of sewing for him.

He had his dad's dark, wavy hair, and Eve had given him a permanent the night before to set off the curl.

"Look at you." She brushed a random lock from his forehead.

"Too hot." Leon pulled at his pants and tilted his head with a crestfallen look, like a puppy. He exhaled a river of discouragement. "I d-don't want to g-g-go."

And René, observing all the pomp at close range, without a stitch of clothing on herself, piped up about taking his place.

"You be quiet," Eve told her. Then she buttoned Leon's vest and adjusted his collar. "Don't worry, Leon. You know where your class is. And I'll be right here."

Leon nodded uncertainly.

"Come on," she said, nudging him out the door.

He ran down the steps, then turned with a mournful look, as if he might just run right back inside, but Eve waved him on.

"There's Jimmy! Go on. See you at lunchtime!"

So Leon disappeared down into the gulch after Jimmy, while Eve and René, naked as the day she was born, waited on the front steps until they saw him waving from the far side of the deep ravine. He'd shed his vest and was dragging it in the dirt behind him, happier now, free.

"Why do I bother?" Eve asked.

But René was busy watching the line of neighbor kids trooping by in their new skirts, patterned knee-highs, polished patent-leather shoes, until a group of older boys with neatly tucked-in shirts and belted pants, laughing and kicking stones, stopped to point and whoop at her.

"Those kids are idiots and ignoramuses," Eve said, turning René so that all the boys had to gawk at was her bare backside. "You have nothing to be ashamed of." But when René turned back around, the boys were still bent together, snickering and cutting their eyes at her. "Run inside," Eve said firmly, stepping between her and the boys, giving her a push. "Don't pay any attention."

Most days after lunch, with Leon at school and Jayne asleep in her bassinet, Eve would find time to give René reading lessons in the old rocker. But not long after Leon had got three stitches above his right eye from running through one of the girls' jump-rope games—getting his feet tangled in the rope and landing on the playground blacktop on his forehead—there was another afternoon call from the nurse. Leon was in the hospital. He'd barreled, one arm extended, straight through the glass door that led from the playground to the gym. The glass had shattered. By the time Eve got to him, he had nearly twenty stitches, up and down his arm, from his wrist to his elbow.

"Seems like your son needs to watch where he's going," the principal said the next day, when Eve called for an explanation.

"How could a door possibly break on a kid's arm?" Eve was trying not to raise her voice. "I mean, what kind of a place is that?"

"We've had that same door for twenty years," the principal replied coolly. "Until now."

When Al got home a few days later, Eve reported what had happened, and Al called Leon into the front room.

"Why don't you watch where you're going?" he scolded. "What's the matter with you? You could hurt someone."

"That's not the point," Eve said, turning sharply on Al. "Nothing's the matter with him. What's the matter with *you*? That's not the point at all!"

Leon held his bandaged arm, swiveling his head back and forth between them.

"*He* got hurt. Twice now on the playground. For crying out loud, Al."

"Seems like you can't hold the whole school responsible for some kid not paying attention to where he's going."

"Just go back to bed, Leon."

"No. You can stay here and learn something."

"Go on," Eve said.

Leon turned and shuffled away.

"If you didn't want my opinion, you shouldn't have asked," Al started.

"I wasn't asking your opinion, for God sakes. I just thought you should know."

"So I don't have one thing to say about it. Is this my house or not? Do I have a say about what goes on around here or not? I'm telling you, he needs to pay attention to where he's going and not go running into glass doors, then crying it's someone else's fault for putting up a door in the first place. That's just asinine."

"You know what's asinine? *You!* That's what's asinine."

"You said it right there, Eve," Al said. "Good point. You win."

Al turned around and left town again, but the phone calls with the school, filled with cross-talk about who was at fault and discussions of conditions for Leon's return to Scotty Philip Elementary, continued. Leon was taller than the other first graders, so that was a problem, and he seemed nervous and distracted, he didn't pay attention.

"We have the other children to consider," the principal warned.

"Meaning *what*?" Eve asked herself again and again as she sorted laundry, cut up potatoes, swept the kitchen, pulled weeds.

So when Leon finally went back to school, Eve signed him up for tap-dancing lessons in the gym with Miss Foley, an older town lady who'd spent a year in Denver in her youth, where she'd acquired, as Al put it, "all manners of airs." But since there was no choice— since no one was going to take her side; since, whatever happened next, Leon was going to end up shouldering the blame; and since there'd be no possible harm in it—Eve figured dancing lessons might be just the thing, might help Leon learn to control his long limbs, help him understand where his physical body ended and other objects, sometimes objects to be avoided, began.

And, it turned out, Leon loved dancing. He loved the music, the patterns of the exercises, the challenge of matching his body to the bright, changing rhythms. Plus, since he was the only boy, the girls were nice to him.

But when Al was home, he wouldn't even pretend to look up from behind his newspaper as Leon showed off a new flap-turn or a tricky jump; nor would he offer the slightest comment when Leon silently moved away to practice his double buffalo out of sight, by himself in the kitchen. He wasn't interested in what he insisted to Eve was "nonsense, pure and simple," and he certainly wasn't going to encourage it.

"That's just a big excuse for you not paying one bit of attention to him. Same as usual," Eve said. Because Al also wasn't interested in helping Leon prepare for the town parade, when all the boys rode their bikes behind the VFW float. Nor did he make a single effort to come to any of Leon's Little League games, even though Leon had won the coveted position of pitcher, which should have been enough to make Al proud. On game days Eve could count on being all by herself, up on the bleachers alongside the fathers of the other boys, and when Leon needed batting practice, it would be her standing in the open field across the road, tossing the ball.

So, on the day of Leon's first dance recital, it wasn't really a surprise that Al got up early and left town, but neither did it go unnoted. Not by Eve.

"You'd think your own father could be here for your special day," she fumed as Leon gathered his tap shoes and silver-sequin-striped pants. "You'd think that wouldn't be too much to ask." She went on from there.

By the time they were ready to leave, Leon looked stricken.

"Don't be nervous," Eve told him, but Leon stayed quiet, holding on to his stomach, and when they got to the auditorium, he vaulted out of the car and ran inside.

René was captured by Leon's dazzling jumps and spins and compli-cated time steps just as much as she was by his heading out the door to school each morning, taking off on his bike in the after-noons, and roaming the fields at will until dinnertime. She cam-paigned to go to dance class with him, but when that didn't work, she started simply standing behind him, following along as he re-hearsed his steps.

"Hey!" Leon would warn, turning to take a swipe at her. Then Eve would call out, "Leave your brother alone. He's trying to prac-tice."

But if Al was there, he'd stop whatever he was doing to watch her. He'd fold his newspaper or set the wrench he was using down on the kitchen counter to take a break. He'd get to laughing and say things like "Well, aren't you just the best little dancer" and "Oh, my. I think they're going to have to put you on TV."

To which, Eve would snort and humph.

"What is it, Eve? You seem to have something to say."

"Oh, I have plenty to say. You know I do."

"No need holding back. We're listening. Why not just say what you mean?"

"I mean you're something, Al. You're something else."

"You don't think René's a good dancer?" Al would wink at René.

"That's not what I said."

"Well, what did you say? You didn't say anything at all, not so far as I can tell. Zippo." He'd laugh like he and René were sharing a joke.

"Of course she's a good dancer, of course she is."

As Eve stretched a hard smile at her, René would freeze, trying to figure a way to leave the room. Leon would have flown outside and hopped on his bike at the first word, but she'd have missed that exit. She'd back away slowly, then casually turn the corner and jet out through the kitchen door. Still, she could hear them.

"That's all I was saying, Eve. I don't know what you think I was trying—"

"Damn right, that's all you were saying. Can't think of anything else that might need saying, can you? When Leon's the one who's taking lessons and really improving. Your son! Can't say a nice word to your own son. Why not? Probably because your mother—!"

"Now, wait just a minute. That's got—"

"You're a grown man, Al. Get over it and say something nice to your son!"

"Don't tell me—! And let's get to the real problem while we're at it. How about how you're raising that boy—with the sequins and the sparkles. For crying out loud, Eve. What good's that going to do him? None. No good! Nothing, just nothing! And I do say nice things."

"Sure, to René. Sure you do. But not to Leon. Not once. And what do you know? You're never around, and you barely give him so much as a look. He likes his dancing. It gives him confidence. Ever think of that? He likes it! You and your mother—there's a mama's boy for you, if that's what you're implying. That's right, Al. Might as well say it. You're the biggest mama's boy I ever laid eyes on, hands down."

Then silence.

"You just have to go running your *big*—"

"Oh, go to hell."

"There it is, Eve. A true feeling and a mouth like a sailor. Have it your way."

"It'll never be my way. Never! That's been clear for a long time. It's your way or else. Isn't that right? Your way or the highway."

René would be sitting around the foundation of the house they'd made so nice, or lying spread-eagle on the grass in their beautiful backyard, or poking around in the garden, but wherever she went, she could hear them. Al would go into the bedroom to pack his suitcase while Eve slammed doors and Jayne started to wail.

"So that's how you're going to take care of it."

"That's right. You're always right." Al would laugh his false, cruel laugh and be out the door without another word.

René would listen as his car pulled away, down the dirt road, and she'd wait, still as stone for a good long time, before she went back inside.

When Al finally came home again, René would be the first to greet him, grabbing his hands, forcing him to put down his suitcase, then balancing on the tops of his cowboy boots and making him dance her around the room. They'd tip back and forth to whatever was on the radio, laughing, crooning along, spinning like a Tilt-A-Whirl.

But soon enough, he and Eve would be back to where they'd left off. So sometimes he'd stay around for a few days, but mostly he'd just empty and repack his bag, slam the front door, and be gone all over again, this time for a week or two.

And gradually, steadily, René was learning.

First, it wasn't like Eve said: she wasn't trying to "steal the spotlight" from Leon. She didn't want to decorate her bike and ride in the town parade; she didn't want to play baseball or scout around the open fields, pitching rocks and pretending to shoot guns; but she did want to dance. And second, Al was right: she could do it. Even without lessons, she was a good dancer. But third, everything was connected like a game of Mousetrap: somehow, whatever it was she wanted would get the ball rolling, and right away Eve and

Al would be at each other's throats, their pitched wrangling running ahead, dropping, weaving, setting off all kinds of bells, felling planks and turning levers until the basket came straight down on Leon.

So you might say she was a spoiled, selfish child, ready to take for herself what rightfully belonged to her brother, regardless of his lost hopes or dashed feelings, his trouble or despair. Or you might say she was just a girl who wanted to learn to dance, or maybe even a girl who'd found a way to hear her father's laughter and see his eyes light up and was determined not to let that go.

Either way, you wouldn't be saying anything that hadn't already been argued—"ad infinitum," as Eve said.

Either way, it was a problem.

5

Flesh and Blood

Philip had one dirt road. It went from the school, on the far side of the western gulch, straight down, then up past the single block of houses, took a sharp right, then ran down again into the southern gulch, to downtown, where it intersected with the town's one paved street, which had a bank, a bar, a drugstore, a diner, a movie theater, and the old-time Philip Hotel.

In René's dreams there were torrential downpours that turned all the gullies into deep pools. The neighbor kids, including Leon, would jump in, but when René tried to join them, the water would rage and churn, chopping itself into white tips and swirling over the banks. Then there'd be a skip—she'd be submerged, pounded by rain, deafened by the water's roar, overpowered by the current and swept out into the flooded gorge, far away from the others.

Sometimes Leon would appear and reach his hand to pull her out, but mostly she'd just startle awake.

It happened again and again, the dream running night after night like a looped film reel.

Drifting off to sleep in her bunk above Leon, anticipating the jump into stormy water, René would imagine gripping the bank more firmly this time or treading more powerfully against the pull of the current, as if the dream were a military drill. She hadn't even turned six yet, but already she knew that whatever came her way, nighttime or not, she was going to have to be brave, she was going to have to buck up and handle it. To start with, she had to figure out how to keep herself out of the riptide in the first place, and dream-drowning in flooded ravines seemed like good practice.

So did sticking her tongue to the aluminum screen doors up and down the block when it was below zero, which she did under the pale light of day. Just as the "wormy Jessup kids" Eve didn't like from next door had promised, her tongue stuck. She had to peel it off slowly, making tight fists in her pockets to endure the burning. But when Leon saw her going from one screen door to the next and ran home to tell, Eve marched out to get her, looking furious, then spread Mercurochrome on her raw tongue and sent her to bed with a hot water bottle and a lecture about not doing the first stupid thing some "goddamn dumb kid" tells you to do.

Then one scorching day in the middle of summer, when all the moms and kids were cooped up in one of the neighbor houses— fans whirring, curtains drawn—and the moms were far too hot to play Wahoo anyway, they came up with a plan. They'd all get into one car and head down to the diner. There'd be air-conditioning, and the moms could have iced tea while the kids got pop.

"Might as well spend some of this Wahoo money," Benny's

mom conceded, using the damp from her forehead to slick her hair back out of her eyes.

So they all squeezed in—René making Benny scoot over and sit on Frankie's lap so she could sit next to an open window—and they headed down the road, into the gully, to the town diner.

"This was a good idee," Hap said, as everyone piled out.

"You could fry an egg," Frankie's mom noted. Then, as Frankie hot-footed it across the burning pavement: "Frankie, why in the *hell* didn't you wear your shoes? Jee-zus Criminy!"

The overhead air conditioner rattled the hanging fluorescent lights and blew a gale through the empty restaurant. Just when they'd all finally settled down—moms at one end of the steel tables they'd pulled together, kids at the other—the diner door blew open and, in a tunnel of shimmering, unwelcome heat, a scraggly old man appeared, bent nearly in half, covered in dirt as though he'd stepped straight out of a cyclone. He wore busted-through cowboy boots, a lopsided hat with a chewed-up brim, and, under his moth-eaten duster, dirt-crusted jeans secured by a rope around his waist. He limped up to the counter, sat on one of the stools, and, keeping his hat and coat on, spun around to take a look.

No one but René seemed to notice him, so he looked straight at her, then chuckled and touched his hat. The few teeth he had left hung like jagged, broken arrowheads from his gum line. Plus, he was missing some fingers. He waved his mangled hand at her table as if casting a spell, then turned back around and took ahold of the cup of hot coffee the waitress had left him. He sipped, spilling on himself, turning every so often to shake his head at her and grin.

At first, René hunkered down in her chair. But after a while, she decided she might as well just sit up and look straight back at him. And it was then that it hit her, right out of the hazy, colorless sky: just like she was looking out from inside herself, that old man was looking out from inside himself.

She let the thought meander in her head, wondering what it would be like to be that old man. She imagined exchanging all her parts with his parts, coming to believe that he might just as soon be sitting at her table in her pink shortie overalls, and she might just as well be at the counter in his dirty jeans and boots, wearing a heavy coat and drinking coffee in the pressing heat, holding her cup with just three fingers. It was possible. It was more than possible. It had come to life in front of her. Just like there was a whole world from her side, there was a whole world from his side; but somehow, at the beginning and end of it all, the two of them were the same: just flesh and blood and feelings.

The old man turned and smiled at her, flashing his ragged teeth like a werewolf, and she tightened her belly and smiled right back. When he'd finished his coffee, he stood up and started past her table. Then, stopping abruptly, digging around in his coat pockets like a mixed-up rodeo clown, he produced a dull nickel, balanced it on his thumbnail, gave her a wink, and flicked it high into the air. The nickel landed in the middle of the table, whirling in tight circles until the arcs widened and it slowed, ringing. The old man laughed and waggled a finger at her, then headed out the door, back into the heat.

After a battle royal over the nickel—with René shrieking even louder than all the rest that it was *her* nickel, the man had pointed at *her,* thrown it to *her;* and with the moms having to jump up and pull their kids off the tabletop, and Eve having to rush to unlock René's grip from Frankie's curls and set her firmly on the ground, saying, "Sorry, sorry. Oh, sorry. What in the *sam* hell?" as she gave René a couple of good, hard swats she wouldn't forget and the other moms dug through their coin purses so that everybody would get a nickel and stop their crying—René went out into the blazing heat and sat by herself on the curb.

The other kids passed her, giving her dirty looks on their way to the drugstore, as she sat staring at the road, sucking on the open scratch on her hand, tasting her blood. At least she had the nickel. She looked up and down the deserted street. Wherever that old man had come from and wherever he'd disappeared to, he hadn't left a trace. It was like he'd risen straight out of the dirt.

Leon came out and sat beside her without saying a word. Then he said, "Don't w-worry."

He'd seen the man smile at her, seen him wink and point his finger as he tossed the nickel.

"It was j-just like you s-said," Leon told her.

And hot as it was, he put his arm around her.

They sat together until the other kids came clambering out of the drugstore with their treats. Then they stood up and headed for the car, where everyone was pressing in, all the kids hollering about who got to sit next to a rolled-down window. What did it matter? Once they got started, the wind was going to be blowing on all of them, just like a heater.

6

Sounding the Bell

Whenever they went to visit her in Fort Pierre, Emma would quickly smooth Leon's hair and turn down his collar, then lunge to deliver a dozen tickling kisses in a single breath to René's cheek and neck. She'd hug René close, laughing as the two of them stumbled ahead into the house, leaving Leon, Al, and Eve, lugging Jayne, to follow.

René would sleep with Emma in her big bed, where they'd be awake long after the rest of the house had gone quiet. She'd let René comb and fix her hair or go through her jewelry box piece by piece. She'd tell René stories of how Grandpa, "now sadly departed," had bought this broach when they'd visited Minneapolis, or how that ivory bracelet with the Chinese carving was something they'd got on a cruise. René had never known her grandpa; he'd had a heart attack and died in a cow pasture, under a burning sun, some years before she was born. "Oh, he'd have loved you," Emma would say in a dreamy voice as René dug through scented storage boxes full of colorful chiffon scarves, or pulled open dresser drawers to get to lace gloves and rhinestone sunglasses.

Emma had been a teacher in a one-room schoolhouse, giving lessons on a single slate no bigger than a picture frame. She'd even potty-trained a second grader, a retarded Indian boy she was happy to have come along to school with all the rest. "And whenever a bat or some creature found its way into our classroom," she'd tell René, "why, I'd simply ask one of the boys to go fetch me the broom." Though she was supposed to be getting into her nightgown, Emma would pretend to strike at the windows and walls, performing a circus-like reenactment in her tension-weary girdle and bra, stopping only to catch her breath from jumping around, laughing. When she'd finally climbed into bed, she'd say, "Now, bats are our friends. They eat mosquitoes and other insects. But sometimes they carry disease."

If it was unbearably hot, which it tended to be in the Fort Pierre summertime, they'd use Emma's "old-time air-conditioning"— soaking their nightgowns in cold water, wringing them out, putting them back on, and running for bed, howling. It was stunning and delicious and "So good for your blood!" Emma would shout, smacking herself all over to get her temperature refigured.

By the time Emma reached to turn out the light, René would be snuggled in close, silently watching the colored stars that flickered and fell behind her closed eyelids as she drifted off to sleep.

They were inseparable.

While Leon played alone in his room or went with Eve and Jayne down to the house by the Bad River to visit Eve's folks, René would wander with Emma out to the far end of the back garden. If they happened into the field beyond the gate and René spied Leon in the road with the older cousins from the other side, digging holes in the dirt with sticks or throwing rocks at a tree or eating gritty, gummy marshmallows, she'd call out and wave.

"Now, what do you want to do that for?" Emma would ask, tsking and taking her hand. "We're having a fine time, aren't we? Here," she'd say, "just taste." She'd pick a strawberry for René and one for herself from the wild vines, piping hot from the sun, and the two would eat where they stood, wide-eyed and mute.

Then they'd gather lettuces—curly, straight, striped—sampling as they went. "Just like a couple of rabbits getting into the garden," Emma would laugh. "Come on now, we've got enough."

Inside, she'd rinse the greens, then heat up bacon fat, vinegar, condensed milk, and sugar for dressing. She'd slice in a red onion, pour the hot dressing over the lettuces, and they'd have wilted lettuce salad with crackers on pastel, etched-glass tea plates, talking about how delicious it was and what a nice day it was and what they might want to do next.

"Maybe you'd like to lie down in the hammock," Emma would say. "We can find something good to read, and I'll bring us some iced tea."

So they'd spend the afternoon in the shade of Emma's big yard, characters in a homespun nineteenth-century idyll. Emma would sit in her metal rocker, drinking tea, while René stretched out in the hammock, suspended between two enormous oaks, swaying over a cool, wide bed of creeping ivy. From time to time, Emma would grab the mesh to give René a swing, or simply reach out and take hold of her hand, and they'd look up together, past the tops of the two big trees, to the endless sweep of sky. And if it was terribly hot, Emma would bring out her Oriental-print fan to keep cool. She'd fan herself, then René, then herself, then René, as René swung close and away, close and away, and they'd both get to giggling, tickled by Emma's complicated gymnastics and just how hard she was working—and for nothing. It was too hot to do anything about it. Anyone could see that.

The problem, which had started earlier—maybe even back before time itself—was that, as Emma was every day bringing René into her heart and holding her as *the beloved,* she was, in the same motion, handily evicting Leon. With every hug and laugh, every smile and bending together of their heads, every scissor project and bedtime story, with every wave of happiness that seemed to lift them both, Leon was being shoved down and out and further away. And the more exiled Leon became, the more Eve looked askance at René.

"*Entitled* is a word that comes to mind," Eve would say to her whenever they were alone, which came to sound to René like the tinkling of a shiny silver bell. *Entitled.* Even when no one was saying it, it was right there, just waiting for someone to pick it up and ring it.

But Leon didn't make a fuss.

"He's sad," Eve would whisper to René whenever she got the chance. "He's hurt."

According to Eve, Leon would lie alone in his bed when they visited Emma, listening to the laughter from the other side of the adjoining wall. Because of René, the nights he'd played Emma's "hired hand"—letting her draw a mustache on him with her eyebrow pencil, then trying on Grandpa's old cowboy hats—were gone. Now he was reduced to running with the cousins who lived in the beat-up trailer down by the Bad River. And seeming to instantly, quietly grasp that there was no longer any room for him, Leon resigned himself to his place, alone in his bed at night, as Emma and René giggled and romped and had "a grand old time."

"They were so close," Eve would remind René at intervals, even long after they were all back home in Philip. "Leon was Emma's precious little gem before you came along. Then she just dropped him in the street like a hot rock. It breaks my heart."

Eve would purse her lips, creasing her forehead into a deep frown, and shake her head as René looked up, feeling her own face tighten in reflection as her body braced against what felt like a slow-motion fall.

7

J.D.

Eve and Al joined the Philip bowling league. Al won the men's tournament at the end of the first season, and all the guys patted him on the back. He came home with a trophy, a bowling man atop a golden column. Eve won "Most Strikes," but their friend Hap took the women's trophy, so Eve came home with only a "First Place" ribbon. "A misnomer if I ever heard one," she said.

On the night of the bowling league banquet—free beer and hot dogs at the lanes—J.D., the manager, came over and congratulated Eve, holding her face in his hands and planting a wet kiss just by the corner of her mouth as Eve brightened and stammered, "Thank you, oh, thank you, J.D., no, no, oh. How sweet!," which was enough to make Al wonder what she did, exactly, on all those nights when he was out of town.

"That J.D.," Al tried on the way home.

Eve laughed. "Good God."

"You two seem to have something special going on," he said, inquiring.

"For Chrissakes, Al. I don't even know him. What in the world."

"Looks like you might know him well enough. Wouldn't want to be knowing a guy much better than that." Al laughed.

"That's not funny. It's not worth talking about. Just be quiet." So they drove.

But at the bowling lanes, Al started to notice J.D. watching Eve. And he started to notice that when Eve saw J.D. looking at her, she blushed. So on the long nights when he was on the road in Montana or Nebraska or over in eastern Wyoming, in yet another stinky motel room on the side of the highway, he began to wonder. He wondered and wondered. He wondered so much that by the time he got home, he'd be convinced.

He'd confront her; she'd deny it. So he'd leave town, have more time to think. Then he'd come back. He'd accuse her; she'd fight him. So he'd leave again. Then one night, arriving home earlier than expected, Al found the kids with a sitter and Eve nowhere in sight.

He sent the girl home and sat by himself in the dark, smoking, until Eve finally came through the door, loaded down with fabrics.

"I didn't know you'd be here, Al," she said, first thing.

"I imagine that's right."

"I've been up to Hap's, helping with some curtains."

"Is that supposed to mean you weren't spending the evening with your *friend*?"

"If I've told you once—" Eve was instantly up to speed.

"Don't lie to me, Eve."

"You're one to talk." She dropped the fabrics onto the kitchen table. "One finger pointing out and three pointing back at yourself. That's what I say. How do I know what you do on the road all the time? I'm guessing it's not all on the up-and-up."

It wasn't any kind of confession, but it was enough to make Al stand and catch her by the shoulder. "I must be the only one in town that doesn't know."

Instead of pulling away, Eve stepped in closer just to scream in his face: "You don't know because there's nothing going on, you *goddamn dumb* son of a bitch!"

Al drew his arm back, and at the same moment, Leon got out of bed and stepped into the hallway. He saw Al's hand come down, saw Eve bend and pull away. He stood, rubbing his eyes as if to clear the scene and start again, as Eve went into her room and shut the door. Then he simply continued to stand there, uncertain, in his printed cowboy pajamas.

"Do whatever it is you need," Al told him roughly, "then get back to bed."

And though in the future Eve would swear it had never happened, insisting that Leon must have dreamed it, Leon would clearly recall that he hadn't continued on to the bathroom that night, as he'd needed to do; instead, he'd turned around and gone straight back to bed, playing the scene over and over in his mind, vowing to remember, vowing to grow up and never forget.

To the great disappointment of their teammates, Eve and Al withdrew from the league. Eve wasn't allowed to go to the bowling alley anymore, not even to meet friends for an afternoon game, which she missed.

"I'm exiled enough, Al, with you gone all the time. I have to do *something* with myself."

"Then find something useful," Al said, not even looking at her.

She shook her head and walked away. No use starting it up.

Then one moonless night, when the world was pitch-black across the long stretch of prairie, nothing but stars—after the dishes were done, the laundry folded, the kids in bed, and with Eve not expecting Al for at least another day or two—a car pulled into the driveway.

Eve inched the drapes apart to have a look and made out what appeared to be J.D., climbing out of the driver's seat and stumbling up the steps.

A knock exploded against the front door. "Evie!"

Eve paused with her hand on the knob. Then she silently turned the bolt and squatted down so he wouldn't be able to see her through the small glass panels.

"Evie!" J.D. knocked harder. He tried the handle.

All her life Eve had hated the name Evie. No one who knew her called her by that name, not more than once.

"Evie, open the door." He was whining, pleading, obviously plastered. "I miss you coming downtown. Why don't you come downtown no more? I don't get to see you no more."

J.D. must have been watching and known that Al was out of town.

Eve waited, perfectly still, at the base of the door. She was barely breathing as J.D. pounded and hollered and pounded again. "Oh, God," she prayed. "Please don't let the kids wake up. Please, please don't let the kids wake up."

"Goddamn it, Evie. Answer the goddamn door!" He was mad now. "I know you're in there!"

Eve waited, trembling, until he suddenly just stopped, tripped back down the steps, and fell into his running car. He sat there awhile. Eve thought maybe he'd passed out, until she heard the engine rev, heard the car back out of the driveway and start down the road.

Al was coming home early, hoping to find a way to make things up. He'd got off the highway, turned the corner, and seen the taillights in his driveway from the end of the block. He saw the brake lights come on, and he watched as J.D. passed him from the opposite direction on Philip's one dirt road.

When he stepped into the house, Eve jumped up from where she'd been sitting in the dark, crying, and fell into his arms. He was stiff and icy, ready to fly against her, but the way she went on—clutching him so tight, sobbing, shaking—he couldn't help but soften and hold her. He kissed the top of her head and sat her down on the couch. "Hush," he said, rocking her. "I'm right here, Eve. Everything's all right now. There, now. That's it. I'm here."

And so it was decided that they were moving on to Rapid City, another ninety miles west, into the foothills of the Black Hills, Paha Sapa, the sacred land of the Indians, "and for good reason," Al said to René, holding her on his lap, taking the time to explain why she was going to have to leave her friends, though she immediately protested that since Eve didn't let her play with the "filthy next-door-neighbor kids," she didn't have any friends, only one, a fat little girl in the house across the alley who got everything René ever wanted, including multiple Barbies with all the outfits and the playhouse and jeep, and white marching boots—with tassels!—plus store-bought cupcakes and root beer floats and little bowls full of candy that she could help herself to whenever she wanted!

Compared to this little town of Philip, Al told her, where the wind blew all day long and the earth was so cracked and dry you had to break your back to grow a single blade of grass, where there didn't seem to be any real friends, and where some people were even willing to try to take what didn't belong to them—but Al had lost his track, and René was squirming, looking more and more alarmed, like she was getting in trouble.

He let her down.

"It's going to be a regular Garden of Eden," he said.

8

Paha Sapa

Al found a house to rent in the foothills above Rapid City, and they drove from Philip in a borrowed, piled-up truck, bouncing along through the Badlands, where the earth fell away into canyons of color-banded, sunbaked rock. They kept going until the prairie grasses started turning green, the highway began to roll, and there they were, rising in the distance—jagged layers of cut-out mountains set off against a perfect Wild West sky.

The Black Hills are older than the Alps, older than the Himalayas. Paha Sapa, Khe Sapa—black mountains rising to meet the heavens, full with pine, flush with rock, abounding in green meadows—pushed up over seventy million years ago, have been occupied by native people for the past ten thousand years, and are full of ghosts, most of them in mourning: ghosts of the Cheyenne, conquered by the Sioux; ghosts of the Lakota, driven out by the whites when gold was discovered and the railroad came through; ghosts of Custer, Sitting Bull, Crazy Horse; ghosts of Calamity Jane, Wild Bill, Jack McCall, Billy the Kid; ghosts of Black Elk, Red Cloud, Kicking Bear, Gall, Rain in the Face, Spotted Tail, Crow King, Hump; ghosts of the Ghost Dancers and Wounded Knee, Standing Rock and Little Bighorn.

The house sat by itself, perched above the twinkling lights of the city, half dug in, with a level drive on the high side to park the car, then three steps down to the back door. In front, where the hill fell sharply to the prairie below and the house looked out over the plains and the city with the Black Hills in the distance, there was a railless rock-and-cement patio with a twenty-foot drop.

Surrounded by the majesty of deep pine forest, ponderosas shooting up on all sides, you could run barefoot across the drive-way, up a small, rocky incline, and enter an enchanted world where the soft bed of pine needles cushioned every step, where perfect pine cones, like ornaments, fell around you, and chunks of rose quartz, shining like pink jewels here and there in the sudden rays of sunlight, bloomed at your feet, some larger than you could carry, where green-and-gray-lichened boulders, higher than your head and older than your greatest-great-grandfather, emerged from the ground, ancient striations slanting to the sky.

René was free to gather rocks and pine cones, find and ford a stream, climb up to the tree house left by the previous tenants, hollering down to Leon about whether it seemed safe or rotted. She could mount a giant outcropping of granite to secure a view of beavers at work, or just lie on the hot cement patio in the sunshine, one eye open for snakes, which seemed, unbelievably, able to climb the steep rock wall that dropped off to the front drive. She gathered quartz, piling it in an empty corner of the living room, and hoarded pine cones until they were spilling off her dresser top and Eve made her take them all back outside.

Leon found an ax and got busy chopping trees and building forts. Whenever René heard his call, she'd scramble up the nearest boulder to see him in a far-off valley, standing proudly at the base of a tender sapling, his foot on the poor thing, which was now prone, undone, Leon's tall, scrawny self looking everything like its simple reflection, its still-upright twin.

When they'd first moved in, the bathtub had been full of dead crickets, three and four deep, and it turned out the house was infested with black widows, so they had to remember to knock their shoes out against a doorframe before putting them on. Al was gone more than ever to keep up with the "big-city rent," and Eve had not a single neighbor, just the darkness of the night, the kids in bed, and two sets of badly tracked sliding glass doors looking out over Rapid City, the Gateway to the American West.

Since Eve was mostly alone in the silence and dark of her house in the woods, before long Al came home with a German shepherd called Chuck. Chuck had to be on a chain. He'd belonged to a rancher who'd wanted to be rid of him because of his constant snarling and barking, which stirred up the cattle, and Al had to admit that he wasn't sure what kind of temperament the dog had or how he'd been treated.

He was to be Leon's dog, Al said. Leon would be responsible for taking care of him, feeding him, training him.

"Not right away," Eve corrected. "I'll manage him to start with," she said to Leon.

Al darkened, did an about-face, and soldiered off to the kitchen.

"And you can take over after we get to know him better. Just in case."

Leon looked crestfallen.

"Just to start with," Eve told him.

Chuck came up to Leon's waist, René's armpit, and over Jayne's head. They all kept their distance for a while, Eve feeding and handling him until she got to liking him so much that she started letting him follow her around while she did her outside chores. And soon she simply turned him loose, so that Chuck was just like any ordinary dog, chasing down rabbits and chipmunks, digging holes up by the house. Then Leon took over the feeding, and Chuck was Leon's dog.

Most days, Chuck would follow Leon into the hills and stand by for the chopping or building until he heard something out of range and took off running. More often than not, he'd be running for the house, where Jayne would once again be out on the front patio, having pulled repeatedly, patiently, at one of the glass doors until she could slip through the opening and toddle out onto the cement. Chuck would take up his post at her side, keeping himself between her and the open ledge that fell sharply to the road below as Jayne made a game of it, running from one side of the patio to the other, Chuck sauntering casually beside her. When she got too near the edge, Chuck would wag his tail and sidle up between her and the drop, using his strong body to block her, panting at her with his big smile, tongue hanging out, as she pounded his back and pulled his hair and screamed. So, while Eve did the washing and cooking, the cleaning and sewing, drove the garbage down the hill and planted flowers around the back steps, Chuck did the babysitting.

The only rule was that Chuck wasn't allowed inside. So that first winter, during the time of year the Indian souvenir calendar left in the kitchen by the previous tenants called "The Moon of Frost in the Tepee," as wind whistled through the cracks in the doors and blew falling snow in icy, slanting sheets, Chuck was on the other side of the glass, huddled under the eaves.

"He's supposed to be outside," Eve would tell them. "That's why he's got that big fur coat on."

Then ice formed on the patio, coated the cement steps, and hung in long, thick cords from the roof to the ground, and ice crusted and dripped from Chuck's muzzle, and every day there were more bloody pawprints up and down the steps to the driveway. Chuck would lean against the sliding glass doors and cry.

"We have to let him in," Leon begged. "He's my dog. I'll c-clean up if he makes a mess, I swear."

So, finally, Eve put down newspapers and old sheets, opened the door, and let Chuck in. Leon got him fresh water, and Chuck lay by the fire and slept and slept. Leon stayed on the couch day and night while Chuck's paws healed, and it looked like Chuck had finally found a real home, until one day, having got into something rotten in the woods, he threw up a lake of pine needles, fur, bones, and bile all over Eve's knitting.

"And *that's* why you do *not* have animals in the house!" Eve cried. "Goddamn it!" She wrinkled her nose and considered the nearly finished purple sweater with white paper dolls holding hands across the front she'd been making for Jayne, now saturated with brownish-green dog vomit. "I'm just going to have to throw it out. After all that work. Shit!"

They'd all heard her counting stitches night after night that winter, and they all, Chuck included, stood frozen and shame-faced as she used an old newspaper to shovel the ruined sweater into a paper bag and throw it in the trash.

"Lord knows I have enough to do without some dumb dog—!"

So Chuck was back outside. And though he still leaned up against the glass at night, gazing longingly, pitifully, toward the fire and what had come to be his place in front of it, there was no use arguing.

After the first few cold nights, Eve agreed to let Leon use an old sleeping bag to make Chuck a bed by the door, and from then on, Leon would be the first one up. They'd wake to find him already outside, bundled in his overcoat, knitted cap pulled down over his ears, curled up with Chuck on the ratty dog bed, fast asleep, his long legs, still in pajama pants, stretched out on the frozen cement.

In Rapid, René and Leon both went to General Beadle Elementary, named after William Henry Harrison Beadle, who'd been appointed surveyor general of Dakota Territory by none other than Ulysses S. Grant. General Beadle had come up with a system for setting aside Dakota land for schools and was a lifetime advocate of education, so they were in good hands, the principal said. There was no mention of this "land for schools" having been secured through the government's policy of cheating Indians out of sovereign reservation territories, so nobody gave it a thought.

Eve drove them to school every morning in her broken-down Chevy, which went forward by lurches and looked like a parboiled turtle. When they got to the drop-off, René would duck beneath the glove box, then quickly lunge out the door and sprint for class.

"I don't want anybody to see me in this junky old car," she said one day when Eve asked what in the hell she was doing.

"And how do you imagine people are going to think you got here, then?"

"Maybe I just sprung up out of the ether," René said. "Like a sprite or a fairy." Her first-grade class had been reading fairy tales.

"Or a mushroom," Eve suggested.

Whenever René got into some kind of trouble on the playground, like with the girl from second grade who wouldn't give her a turn on the swings, or with Timmy, who made her suck on his marbles to get in the game, then told her he'd peed on them, she ran to the barrier between the upper- and lower-grade playgrounds and called out for Leon. And Leon came down.

"Timmy peed on the marbles!" was all she needed to say.

"Okay," Leon said. "I'll be r-right back," he called over his shoulder as the other boys protested.

"Over here." She led him to where she and Timmy had been quarreling.

"Hi, Timmy," Leon said, towering over the younger kids. "How you doing?"

René thought Leon was too slow in getting to the point, but he was a diplomat—patient and willing to see all sides.

Timmy glowered at René and kicked the gravel with his toe.

"You guys should be n-nice to each other," Leon finally said.

Timmy bent his neck to look up.

"You didn't p-pee on those marbles, did you?" Leon said.

"I didn't do it," Timmy admitted. "I only said it."

"Okay," Leon said. " 'Cause René likes you."

René glared at Timmy so he didn't get the wrong idea. Eve had warned her not to play with Timmy because Timmy was Indian and might give her worms or scabies. But Timmy was actually only half Indian. He lived in one of the underground tar-topped houses right across the street from the school, and mostly they were good pals.

"She steals my marbles," Timmy said.

René had won some of Timmy's marbles, but Timmy was an Indian giver and he wanted them back. They were in constant negotiations.

"She takes them and she doesn't give them back," he said.

"What if she promises not to take your marbles? Do you p-promise?" Leon looked at René. It was clear he wanted to get back to his game.

"I don't take them," she said, looking at Timmy. "I *win* them."

She'd won a few, and she'd taken a few.

"If you want to play, you have to p-promise not to take his marbles," Leon said.

"Promise," she muttered.

"Tell Timmy."

"Promise. I won't take your marbles."

"Okay," Timmy said, looking at his shoes.

"Okay, g-good job," Leon said, and he touched Timmy's shoulder, patted René on the back, then tore off to the upper terrace, where the other boys were calling for him to hurry up before the bell rang.

Eve did her shopping in the Indian part of town, where the dented canned goods were stacked on open plyboard shelves, still in their delivery boxes. It was cheap. She could get an oversized box of powdered milk, an enormous bag of puffed rice, an extra-large block of Velveeta, and a case of pork 'n' beans for four dollars and twenty-nine cents, so even though these were tough times—with the cost of the move and Al needing to be on the road all the time, taking more and more risk borrowing from the banks to purchase cattle—they had enough. They ate pork 'n' beans for dinner, sometimes with chicken legs, sometimes with potatoes or carrots or hard-boiled eggs, depending on what Prairie Market had on sale. They ate puffed rice with watery powdered milk and sugar every morning, and at night, too, if they wanted a bedtime snack.

On the prairie just below them were a few broken-down trailers set at random in the tall grass. "Don't you ever go down there," Eve warned. "It's all Indians, and they don't like people coming around."

But René was beginning to mistrust everything Eve said, as if Eve were purposely inverting the truth, saying things backward and upside-down just for her. So she'd make a point of sneaking down to the flatlands, following the hill around the house to the little car bridge someone had put up across the deep wash, careful to match her stride to the planks of nailed lumber so she didn't get a foot stuck in one of the narrow divides. As soon as she reached the meadow, there'd be the rising scent of sage and sweetgrass. There were distant barking dogs and even a shaggy brown pony with a bowed back that seemed to wander at will. She'd hide in the brush like a tracker, trying to see for herself if there were really any Indians down there.

The trailer closest to the road was a rusty silver bubble with a long-abandoned hitch and seemed to have only one wrinkled old man inside. He'd come out shirtless, in jeans and a black hat with a rainbow-beaded hatband, a single eagle feather trailing down his back on a long leather string. He'd leave the door open on its hinges, sit on his metal trailer step, and smoke.

"Why don't Indians like us?" René asked one day as Eve was bent, mopping the kitchen.

"They like their own," Eve said. "Everybody's like that. Everybody likes their own."

"Why don't we like Indians? They were here first. It's their land."

"It was," Eve said, "but it's not anymore. And it's not that we don't like them, it's just that they're different. They don't take care of things."

That wrinkled old man didn't seem all that different. He was just smoking on his step, looking off to nowhere, like Al sometimes did.

"And they're lazy," Eve went on, out of breath, losing herself. "They're always looking for a handout. They're just not willing to work hard like the rest of us. They'd rather drink their firewater," she said. Then she stopped and looked at René. "How'd you get me on that? Aren't you supposed to be cleaning your room?"

René smiled, caught.

"Just like an Indian," Eve would scold whenever René balked at her chores. Because wasn't she lazy? Didn't she prefer soft, dirty sheets to scratchy clean ones? Didn't she always argue about making her bed in the first place, since she was just going to get back into it sooner than later, about cleaning out her closet, which was going to be all mixed up again in a day or two anyway? More than once Eve had told her, "You want to live like an Indian? Fine. When you get your own house, you can go ahead and live like a Comanche for all I care. But not in my house."

"Go on," Eve said to her this time. "Get going. And don't let me catch you down in that valley," she called as René ran up the stairs.

"I won't," René called back, more than happy to leave it at that.

9

Right Foot Out

Eve found a place for Leon to continue his dance lessons—Lois Mann's Tap 'N' Tune—and pretty soon René was in Miss Mann's dance school, too, in the Tiny Tykes class, learning not just shuffle ball-change but gymnastic moves even Leon didn't know, like kick-overs, walkovers, chest rolls, and one-handed cartwheels. She excelled at anything that involved hyperextending the spine and could memorize steps almost instantly. She'd get bored and tap her way through an entire routine as Miss Mann tried to break it down and explain it—"one more time, all over again"—to the kids who still weren't getting it. Miss Mann kept telling René to stand still, but she was as frustrated with those stragglers as René was.

For their spring recital, Tap 'N' Tune was going to be the special guest on *Mabel's Open House,* the local TV talk show, and one day while Leon was busy practicing his solo at home, Eve got a call from Miss Mann saying that René was going to have a solo, too. René figured Leon would be mad at her for "always stepping in his sunshine," as Eve said, but he didn't care. He was planning a party for his school friends. They were going to take a record player onto the cement patio so they could dance grown-up style. Eve had been giving him lessons in the waltz and the Texas two-step, and Leon had recruited René to call "Snowball!" so kids would have to change partners. He told her again and again that when she saw him dancing with Cindy, the girl he liked, she shouldn't call "Snowball!" for a long time.

"A *really* long time," he said, holding her by the shoulders so she'd be sure to pay attention. "Just w-watch me. I'll t-tell you when."

When recital day finally arrived, they drove to the television studio and Eve hauled their costumes up a steep flight of stairs to the lobby, where the station had its logo—the rugged profile of a stately Lakota chief in full-feather headdress superimposed over Mount Rushmore and surrounded by bull's-eyes—painted on a far wall. They were shown to what their escort called the "ladies'-room-plus-dressing-room," and René put on the glittery pink-checked outfit Eve had sewn for her. Eve pinned an oversized matching bow into René's hair, then leaned her back in an old barber's chair and drew on eyeliner, patted her cheeks with rouge, and dabbed on lipstick. When they were ready, they pushed through a heavy black door into the cavernous television studio. There were inverted-washtub lights blazing overhead, and there was Mabel herself, just like they always saw her on TV, now sitting on her sofa, chatting with Miss Mann.

Miss Mann gave René a frantic wink, then Mabel introduced

her, and René stepped out under the lights. When her music started, she sang and danced with everything she had.

First you put your two knees close up tight,
You sway 'em to the left and you sway 'em to the right—

René threw herself into the dance section, ending it all with a contortionist's chest roll—lobbing both legs over her head and rolling on her turned cheek to one knee. She hadn't dropped a line or missed a step. Mabel and Miss Mann gasped and applauded while Eve, standing behind the camera, gave her a big thumbs-up.

Leon was next. He stepped out onto the floor in his top hat and vest. He had on a nervous grin until his music started; then he let his top hat tumble down his arm, caught it in his fingertips, snapped it back up onto his head, and made an easy slide into his soft-shoe number. He glided through the routine with so much elegance and grace you'd have thought the studio was a grand ballroom out of a Fred Astaire movie. When it came time for the wings—the new step he'd been practicing endlessly on the kitchen linoleum—Leon nailed it and went straight into a series of barrel jumps, then a grapevine into two double turns, and a sharp finish, hat in hand. He was brilliant and natural, a joyful, generous dancer, and everyone could feel it. Mabel and Miss Mann exploded in applause while Eve, René, and even the cameraman clapped along.

Miss Mann had already said she shouldn't be teaching him, that he should move on to another teacher in town, one who could instruct him more seriously.

"He's too talented," she'd said, ruffling Leon's thick hair as he screwed his face into a goofy smile. "He needs to study ballet. Then he can do any kind of dance he wants."

So Eve enrolled Leon and René in Rapid City's one serious dance school: the Academy of Ballet. There'd be no more gymnastics, no more tap dancing or musical numbers, no breaks for graham crackers and Kool-Aid. From what René could gather, there'd be nothing but hard work and high expectations, but it was the only place to really learn to dance.

Leon kept saying he was nervous. "It's gonna be hard," he'd say. "You w-wait."

"Don't be such a chicken," René would yell, after she'd made sure she had a good head start. Leon didn't like being called chicken, but as long as René could get him to run far enough, the mad would run right out of him. He might catch her and put her in a headlock, but they'd end up racing back to the house, René hollering about how Leon had hit her and him not even bothering to deny it as he reached his long arms to take phony swipes that grazed her ears or mussed her hair, until Eve finally told René to be quiet and quit squealing on her brother.

"Time to set the table," she'd say. "Get busy. And Leon, you take out that trash." To which they'd give a collective groan.

Girls wore dresses to Leon's party and boys wore ties. Leon wore black pants and a pressed white shirt with a snap-on red plaid bow tie. The record player was out on the patio, along with a table of cheese puffs, M&M's, raspberry Kool-Aid, and Vienna sausages on toothpicks. Since René had been given an official role, she put on her lime-sherbet-colored party dress over her shorts.

The girls arrived in a group and stood at one end of the patio while the boys huddled together at the other. Then Eve came out, paired them up, and gave a short dance lesson, and when the music came on, René took her seat by the record player and watched for Leon's signals. It was fun to call "Snowball!" and see the older kids panic and scramble for a new partner.

Suddenly Leon was dancing with a blond girl in a bright blue dress. He looked at René and raised his eyebrows.

"Snowball!" René yelled, and instantly saw her mistake.

Leon turned sharply and stepped away from the group as he let the girl go.

"That was *her*!" he whispered, frantic. "What are you d-doing? I t-told you—"

"How could I know? I thought you wanted—"

"No. You were supposed to w-wait a long time, remember? Jeez."

"Okay," she said. "Just try again."

"I'll never g-g-get her again," he moaned.

"She's right there," René said, pointing.

Leon edged back into the group and René cried, "Snowball!" But Leon ended up with the girl next to Cindy. "Snowball! Snowball!" she called, but Leon kept going the wrong way around the circle, and some of the kids were getting tired of dancing and had started to break off for the snack table.

Pretty soon all the girls were on one side of the patio again, and all the boys were on the other, and Leon had not danced with Cindy but for those first fleeting moments. There were a few forays back and forth, kids from one group going across to the other like emissaries sent to negotiate, but after that, their rides starting showing up and everybody went home.

"Nice party," Eve said happily, dumping the uneaten chips back into their bags.

"Yeah," Leon said. He was disappointed. "Thanks," he said.

"Sure, honey," Eve said. "We'll have to do it again sometime."

"That's okay," Leon said, and he went up to his room to get out of his good clothes. Then he and Chuck launched back into the woods.

10

Outnumbered, Surrounded

Eve got a call from Al. He'd invited an "important rancher" from Montana for dinner. They were on the road and would be arriving soon, so Eve should get some dinner ready, he said.

"Of course at the last *damn* minute. Can't imagine what in the *sam hell* he thinks I can just cook up on the spot like that." She started banging around the kitchen, frantically defrosting chicken in hot water, digging through her vegetable drawer. She got down flour and sugar, soda and salt, and checked to see if she had any frozen strawberries. "And when am I supposed to get my*self* ready, I'd like to know. God knows I need to wash my hair. You make sure Jayne is dressed, and take a bath, and pick up your room," she called to René. "And Leon, pick up this front room, and get out the vacuum, and help me get the extension in the table."

They were all in a panic.

"No doubt they'll be here before we can get it all done," Eve fretted. "Soon as I get this meat in the oven, we'll do the table. And maybe I'll have just enough time to drag a comb through my hair."

She flew, and when Al and the important rancher and his wife pulled up, forty-five minutes later, everything was ready: the chicken was in the oven, the table was set, Eve had on a pretty dress and fancy apron, with her hair pinned back, and the kids had clean clothes, freshly washed faces, and real smiles at the excitement of company. Al had even brought home a bottle of chokecherry wine from some farmer friend of his, and Eve walked right over and gave him a kiss.

The grown-ups sat in the living room and talked, drinking the sweet wine and commenting on the beautiful view, the twinkling lights of the city. The doors were wide open, letting in the fresh, pine-heavy air. It felt cozy and comfortable and safe with so many people talking so nicely, with Eve and Al so cheerful, laughing at the important rancher's jokes, and Al telling some good ones of his own.

Dinner went off without a hitch. There was oven-fried chicken, mashed potatoes and gravy, carrots and peas in ginger sauce, salad with homemade dressing, and cranberry gel. René couldn't help but wonder where all this food had come from. Before Al had called, it was looking like they were going to have hot dogs, pork 'n' beans, and carrots for dinner again.

Jayne got down from the table first and went out onto the patio with Chuck. Then Leon got up to follow.

"Get back here and clear your plate, Leon," Al called after him.

Leon was on his way back to the table when Eve grabbed his arm and pulled him close. "Leon had a solo tap dance on television, right here in Rapid," she said to the company.

"So did I," René put in, and Al smiled.

Leon shrugged, embarrassed, then glanced up at Al, who immediately dropped his head to examine his napkin.

"He's doing such great things," Eve went on, hugging Leon closer. "His teacher says he has a natural talent. And this year, he's going to start taking ballet lessons."

"My," the rancher's wife said, blinking. "Well, isn't that nice."

The rancher looked to Al, who continued fussing with his napkin as if he were considering reweaving it.

"And I see your big dog out there," the rancher's wife went on. "Did you know your dad got that dog from a neighbor of ours? Is he being a good dog for you all?"

Leon nodded. "I taught him some tricks," he said shyly. "Well, not t-t-tricks, but things he can do. Like s-sit, stay. Just things."

"Why not show us?" the rancher said.

Al raised his head.

"I'd love to see that, Al. I would. Why, I hear tell that dog was such a nuisance—"

So Leon brought Chuck inside, with Jayne following after. He held a piece of leftover chicken and said, "Sit," and Chuck sat, then "Shake," and Chuck lifted a paw.

The rancher chuckled, and Al started to grin.

"Down," Leon said, and Chuck lay down. "Okay, Chuck," Leon said. "Stay!"

Leon walked around the table three times before coming back to Chuck and finally giving him the chicken, which made the rancher and his wife laugh. Eve laughed and applauded, while Al laughed and kind of blushed.

Then Leon ran to clear his place, like Al had told him, stumbled over Eve's chair leg, and fell into the table where his plate was sitting, just a fraction off the edge. He hit the plate with his open hand and sent chicken, bones, peas, bits of potato, and cranberry flying into the air, then falling and spilling over the carpet, some even splattering onto the rancher's wife. Chuck grabbed a leg bone and took off out the door as Leon stammered and dropped to pick the greasy bits of food out of the rug, and the rancher's wife started and gasped, and the rancher said, "My heavens!"

"Oh, sorry, so sorry," Eve said. "Here—" She jumped up and got a damp cloth for the rancher's wife, who dabbed at the shoulder of her dress.

"Jesus Christ," Al said, his face on fire. "Damn dumb Indian."

"Oh, now, Al," the rancher said, laughing.

Eve threw her napkin onto the table with a snap, then got down on her knees to help Leon with the cleaning. "Go on. I'll get this," she said when they'd gathered most of it. "Go ahead outside."

"Accidents happen," the rancher's wife put in. "I know with our boys it was one thing after another."

Al gave a half-hearted grunt of agreement, Leon went outside, Eve retired to the kitchen, and the room went terribly quiet.

After a long moment that felt as if an eclipse had darkened the surface of the earth, René said, "I can do a walkover."

Al looked at her, vacant and pale.

"And what on earth is a walkover?" the rancher's wife said, as if she were wondering what indecency was going to be perpetrated against them next.

"I have no idea," Al said, looking at the important company as though he'd just awakened to the sound of shattering crystal.

René got up and unloaded her entire repertoire of gymnastics: a walkover, then a one-handed cartwheel, a headstand, an arching chest roll, the splits, a backbend, a back walkover, and a headstand with the splits.

As she was going along, Al began to get his color back, and the rancher and his wife began to nod their heads, until everyone seemed pretty darned cheerful again.

"Dessert?" Eve said, coming back from the kitchen, her eyes looking almost like she hadn't been crying but for one light streak of mascara. She was right on cue with a beautiful strawberry short-cake, complete with whipped cream.

Whipped cream? René thought. *Where'd she get that?*

Leon was out on the patio, sitting on the ledge, his legs hanging down to nowhere, his arm around Chuck. René went out to get him.

"Mom made your favorite," she said.

"I don't want any," he said quietly.

"Come on."

"I'm not hungry," he said.

So she left him, and he sat by himself, looking out at the dark, starry night as the rest of the company shared in dessert.

As the years went by, Leon would find himself sitting on a ledge like that again and again, staring into some endless darkness, wondering how the ground beneath him could shift so suddenly, how he could be so easily cast out, dismissed, discarded for something he hadn't meant to do and didn't know how to fix.

Even as a grown man—drunk or recuperating from a week-long bender, or fresh out of rehab with his hair slicked back and so much cologne you could feel his aching, or homeless, living in a waterlogged tent by the river, roaming the streets, getting singled out for his dark hair and Native features and beaten up by a gang of teenagers, or back at home, trying to make a fresh start as a "good Christian man"—he would think of it as a well.

"You know how you keep going back to the well and the well is always dry?" he said to René maybe a hundred times as the years unfolded, their heads bowed over coffee and the ashtray he was fill-ing, each looking into the palms of their hands as if they might be able to trace their life stories backward. "It's like that," he'd say. He'd hang his head ponderously low, shaking it back and forth. "It's no use going back to a dry well," he'd say. "That's what it's like." And he'd pause, and without the slightest hint of animosity, just wanting to be clear, he'd make a gesture toward his heart: "For me."

Too many times to count, René had thought of telling Leon he needed to fight, to claim his place, to take what he wanted and never give it up, no matter who it hurt or what was lost. He needed to get for himself what they wouldn't give him, she wanted to say. But there was never a good time to say something like that to Leon, not without feeling like you were simply piling on.

After the important rancher and his wife had left, with Eve and Al waving their goodbyes, Eve came in, sent the kids to bed, and said, "There. We did what you wanted. Now why don't you just go."

"What I wanted? What *I* wanted? Well, for crying out loud, you think I wanted food flung in our guests' faces? For God sakes, Eve, what *I* wanted? Or 'Leon's taking ballet lessons.' How about that? *That* makes an impression. That's an impression, you bet."

Eve stomped off to clear the table. "You heard me," she said.

"Those people mean business for me, Eve, and food for your big mouth. You know how many head of cattle that man moves in a month? In a year? No! No, you don't! Because everything's just given to you, no questions."

"No questions? I get nothing but questions—questions and ac-cusations. No matter what I do! No matter how I work and sacri-fice and do without! Nothing's ever good enough for you, is it, Al? Nothing's ever just right, not even your own son."

"Jesus."

"*Jesus* is right!" Eve was crying in the kitchen, slamming dishes into the sink. "He's your son, Al. Your *son*. And you can't treat him as well as you would a stranger. He's just trying—"

"Trying to what? Trying to ruin the carpet so we'll have to pay good money to replace it? Trying to embarrass me in front of— with all this ridiculous ballet talk. That's your fault, Eve. That's your doing."

"Trying to impress you!" Eve hissed. "Could you be so blind? He's trying to make you proud of him!"

"Oh, why, yes. Yes, yes. Of course," Al mocked.

And on it went, up and up, Eve sobbing and screaming, Al holding his ground, the two of them battling into the wee hours as the kids, perhaps, God willing, finally succumbed to the quiet, the peace of sleep.

When René got up in the morning, Al was sitting at the big table, behind his paper, and Eve was in the kitchen, stirring eggs and sipping coffee. No one was talking. Leon had already escaped to the woods. Jayne and René got up to the table.

"And how are the girls this morning?" Al said, cheerful-like.

"Good," René said for both of them.

Eve put the eggs on the table, then went back to the kitchen, leaned against the counter, and lit a cigarette. "René," she said, obviously furious, "when you finish your breakfast, you can go clean out your drawers and vacuum your closet."

"But—"

"No buts. And you can plan on helping me all day today, no complaining."

Al gave her twinkling, buddy-buddy eyes to say, *Watch out. Looks like there's gonna be hell to pay today,* which she both did and did not appreciate.

At church, which they attended at random intervals, the Sunday school teacher often spoke of sacrifice, of how Christ had given his last breath to those who opposed him, with prayers for their salvation. So, the teacher said, the path of Christian faith involved accepting everything that came your way, all the suffering and hatred and cruelty, without animosity or anger or resistance. But René wasn't like that, and neither was anyone she knew.

The church put together Christmas boxes filled with canned hams, homemade cookies, and old coats to give to the Indians, but that didn't seem like much. Hadn't they taken the Indians' sacred land? And weren't they living on it, spreading out to their heart's content without the least hesitation or regret? Brutality and force had got them what they wanted, and it certainly looked like they meant to keep it. You couldn't make a story of sacrifice out of that.

Some of the Indian kids whose grandparents and great-grandparents had survived the frontier battles were in René's Sunday school class. Their families had been starved and murdered, imprisoned on reservations, yet they folded their hands and bowed their heads just like the white kids, which made René wonder if they weren't the real Christians, the ones who knew what it meant to have faith, what it meant to love God in spite of a smoldering pit of loss.

She'd seen the pictures at the Indian Museum downtown. Right alongside the beaded moccasins and leather loincloths were old black-and-white photos of Indians frozen in pools of their own blood, or lying in disarray, limbs twisted at impossible angles, mouths eternally open, defunct flesh and scant clothing woven into snowbanks.

The whole arrangement put René in mind of a bottomless pool of hurt. Was she really living under the watchful eye of a tender, loving God, a God of mercy and forgiveness and protection? Then what about the Indians? And what about Leon? Because as far as René could tell, Leon was in a fight just like the Indians—a fight he hadn't asked for, didn't understand, and couldn't win. Just like the Indians, Leon was overmatched. He was going to lose, and it wasn't going to be fair or just or right.

But when it came to sacrificing something for Leon, it always seemed to René like there was an answer she couldn't remember or that she'd never known in the first place. She didn't know what to do. How was she supposed to help him? There were no instructions, no directions, no back passageways or hidden doorways opening into the sudden daylight of a clear solution. And mostly, she was watching out for her own skin.

From time to time she'd stop and scan the horizon, but nothing—nothing inside or out—was giving up any secrets.

Part Two

11

To Ripen, to Bring
to Fruition

It was a miracle of circumstances, involving things as far off as the Russian Revolution and two World Wars, that classical ballet in the tradition of Diaghilev had found its way to the frontier town of Rapid City, South Dakota. But there it was: the Academy of Ballet, founded by former Ballet Russe de Monte Carlo corps de ballet member Helen Gilbert. She had white hair that stood up around her head like a powdered-sugar halo, turned-out feet, shot ankles, arthritis in her hips and knees, and a waddle like a sea lion. She carried a stick around the classroom for tapping out the beat on the sprung wooden floor, poking some innocent's jutting-out ribs, or swatting an untucked behind. She weighed about two hundred and fifty pounds, having married, got pregnant, gained weight, and never got her body back. Plus, she was a big eater.

"Dancers use up a lot of energy," she'd say. "When you stop dancing, watch out. Everything changes but your appetite."

She'd sit on her stool at the back of the class, surveying the young dancers at the barre. "Why, after all this time," she'd say, stopping the music, coming over to jab some little girl in the stomach and push down her hips, "do you still have your great big butt hanging out? Now tuck it in like you're pinching a penny! And pull up. There." Or, like an empress, waving her stick menacingly to indicate the entire landscape, everyone as far as she could see: "I have never in all my life seen the kind of pig slop you girls are dishing up today. Suuuu-ey!" she'd squeal. "Now do it again, and pay attention! Watch yourselves! Focus, balance, concentrate! Leave the pig slop for the pigs!"

René was in Beginners, Leon in Advanced Beginners, and they all, Eve and Jayne included, started falling in love with the pure force, the aliveness, that was Mrs. G.

Leon's class met three times a week, and René's met twice. It was a lot of driving for Eve—down the hill, then all the way through town, out past the Canyon Lake Club—and she didn't want to make the round-trip twice in a single night, so she'd bring Jayne and some knitting or a sewing project that required handwork and sit in the waiting room until classes were finished.

Mrs. G didn't allow anyone to watch, but Eve would sometimes peer through a crack in the doorway. And as Helen Gilbert turned her wrath on some kid over a bungled combination or a lazy turnout, Eve would reminisce about being a girl down on the Bad River, about how the one thing she'd wished for most of all was to learn to play the piano. Though she knew it wasn't something her folks would even consider, not with seven children to raise—her father tending the back roads for the county, her mother wrung out from housework that seemed to come to nothing—still she'd wanted it.

She didn't hold anything against her parents—Lord knows, they'd had it hard enough—but if she had, it would have been that she'd got no lessons of any kind: no piano lessons, no dancing lessons, no language or embroidery or sewing lessons.

What she had got was a summer job working a farm near Hayes, South Dakota. She'd had to ride her pony, following the railroad tracks morning to night to get there. And though she'd packed herself a lunch, planning to stop for a picnic, the dumb thing had bucked her off twice on the way. She'd had to discipline him each time, then hold tight to the reins so he couldn't turn his head to bite her when she got back on. And after the second throw, which happened when the train came by, sounding its whistle and scaring her pony so badly that she had to chase him, limping through the open field until he'd settled down enough to let her come near, she couldn't risk stopping for lunch. She was twelve years old, by herself, and far out in the country. There wasn't going to be anybody to help her. She bit her lip, doubled the reins around her hands, and gave that pony a stiff boot.

She got herself all the way to the farmhouse, where the wife was sick, the farmer was in the fields, and the little kids were desperately in need of just about everything. She caught chickens and wrung their necks, bled them out, plucked and fried them for dinner. She killed three rattlesnakes in the barn, chopping off their heads with a garden hoe because the little ones couldn't play in the yard with a nest of rattlers nearby. She bathed the kids and nursed the wife—made her broths and mashed her food, brought her cool cloths and clean sheets. She stayed out there all summer. She was lucky that when school started, she got to come home and go into the seventh grade. She'd always done well in school, ended up class president, head of journalism club, valedictorian, so it was good of her folks to give her that chance. She hadn't had to keep on doing farm work. Some of the less fortunate ones had, but then, some hadn't wanted anything different.

After class, Eve would sit and chat with Mrs. G while the kids got changed into street clothes. Since Leon was the only boy—which meant the girls would have to let him through their dressing room, into the bathroom, to change, and he couldn't come out again until every girl was dressed and they gave him the signal—it took a while. So Eve and Helen Gilbert got to be friends.

Helen would tell Eve about her time in vaudeville, her stint with Ballet Russe, how she had friends who were still traveling the world, how if she hadn't got distracted with getting married and all that nonsense—ha-ha-ha. They both knew that story.

They'd get to chatting so much that Eve would always be the last one out of the studio. Other moms would poke their heads in to say hello, or just sit in their cars waiting for their kids to come out, but Eve and Mrs. G would go on and on.

And Mrs. G was thrilled to have Leon. "We need boys," she'd say. "If we could get more boys like Leon, then we could really do something."

Because Helen Gilbert had dreams and, like a shaman or a fairy godmother, she could make things happen. She had the charisma of someone who really knew things: she'd walked the streets of London and Paris and danced at their opera houses; she'd wandered the canals of Copenhagen and Saint Petersburg and performed for their monarchs and statesmen. And she made it clear that, though it rose and shaped itself from the basest limits of our existence—from sweat and bleeding blisters, from the inescapable force of gravity, from the endlessly circumscribed range of the body—ballet was nothing less than the one pure expression of humankind's ability to transcend, to make this coarse material realm

at once central, ethereal, and fully luminous, as if the very word—
ballet—meant nothing less than "to ripen, to bring to fruition."

Eve would get into such lengthy discussions with Mrs. G that
when they were all finally dragging back to the car in the pitch
black, she'd have to apologize. "Sorry," she'd say to the kids. "She
gets to talking and I just can't get away."

But they didn't mind. As Mrs. G went on about how dance sur-
passed all other art forms, how it lifted one beyond the mundane,
they were all ears.

"It's not like playing the cello," Mrs. G would start. "If you
want to play the cello, the cello's right there. You can just sit down
and learn to play it, right? But with ballet, you have to build your
instrument. You have to build your body. And you have to build it
in the right way before you can even begin to learn to use it. If you
do it right, it'll take you places you can't even dream of. And I don't
mean just different towns and cities—*inside* places, like that place
inside all of us that can fly!" She'd laugh, elated; then her face
would darken and contract, and she'd reverse direction without
even slowing down. "It takes determination and years of hard
work," she'd say. "It can be the doorway to everything beautiful,
sure, but you have to be *so* dedicated."

They listened. And as she spoke, their world expanded and became so brightly lit that their ordinary sky began to crack and chip
and fall away like the outgrown shell of a baby bird, and they could
see themselves emerging into this new order, this shining promised
land on the far other side of anything they'd ever known.

"If you don't build your body correctly, you won't be able to
take a single step with grace and purpose. But if you do, by God,
you could weigh five hundred pounds and still be a star. Look at
me." She'd stand up from the high stool at her desk and demonstrate a few simple steps—a port de bras or révérence or chassé,
pas de bourrée. And she was right: she was glorious.

"Too bad she can't take off some of that weight," Eve would say when they were back in the car. "It must make her terribly uncomfortable."

Then late one night, Mrs. G started talking about having a ballet class for the moms, which Eve was all in favor of, saying she'd be the first one to sign up.

"I can organize it," Eve said. "Just give me a list of who might be interested and I'll give them a call."

"You don't mind?"

"Not a bit. It'd be fun. It'll give me something to do while the kids are at school."

They both laughed.

"If you want to," Helen said.

"I can't wait. Really. I'd love to."

And just like that, they were partners.

Eve got the adult class going with all the zeal of the converted, and after only a few months, there was a write-up about Helen Gilbert and the Academy of Ballet in the R.C. *Gazette,* along with a picture of all the moms lined up at the barre in leotards and tights, their hair carefully sprayed into matching high bouffants. And somewhere between the pliés, the port de bras combinations, and the coffee klatches that followed, they started coming up with big ideas.

Mrs. G wanted her ballet school to put on *The Nutcracker.* They could do it at the local high school, she said. She was already the choreographer for the school productions, so she could arrange it. Eve could design the costumes and do the parent organizing, and everyone could pitch in with sewing, shoe dyeing, set painting, and carpooling to classes and rehearsals. If they all worked together and the kids worked hard—"*If,*" Mrs. G repeated firmly—they might just do something that had never been done before.

"Just imagine. A Snow Queen in a glimmering white tutu sailing through the air in a grand jeté to piqué arabesque," Mrs. G said—all of which she demonstrated in grand style with her head and arms—"right here at the Rapid City High School Auditorium. Nobody'll believe it." She laughed.

The choreography was in her head, and she could simplify it, she said, raising her eyebrows and letting her eyes roll. "As needed."

They dove in, forming parent committees and typing up phone trees. Helen drew sketches of costumes and handed them off to Eve, who tried to figure out how on earth she was ever going to get them made, especially with this group of women, some of whom had never done anything beyond hemming a pair of pants or sewing on a button. She made one pattern after the next, trying to find something everyone could get right so that she wouldn't end up having to rip out all the costumes backstage at the last minute and stitch them back together herself. She even came up with an idea for the Mouse King's headpiece from a craft magazine that appeared in the mail like a missive from heaven: papier-mâché.

Helen Gilbert was thrilled. "We're going to knock the socks off this little Podunk town, Eve, ready or not," she said one night after class. "We're going to give them something they've never even dreamed of." And after they'd had a long, nervous laugh, she added, growing serious, "Maybe we can have it all set by next year, Eve. Maybe. God willing."

It wasn't going to be easy, and it would take time, but they'd already taken the first steps. They were really going to do it.

12

Cheating Gravity

That fall Eve decided she'd had enough of living in the hills, spending all her money on gas, and they moved down from the mountain and into town, to a two-story house in a real neighborhood, across the street from a wooded field and the wide expanse of the Congregational church parking lot. Asphalt covered the entire hilltop the church had bulldozed, so there was plenty of room for Leon to go-kart, bike-ride, even practice driving a stick shift.

René would take off across their backyard for school, giving Chuck a pat as he milled in circles around the one big tree, then continue past the detached garage and rusty swing set. If the weather was just right, there'd be a million grasshoppers on the trail leading down to the neighbor's yard. She'd run screaming as they flew, latching onto her knee-highs or bare legs. But after that, the world would open into a wonderland.

She'd walk Clark Street until it curved to trace the bottom of the hillside, then scrabble up a steep, crumbling sandstone embankment to keep from going around the long block, cut through backyards to reach the crest of the hill, and follow the lightly worn footpath that ran through the prairie scrub. She carried her books and notebooks, but she never hurried. She'd stop to pick a handful of sage and breathe the deep perfume, just standing, looking out at the sky. And if there was rhubarb growing wild or green peas hanging over someone's fence, she'd linger, peeling the thin skin off the rhubarb stalk and biting into the tart fruit, or opening the peas at the seam and tipping her head back to pop them into her mouth. She'd take a detour to avoid a barking dog, kicking away any loose stones, feeling her way forward like her ancestors, the pioneers.

Not all that long ago, her very own great-grandfather had stopped somewhere not so far from here, right in the middle of Indian country, in what was now called Canning, South Dakota. He'd planted ten thousand trees to settle his claim. "We had peach trees and plum trees, apricots, crab apples. Ten thousand," she could hear Emma gasping. "Just imagine!"

From there René's grandma would plunge headlong into how the whole town would gather at their place every Fourth of July for a picnic because of the lovely shade; how the women would wear new summer dresses and bring dishes to pass—including grape and chokecherry pies; how her father's first wife had died from the hardships but his second wife, René's great-grandmother, had been as strong and steady as one of the big oaks. She'd been a nurse, and Emma would go on to tell René about the year a deadly pneumonia had come around to Fort Pierre, back when René's dad was still a small child. Most people had flocked to the hospital, where, in an effort to combat burning fevers, doctors were throwing open windows in the middle of winter—and at the very mention of this, Emma's brows would fly up in alarm. It was because of René's great-grandmother, the knowledge and skill she'd passed along, that Emma knew better than to let some doctor set a cold breeze on a soaring temperature. She'd kept her young family at home, sealed up the house against the slightest draft, coated chests and backs with mustard plasters, changed sweated bedsheets, brought hot broths and extra blankets, and prayed for salvation. And while the folks who'd run to the hospital were "dropping like flies," she'd tell René, every last one in her house had pulled through. "Which is the reason you're here today and I can get to tell you this," she'd say, her look of consternation finally giving way to a smile. Then she'd sigh. "So many died that year. No sooner would a person set foot in the hospital than they'd drop dead." Emma would shake her head, still disgusted, remembering.

And as René walked along to school, the prairie would seem to teem with those who'd come before, who'd made their way through this endless sea of cactus and yucca, outcroppings and wash-out gullies, just like the great explorers—by being tough and sharp and willing to stand apart. Even all alone in the middle of that wide open emptiness, René would feel she was in the midst of a bustle, the call of the meadowlark just adding to the general hubbub as a single billowy cloud sailed above her, high in the boundless sky, until she arrived at Lincoln Elementary in plenty of time for class.

In the third grade there was a new reading program students could complete at their own pace, with a chart on the wall to record each one's progress. René loved having her name up there and made sure to keep ahold of her lead. On the playground, she challenged kids to cartwheels and splits, to backbends and tricks on the monkey bars. On the uneven bars, she was the only one who could drop backward or forward and do an uninterrupted series of spins, her long hair flying behind her like a victory banner. And at Four

Square, she won so often the other girls started whispering that she was cheating.

"There's no way to cheat," René yelled at the ringleader when the girl finally accused her to her face. "Besides, you don't have to cheat to win a stupid game like that."

"You really think you're something special, don't you?" the girl said, which made no sense to René. Of course she thought she was something special. "You're so conceited," the girl went on. "That's what my mom says. She says you think you're the cat's pajamas."

Her mom? Cat's pajamas? René went inside to read.

Later that day, in music class, the teacher put Saint-Saëns's *Danse Macabre* on the school phonograph and told the students to draw whatever came into their minds. So René gave free rein to the whirling visions of dancers Mrs. G was constantly describing in ballet class—images of agility and accomplishment, of dancers executing heartbreaking feats of athleticism and artistry, which had instantly taken hold of René's imagination. She drew a mummy in high double pas de chat suspended weightless over a gravestone, and another in piqué arabesque, her impossibly long leg extending far above her head, pointing to the moon. She drew ghostly whirling dervishes in a line, en pointe, and vampires flying between mountains in distant grand jetés. And as the teacher held René's drawing in front of the class to extol its virtues, the same Four Square accuser from the playground smirked and coughed and said something to her nearby companions that made them all laugh behind their hands, which gave René plenty of reason to scowl, fiercely and openly, at the lot of them.

Eve went to the school for parent-teacher conferences and came home looking rattled. She threw her purse onto the kitchen table, then dropped into a chair and rummaged around for a cigarette.

René had been waiting—fidgeting, arranging herself, trying to remain poised and humble for the inevitable showering of praise. But now she felt a wave of something else entirely coming for her.

"I don't want you paying one bit of attention to those small-minded dullards," Eve started. "I've known their type all my life!" She lit a cigarette and took a long, deep drag. "You did great," she said, shaking her head. "Really. Your teacher said all kinds of nice things about you."

René hesitated. "Like what?"

Eve looked at her, seeming to take her measure.

"Well, the first thing she said was"—Eve effortlessly pitched her voice into a high, mocking register—" 'The other girls in class have mentioned, and I've noticed myself, that René is very proud of her long hair.' Can you imagine?" Eve rolled her eyes as she knocked the ash off her cigarette. "I just told her, 'Yes, I'm sure she *is* proud of her long hair. It's very beautiful!' What a dope! She clammed up after that and went over your schoolwork, which was perfect, excellent. Truly. You're doing such a good job, honey. Just keep doing what you're doing. I'm so proud of you." She stabbed out her cigarette. "Don't worry about it," she said. "I shouldn't have said anything. Don't even think about it." Then she marched up the stairs to change out of her good clothes before starting dinner.

René was stunned. So it wasn't just the other girls and their mothers, it was also her teacher. Everyone seemed to be in agreement about their general dislike of her. She was being talked about by the other girls and their mothers, by the other girls and her own teacher. And she started to consider that maybe there was something *off* about her. She felt she understood it instantly, intuitively, as if she'd known it all along. She was abrasive and arrogant. She was bossy, overbearing, driven. She was everything her own mother had ever accused her of.

For the next few days, back at school, René was quiet and, for the first time, unsure. But in her chest she could feel something like a caged animal beginning to growl and pace. It got louder and more insistent, roaring through the bars of its cage until she was forced to turn and look at it, to face it and listen to it, and she found that it had something important, something pivotal, to convey to her. And she came to a decision.

If they were going to stand against her, they'd soon find out that she was going to win. As far as René was concerned, this was going to be full-on War.

She dressed in her best clothes and brushed her hair to gleaming. She surged ahead in the reading challenge, completing levels three, four, five, and half of six before her teacher stood over her, pinching her shoulder with a sharp, bony claw, and said, "What are you up to? There's no more room on the wall."

René just looked at her. *So what?* she didn't say.

"Find something else to do during reading time," the teacher told her.

She used recess to practice leaps and arabesques on the playground, and she did handstands, cartwheels, walkovers, splits on the grass, letting out the stops, taunting the girls to distraction and drawing the attention of the boys.

The girls would huddle in a group, heads bent together, and if René walked anywhere near them, they'd turn and go the other way, looking over their shoulders.

"No more pretending to be friends," René told herself. "No more hoping they might like me." She followed them coldly and openly, pushing them into different corners of the playground as if she were herding sheep. "Baa," she bleated at them under her breath as they moved away. "Coming through."

Then one afternoon, Eve appeared at her classroom door.

"What are you doing here?" René said, running to greet her.

The other girls cut their eyes at her, exchanging sharp glances.

"I don't know," Eve whispered. "I got a call." She raised her eyebrows and gave René a *you know what I think of these bozos* look.

At home that night, René couldn't get the whole story, but from what she did get, it seemed that the girls had started visiting the school counselor just to complain about her—about how conceited and stuck-up she was, how she showed off all the time, how she was mean to them. On and on. Nothing new. But they were widening the circle, raising the stakes.

"Don't pay one bit of attention," Eve told her. "They're jealous. They're so jealous, they can't see straight."

It didn't seem to René that they were jealous; it seemed that they were mad, as if they felt that, from the very beginning, she'd been shellacking them in class and on the playground out of spite. It didn't make any sense. What was she supposed to do? Cut her hair because theirs wasn't as long? Keep herself to a single spin on the bars because the best of them could manage only two? Misspell all the spelling words on purpose? Just how self-annihilating did she have to be to avoid crushing these delicate prairie flowers?

"You bend over backwards for those girls. I've seen you," Eve went on. "Time and time again."

René didn't think she'd ever "bent over backwards" for any of them, but before this all started, she'd at least tried to fit in. She'd joined their after-school Bible club and memorized verses, reciting without a single fault, and she'd gone along to the Y whenever any of them invited her for free "open-swim" night, showing them water ballet moves and doing fancy dives off the low board. Who were these girls anyway, and why didn't they like her? Because she was good at things? Wasn't that the point? Weren't they supposed to be trying to be good at things?

"They're dying of jealousy," Eve was saying. "They're a bunch of mean little dopes, and they're trying to punish you for doing your best. It's absurd. And the teachers are no better," she said. "Ridiculous. They should be helping you, and instead they want to pull you down to their small-town, know-nothing level."

Then Eve stopped and looked at René so intently that René couldn't help but fix herself in place and listen.

"No one should ever have to give up what they want just to make someone else happy," Eve said. "You remember that. If you let them take it away, you can count on the fact that you're never going to get it back. Believe me. That much I know from experience. Firsthand." She paused. "If I were you, I'd just as soon stay away from the whole lot of them," she said. "Good riddance. That's what I'd say."

So it seemed that, from a certain perspective, René had succeeded in sailing right past those dull, ordinary, homespun girls, flying out to where they couldn't follow, far beyond the edges of their shrunken little maps, and good riddance it was. Good riddance to girlfriends, good riddance to playmates, good riddance to shared secrets and putting on each other's fingernail polish, good riddance to Saturday walks downtown with a dollar to spend, good riddance to long summer swim days, good riddance to all that junk. Good riddance to bad rubbish.

13

Laana

Laana Folger lived in the house just below René's, and though René passed alongside Laana's fence every day on her way to school, she never asked Laana to walk with her. Laana had greasy hair that fell in strings, and she was tall, which she tried to hide by stooping like an old lady. She was slow in everything, and René didn't want to be seen with her. Besides, René liked to walk by herself.

Laana started coming up to the far corner of René's yard and standing there queerly, brushing her hands through the swollen tops of the tall prairie grass, letting the grasshoppers perch on her skin and clothing as she watched René's house, looking every bit like she was trying to see right through the walls. When René asked Eve why Laana was just standing there, staring, Eve said that maybe she wanted to be friends, that maybe it would be nice of René to invite her up. So René did. They played outside, they played at Laana's house, and they played at René's house. But they never played at school. At school, they didn't even talk. There was one retarded boy in their class whose limbs bent at crazy angles and whose head and eyes rolled back and forth in unpredictable arcs as he walked his crazy walk around the playground, and there was Laana.

At Laana's house, there were dried-up dog and cat poops everywhere—piled under the sofas, scattered under the beds, in the corners of every room, sometimes right on the front doormat as you came in. Most of them were hard as rocks and gray or green, but some were fresh. After you'd caught a whiff of it, you could smell Laana's house from outside as you passed by on the road.

Her dad was home all the time, it seemed, sitting on the toilet, reading the newspaper with the door open. And everyone yelled. Even Laana. Once she got inside, her shyness dropped away.

"Shut the door, Dad! God! We have company!" she'd shout if they happened to spy him on the john during a game of jacks or while they were cutting out snowflakes. She'd stomp over and slam the door. But even as she returned to their game, the door would begin to slowly creak open on its hinges until it was just as wide open as before, her dad still sitting there, rustling his newspaper, turning the page.

"See, Lalee," he'd say. "It don't stay shut. It ain't my fault."

"God, Dad. God!" Laana would scream, throwing down whatever they were doing.

"We can go to my house," René would whisper.

At René's house, they'd organize the old *National Geographic*s René's grandma had given them, or try on René's mom's necklaces, or hold up sections of a new dress Eve was making and strike poses in the mirror. Or René would try to teach Laana to do a backbend, or a changement, or just to point her toe, all to no avail. But no matter what they did, Laana would gaze at René starstruck, her eyes moist and dreamy as the rest of her face hung slack.

Since Laana wanted to do everything René did, she started taking ballet lessons with Mrs. G, which René thought was unfortunate, being that Laana was so awkward in general. And once, just after René had worn a new, store-bought pantsuit to school—red, blue, and cream checked bell bottoms with a metallic thread, like tinsel, woven through, and a matching navy vest with silver buttons—there was Laana, standing on her front steps, about to head out to school in the exact same outfit, except with the red vest instead of the blue, her mom behind her, pulling her hair into a high ponytail. René stared in astonishment as she passed the house.

"Laana liked your outfit so much," Laana's mom called out. "She had to get one just like it. But see? She got the red vest so it don't match exactly. Imitation is the highest form of flattery. That's what they say."

René hurried past, not responding. This was going to cost her. This was going to give those other girls something to throw at her. At the very least, she could never wear her new pantsuit, not ever again.

"You want a ride?" Laana's mom hollered after her. "You're gonna be late."

René shook her head and kept walking.

"Ain't no big thing, little missy," she bellowed. "You keep on worrying yourself like that and you're gonna have ulcers before you turn thirteen, you know it?"

René put her head down and picked up the pace. She was almost out of range.

⌣

Laana's mom was kind of a bombshell. She had bottled blond hair that poofed around her head, then cascaded to her shoulders in feathery waves. She had a groovy record collection and was actually cool, like a swinger or a housewife you might see in a magazine. When the house was empty, René and Laana would kick the dog turds under the couch and play her records, making up dances in the living room.

Laana's mom and dad were always having cookouts in their crappy backyard, wearing stained parkas as they fired up the old grill and mixing cocktails for themselves in unwashed shakers. Their house was a crazy quilt of filth. Anything and everything was fine with them. They had TV dinners as a family, and sometimes, if she felt so inclined, Laana's mom would bend down and pick up one of the dog or cat poops with a Kleenex, throw it in the kitchen garbage, then go back to buttering a piece of toast or opening a box of crackers without even washing her hands.

Eve went down to have coffee with her one day, just to be neighborly. When she got home, she bent forward, leaning heavily against the kitchen table, one hand on her stomach, and said, "Oh, God. I think I'm going to be sick."

After that, whenever Laana came over, Eve would find a way to whisper things offhand to René, like "I don't think you'd be friends with her if she didn't live so close, do you?" or "She's just not up to your level, is she. Poor thing. Good grief. She's pretty dull, don't you think?"

"She's okay," René would counter, defending Laana even though she agreed, had agreed from the very beginning.

"I just don't see how people can live like that," Eve would confess once Laana had gone.

"It's not her fault," René would say.

But each time Laana came around, René would feel herself succumbing more fully to Eve's point of view. Eve was right. Spending time with Laana was like spending time with a stuffed animal or a rag doll. Plus, Laana had started shadowing her on the playground, gazing at her longingly from across the gravel lot, making small motions as if to test the possibility of approach. Nothing good was going to come of it. And suddenly Laana just didn't seem like someone worth hanging out with anymore.

Good riddance.

14

Unintended Disfigurement

For some reason no one could comprehend, Leon had started pulling out his hair. He'd pulled out all of his eyelashes and both of his eyebrows, and now he was pulling out the hair on top of his head. His forehead was eerily bald, the rims of his eyelids were exposed, swollen and raw, and there was a gleaming white bald spot widening on the crown of his head, like a shiny teacup saucer or a crop circle, surrounded on all sides by his thick, dark God-given hair.

He'd had to switch schools when they'd moved down from the hill. He'd started junior high as a new kid, at a school across town from all his friends, but that didn't seem like enough of a reason, Eve said.

"Keep your hands off it, Leon," she told him over and over. "Don't pick."

Life went along smoothly enough when Al wasn't home, which was most of the time. But when Al showed up, there'd be blazing arguments: "Leon—" this and "Leon—" that, and "Leon's hair—" this and "Leon's hair—" that, and "Leon's friends—" this and "Leon's dancing—" that, followed by "Well, you did—" this, and "You did—" that, and "You never spend any time, so what do you expect?" and "Just who do you think you are?" and "Are you just plain blind or are you retarded?" and "You can just go to hell!," sometimes with tears, sometimes with door-slamming, always deep into the night.

René would lie in bed, with Jayne in the bed next to hers, and keep watch out her window at the blinking red lights of the radio tower, listening as Eve and Al went on and on. Then, after two or three days of cold, silent glares between them—with no telling when the booby trap of a wrong word or a spilled glass of milk or an unfinished homework assignment was going to set off another round—and after long nights filled with skirmishes and reversals, great mountains of ammo plied into endless histrionics, Al would repack his suitcase and be off to look at cattle in Montana or Wyoming or "over east." And they'd only have to endure Eve's foul mood and aggravated replays for a few days before everything finally settled back into the regular routine, and there'd be some peace until the next time.

One of the many repercussions was Eve's belief that Al likely had another family—one he was spending time with and "squandering good money on"—probably somewhere up in Montana.

"I wonder if they know about us," she'd say, leaving the kids to conjure their counterparts—clean, quiet children with good manners and all the hair on their heads.

"I'd be almost sure of it," Eve would add, "if he wasn't such a god-damned tightwad."

Even after Eve and Al had spent an entire lifetime together—

often ending weeks and months of battle by wordlessly calling a truce and taking sandwiches to Canyon Lake Park, where they'd feed their crusts to the ducks and geese, then sit quietly, side by side, like any old couple, holding hands and listening to the water run over the spillway—in the days just after Al's funeral, Eve was still waiting for her mirror self, her double, Al's other wife, to step through the door, to claim her right and place, with unknown grown children lining up behind her to inherit. Even as Al's IRAs and brokerage accounts were renamed and transferred, his death record settled, his headstone finalized, carved, and placed, though Eve would sometimes become misty, other times she'd shift uneasily in her chair and cock her head warily to one side, waiting for the doorbell to sound or the phone to ring, as if the threat were still hanging heavy in the air, maybe finally ripe enough to drop.

When Leon and René were grown-ups, years after Leon had received his dual diagnosis—alcoholic/chemically dependent and bipolar—he was astonished to receive an additional diagnosis of post-traumatic stress disorder.

"It's like we grew up in a war zone," he told René. He laughed. "God. Jesus." He got serious. "I'm not kidding," he said.

René had no choice but to agree. Though she could remember times when she'd come home from school prepared for another knock-down-drag-out, only to find her parents lying together on the sofa in their work clothes, face-to-face, enclosed in each other's arms and fast asleep, still every therapist she'd seen over the past two decades had come to the same conclusion. She'd had the DSM-III code in her chart from way back.

"Jayne, too," Leon said.

Jayne had always seemed steadier than either of them, as though she'd somehow stayed above the fray. René thought perhaps her sweet, cheerful nature had protected her in a way that René's drive and Leon's willingness to take a fall had not. But lately Jayne had been having a hard time. Though she had everything anyone could hope for, she said—a job, a house, a good husband, sweet kids—there'd been about three months now when she just couldn't stop crying, and she didn't know why.

Since they were spending nearly all of their free time at the ballet studio, taking classes with Mrs. G, Leon and René progressed quickly through the ranks.

"Faster than a speeding bullet," Leon said on their way to the car after Mrs. G had given him yet another promotion, to the Advanced class this time. "See ya, sucker!" He sailed the airplane of his hand across the top of René's head, spreading his fingers in an aerial explosion. *"Boom!"*

But then, since Eve had to drive Leon five nights a week anyway, Mrs. G said that René was "close enough," so she might as well come along.

"Sucker, yourself," she said to him just before class. "Boom!"

He laughed and shooed her away as if swatting a gnat.

René got her first pointe shoes and marveled at the stiffness of them, at how she couldn't push her ankles far enough forward to get over onto the tops of them, and at the constantly shifting colors of pain.

And shortly after that, Mrs. G asked Eve if René might be willing to demonstrate for her Beginners and Intermediate classes. So every Saturday René would do her best, standing on her own at the portable barre in the center of the studio, performing whatever combinations Mrs. G called out, as perfectly as she could manage, reveling in her new, exalted status.

When she was finished demonstrating for all the lower classes, she'd take her place in the new partnering class Mrs. G had started in preparation for *The Nutcracker*. There was another boy now, Joey. So Mrs. G paired René with Joey, and Leon with a lovely girl just his age, Catherine.

Catherine was pale and freckled, with thick, yellow braids and a conspiratorial smile that made you feel like any minute the two of you were going to be sitting down to share your deepest secrets. Her family owned the largest actual gold mine in the Black Hills and was easily the wealthiest family in town. They had a swimming pool, a tennis court, a private zip line, and endless property in the hills, with housekeepers and cooks, groundskeepers and drivers, even an antique yellow motorcycle with a sidecar, which her dad sometimes drove around town, wearing an old leather helmet and strap-on vintage aviators just for fun. And, likely because René had been badgering her for an invitation, Catherine asked the pas de deux partners over to her house one day for lunch.

They arrived in the morning, remnants of a disappearing mist still lacing the treetops. While Leon and Joey went off to ride the zip line, Catherine and René sat by the pool, taking in the early Indian-summer sunshine. Catherine asked René if she'd ever carved someone's initials into her skin, and when René shook her head, Catherine got out two straight pins and showed her how to get started, first making little pinprick dots, then scraping between them, connecting the dots to make a line, then a letter. They both got to work, but when René looked over, Catherine was carving *JB*, for Joey Baker, into her thigh. René was carving *JB* too, because she certainly couldn't carve her own brother's initials into her leg.

"You should do Leon's," she told Catherine.

"No," Catherine said, not even looking up.

"Why not?"

In Pas de Deux class, Leon and Catherine were a perfect pair, their bodies matched like shadows. Catherine would spin and Leon would guide her lightly with just his fingertips, lending her speed and balance. Or Catherine would jump and Leon would lift her as she secured herself against him, letting his firm, strong hands handle her however he needed to. And, like René, Catherine could run at Leon and leap, and he'd catch her mid-flight, taking her into the next step or turn without the slightest hitch, with simple, continuous motion. They were a natural couple.

"Don't you like him?"

"I like him," she said, noncommittal. "But I *like* Joey."

"But we can't both put *JB*."

René was reeling, partly from the pain and beads of blood, partly from the way she was putting everything on the line, ruining her one chance to be friends with Catherine by making a fuss over the boys' initials, and partly from thinking how Leon would feel when he saw that they'd permanently branded themselves for the boy they liked best and no one had chosen him.

Catherine just shrugged and kept going. "Let's go get a snack," she said when they were done. "And we should put some alcohol on these."

So they went inside.

There was a sign on her enormous refrigerator door: TRESPASSERS WILL BE PROSECUTED!

René read "Persecuted," and could only think of being condemned and nailed to a cross, which was a turn the day seemed to be taking on its own.

"What does that mean?" she asked, feeling like a dumb baby. Something about the depth of Catherine's privilege and the solid foundation of her superiority had undone her.

"Oh, God," Catherine giggled, not answering. And though René was still in the dark, she made herself laugh like she was in on it.

The minute they tugged open the refrigerator, a woman in a white nurse's dress was at their side. "You sweethearts want something to eat right now?" she said. "I'm just making your lunch. Can you wait five minutes?"

"Sure, Molly," Catherine said. "We can wait." Then she looked at René like she was beginning to wonder what to do with her. "Let's go to my room," she said.

"Was that your mom?" René whispered as they took off down some steps.

Catherine didn't answer. She just turned and looked at René as if that was the most totally asinine question she'd ever heard in her life.

René followed her through the marble foyer, which had a wide upper-level balcony with an elaborately carved wooden railing, then down through a dark, interior hallway that seemed to go on forever. Along the way, Catherine pointed out rooms.

"There's the pool room, there's Daddy's library and office, there's the music room, here's a bathroom, there's the den."

Then they continued up some steps, turned a corner, and went through her bedroom, which had a pink canopy bed trimmed with tiny, dangling pom-poms, and into her bathroom, which had double sinks and multiple full-length mirrors. Catherine got down some alcohol, and they swabbed their new cuts.

"I wonder if they'll notice," Catherine said, her eyes shining.

René kept quiet. She hoped not. She hoped against hope that they would not.

They all had lunch together at a little table someone had set up under a tree in Catherine's back garden. There was a crystal pitcher of lemonade and tuna fish sandwiches on gold-rimmed china, along with potato chips, celery sticks, watermelon slices, and hand-churned strawberry ice cream with homemade chocolate-chip cookies.

They joked and laughed and ate everything in front of them, but the whole thing made René sad. Sad for herself, since it seemed clear that she would never have Catherine as a friend, and beyond that, she would certainly never have any of the cool things Catherine had. And sad for Leon. He liked Catherine. He liked her all-over freckled face and the way her yellow hair curled out from her thick braids. He liked her warm smile and the way he was accustomed to being near her, already adept at handling her, holding her. But whenever he was around her outside of the ballet studio, he couldn't seem to keep himself from smiling and acting shy, the confidence he had when they danced together apparently lost, or maybe just hidden away, waiting for some music to start. And as he sat at their glamorous summer lunch table, grinning at her, with no eyebrows or eyelashes and a big white bald spot gleaming like a searchlight from the top of his head, it was all too clear. None of this, none of what was here today, would ever be his. Not Catherine, not the swimming pool, not the high-flying zip line, not the trails through the woods, or the library, or the happy, carefree afternoon. Catherine was nice to him because she was rich and sweet and had good manners. But she had *JB* cut deep into her thigh, just like René did. And even if Leon didn't notice right away, it would be a while before the newly scabbed initials healed over.

The whole thing made René feel like a traitor.

They were waiting in the shade by the front door, under the stone portico with the second-floor terrace overhead, as Eve's old Chevy turned in at the bottom of Catherine's long driveway. It made its way around the circular drive and came to a stop just after the first set of pillars, brakes squealing. They piled in, and Eve took off, Catherine waving them goodbye.

"Did you have a nice time?" Eve asked.

"Yeah," Joey said.

"It was fun," René said, feeling the edgy magic of the afternoon and the long shot of having Catherine as her new friend already far behind her.

"It was okay," Leon said, looking disappointed and hopeless.

Joey gave Eve the whole explanation of the day, answering all her questions about how many cars were in Catherine's garage, and how big the swimming pool was, and how the maids were dressed. He couldn't help her with what Catherine's mom was wearing because no one had seen her. They'd seen her dad. He'd helped Joey and Leon get set up on the zip line, and he'd turned René on her side and tickled her, pretending to draw a bow across her belly when Catherine begged him to "play the violin." But they hadn't seen her mom.

"I hear she does all her shopping in Denver and Minneapolis," Eve said. "She buys fur coats and diamond earrings and all the latest styles." Eve was giddy. "Can you imagine?"

But they were tired. They'd spent the whole day imagining.

So after they dropped Joey off, they drove the rest of the way home in silence.

15

Where There's Water

Late one evening Mrs. G called, frantic.

"Oh, Eve," she said, "I'm so sorry. I've made a terrible mistake. Just terrible."

"What is it?" Eve said. They'd all just got home from ballet class and were having a bite to eat, Leon with his head down over his soup bowl.

"Oh, I can hardly say it." She paused.

"I'm sure it's not as bad as all that, Helen." Eve waited.

"Well, you know how some of the boys are wearing their hair in all kinds of crazy styles? Mohawks, shags, Afros, what have you—"

Eve took hold of the kitchen counter.

"Oh, Eve. I just figured Leon was doing his hair according to some new fad, and I said something to him in class about his 'wacky new hairdo.'" She took a breath. "I knew right away when I saw the look on his face. What a terrible mistake."

"It's bound to happen," Eve said in her best voice.

"Eve—? Is everything okay with Leon?"

Eve cleared her throat. "Can I give you a call later? We're right in the middle of dinner."

"Of course," Helen said. "Of course. I'm sorry. Please tell him. I love Leon. He's my buddy. I'd never do anything to hurt him. I hope he knows that. Please tell him how sorry I am."

"I will," Eve said, and she hung up and went straight to the other end of the house, to the family room, where Al was sitting, having finished his dinner earlier—"at dinnertime," he'd felt compelled to point out—and she fell into a chair.

Al was watching *Lawrence Welk* and eating ice cream, but when Eve came in, he looked up to see about her. And though his favorite clarinetist was bubbling a tune from the bandstand, he put down his spoon, set his bowl on the side table, and reached out to touch her arm.

"What is it, Eve?" he said.

As his hand settled on her forearm, Eve could hear the tenderness in his voice and feel the sudden weight of his concern, and she gasped and leaned toward him. She needed him, and he was there. He was right there when she needed him most. And her heart opened, just like a flower trusting in the warmth of sunshine opens to the light.

"Helen Gilbert called," Eve said, and she started to cry. "It's just terrible, Al. I don't know what to do."

"Well, now," Al said, patting her arm. "I'm sure it's not all that bad."

"It *is* that bad," she said, blubbering. "It's Leon's hair business." She wiped her eyes. "She didn't mean to, but she embarrassed him in front of the whole class today. She didn't mean it. She's so good to him."

Al paused and sank back a little. Then he said, "A person can't take everything on his own shoulders, Eve. You can't keep taking everything on yourself. At some point, Leon's going to have to take responsibility. You've talked to him again and again. I know you have."

"But it's so hard for him," Eve said. "Maybe we could do something—" She hesitated, wary, sitting up. "At least try something different." She paused again and dried her eyes before venturing headlong. "The Jensens thought maybe a psychiatrist—"

"The Jensens?"

"Yes, the Jensens," Eve said firmly, knowing full well what Al was getting at. According to Al, Eve would take the advice of her bridge buddy Doc Jensen over anyone's, even his, and for no reason other than the fact that Jensen was an optometrist and had a couple of letters after his name. "Not even an M.D.," Al would remind her, and not a very good eye doctor, either, from what he claimed to hear around town.

"Oh, for crying out loud," Al started. "The Jensens, the Jensens. I'm not going to send Leon to some voodoo head shrinker just because Doc Jensen has an opinion about it. Do you know how much that would cost? That's ridiculous." He took his hand back and picked up his ice cream bowl. "We're not looking for angles to get rid of our money, Eve. Contrary to what you seem to believe. I work hard every day. And we certainly don't have the kind of insurance the Jensens have. I guarantee you that! We just can't afford it."

"I know," Eve said, defeated by something deeper than their disagreement about the Jensens. She sighed. "What are we going to do, Al? If it keeps up—"

"I'll tell you what Jeb Bickman down in New Underwood says," Al continued, citing a friend of his own, one he knew Eve would never stoop to agree with just because Jeb had run a farm all his life—as if all that impossible hard work were nothing, less than nothing. "He says if it was his son, he'd take him straight to the woodshed. He says every time I see that Leon's been pulling out his hair, I should give him a taste of the strap. That's his idea. He says anyone who's had a taste of that will not want to repeat it. And he knows." Al paused, dropping his head at the thought. "It would make him think twice, I bet. I do believe that."

"Oh, Al, no. No. That's a terrible idea. I'd never allow it. Never."

"It's not a terrible idea if it works," Al said. "If it did work, we'd both be happy for it, we'd all be happy for it in the end."

Eve just shook her head.

"I don't like it either," Al said. "Not any more than you do."

They both looked to the TV, to Bobby and Cissy dancing a quickstep, and Al stood up to take his empty bowl to the kitchen. As he passed between Eve and the television set, he turned to her and did a little hop, skip, slide combination that almost made Eve laugh. She smiled and shook her head at him, which was enough. He laughed.

"Want some ice cream?" he said, turning the corner.

She shook her head as she blew her nose. "No, Al. No, thanks."

That winter they joined a carpool to ballet so that Eve didn't have to drive every day. It was crowded and smelly and chatty, and mostly René was late getting ready, so there'd be a car in the driveway after school every day, honking for them to hurry up. The kids were tired and grouchy, and whenever it was their turn, the moms felt put out about having to drive.

One of the moms had a small hatchback, so whenever it was her day to drive, Leon had to ride behind the backseat, basically in the trunk. He was scrunched in there one night after dance class, as usual, his body bent like a contortionist's, when something René couldn't decipher started up between him and the girl whose mother was driving. Was it something about his eyebrows and eyelashes missing or his freaky-looking bald spot? Maybe repaid with a shot about the girl's ridiculous open-crocheted gloves, which couldn't have possibly kept her hands warm, or about all her whining in spite of being up in the front seat, right next to the heater? Whatever it was, suddenly the mom slammed on her brakes and the car came to a screeching halt in the middle of a dirt road, well before their turn onto Clark Street. It jolted them all forward in their seats, and Leon barely caught himself against the rear seatback.

"That's about enough outta you, *Mister Ballerina*!" the mom screamed at Leon, catching him in the rearview mirror. "Now get out! Get out of my car! You can walk home."

It was dark. There was snow on the ground and thick patches of ice on the cracked sidewalks. It was deep winter, and they'd all just danced a full class of jumping combinations as Mrs. G talked about *ballon* and how professionals hardly make a sound when they land, even from the greatest of heights, how they use the power of their breath and the strength of their legs to keep them, paradoxically, aloft and light. Leon and Joey had attempted single tours and double tours to one knee over and over again for at least half an hour straight. There was no one in that car who wasn't bruised and clammy and still sweating.

René could see that Leon was stunned, bushwhacked, but he opened the hatchback and started to climb out.

"Hey," she said, startling from her exhausted stupor. "Hey, don't!" she called to him.

But Leon was already gone.

"You wanna get out, too?" the mom suddenly growled at her.

Like a small animal startled by a sharp noise or a bright light, she didn't move. She needed a minute to think about it. But as soon as Leon closed the trunk, the mom tore off, throwing gravel.

René turned back to see Leon tucking his head into the wind. He was still in his ballet slippers and tights. The mom had been honking for him after class, and Leon had grabbed his clothes as he came running out to the car, but he'd forgotten to change his shoes. He'd left his street shoes back at the ballet studio. René turned and watched as Leon bent against the night, struggling forward on the icy cement in his thin dance slippers until, sinking farther and farther into the darkness, he finally disappeared against the black horizon.

I should've got out with him, she thought. *If she was going to do something like that, I should've gone with him.* But she was tired, and she didn't want to walk in the cold, and it had all happened so fast. Still, she shouldn't have let him get out like that. She thought that over and over.

When the carpool finally stopped at her house, René ran inside and told Eve. But when Leon came through the door, he ignored all of Eve's questions, went straight up the stairs to his room, and didn't come out.

And as René sat in her bed that night, looking across the hall at Leon's closed bedroom door, she couldn't help but wonder where all the hurt and anger went after something like that. Did it just disappear as a person grew older, dissolving in a mist of resignation and forgetfulness? Or did it crystallize, so that you carried it with you, building layer upon layer as the years went by, each incident adding to a more solid core of pain, until you came to face the world more rock than flesh?

As she lay in her warm bed, one thing became clear: she hadn't got out of it simply by staying in the car. Watching Leon trudge through the snow in his ballet slippers, seeing him slip and catch himself on the icy pavement, had made her just as miserable as if she'd got out herself and gone with him—maybe more. And she began to feel that these random torments—which seemed to shift and change shape arbitrarily, like the fleeting pictures made by colored shards in the turning of a kaleidoscope—were going to follow her no matter how slyly she angled to avoid them. She hadn't won anything by staying in the car, but she'd lost something—something, she could now see, she wasn't going to be able to get back.

So she lay quietly, closing her eyes.

There was nothing to do about it.

And as the misery and self-loathing began to subside, there was once again the familiar open space of her breathing and heartbeat, which seemed to have been continuing all along at the very bottom of everything, like a pristine spring, unable to keep itself from eventually rising up, or like the first few bars of music at the beginning of a combination in dance class, signaling a whole new chance. It didn't make any sense, but there it was. Right there. So close she could feel it, could know it without being able to name it. In spite of everything, she could turn her mind and feel her world quietly, patiently waiting for her to come around. But now, welling up alongside that fresh, welcome hope of a brand-new start, she felt a confusion that was something like being lost.

"If you ever do get lost," Al had always told her, "just look for a stream. Where there's water, sooner or later there's going to be a town."

Though there wasn't going to be a stream, and she wasn't looking for a town, the instructions circled in her head like an unsolvable riddle until she finally fell asleep.

16

Welcome the New Order

By the time she'd turned ten, René didn't walk. Anywhere. If she needed to get from the kitchen to the family room, she'd just make up a combination—maybe a quick relevé, then chassé, pas de bourrée, grand jeté, grand jeté, chaîné turns to arabesque—and she'd be there. When she was on the move, no one could stop her. Leon and Jayne would jump aside as she spun through a doorway or leapt across the landing at the bottom of the steps, and if Eve and Al were locked in a quarrel, she'd sail right past, spinning like a twister, calling "Sorry!" as they stepped out of her way.

It helped that there was very little furniture and bare wood floors. In the dining room was the collapsible maple table Al had bought Eve for their anniversary. They'd left Jayne and René with a sitter and Leon with one of his Little League friends and driven to the factory in Minnesota to pick it out. Eve kept both sides folded down and pushed it up against a far wall. She put a protective tablecloth over it and placed a bouquet of artificial flowers in the narrow center of the tabletop, and though they brought it out only twice a year, for Christmas and Thanksgiving, whenever she dusted, she took the time to polish it to a sheen. And there was the new Hammond organ, with the countless pedals, buttons, levers, and pegs, fitted into the dining room alcove. Al had bought that for her too, after one of their endless discussions had turned to the things she'd always wanted but never got. Now Eve was taking ballet lessons, organ lessons, making all the costumes for *The Nutcracker,* and volunteer-teaching the little kids' Pre-Ballet class for Mrs. G.

"Far as I can tell, the money's going out, out, out," Al would sometimes complain, but when Eve looked at him, searching for the man who'd bought her all those things in the first place, he'd add, "And why not? Why—not," just trying to keep his mouth shut.

In the living room there was only a slim sofa and two small side tables, all pushed back against the wall opposite the front window, so the way was clear. And around the corner, as you entered the family room, Eve's sewing machine took up just one side of the wide hallway that led to Emma's old rocker, a yard-sale couch, and a television with tinfoil rabbit ears. When René got to the far end of that last room, she had to stop and either sit and watch TV or deliver her message or do the chore she'd been sent to do, if she could remember what it was, then turn around and make her way back with a brand-new combination—maybe a single pirouette, then tombé, pas de bourrée, glissade, glissade, pas de chat, pas de chat, run, run, run, leap!—whatever she wanted, nothing and no one to stop her.

⁓

Leon's baseball season came to a close with a letter saying he'd been selected to pitch for the Rapid City All-Star team. Al was out of town, so the rest of them went to the game without him, René and Jayne dragging back and forth to the busy concession stand for yard-long licorices and autumn snow cones as Eve screamed her lungs out from the bleachers and ran down to the high chain-link fence to fight the ump on calls. But Leon's team lost to Sturgis, which somehow made Al's absence more acceptable to everybody.

Then one day, Mrs. G started casting for *The Nutcracker*. Leon, Joey, Catherine, and René had multiple roles. Leon and Joey would be Russians, then partner René and Catherine for the Candy Canes; Leon would be the Mouse King and Joey a soldier; René would dance the Mechanical Doll, and Catherine the Harlequin; and they'd both be Snowflakes as well as Chinese emissaries to the Land of the Sugar Plum Fairy. Even Eve was given a part: Mother Ginger. She started making herself a hoop skirt wide enough to cover all the students in her Pre-Ballet class. So far it was just a wire frame held together with cloth ties, so when Eve put it on, they could see all the little kids, including Jayne, crouching around her feet as though they were sitting under an enormous see-through umbrella. The kids would scoot along on the floor as Eve walked, and when she lifted her skirt, they'd pop out and scatter, squatting and jumping like lost little jack-in-the-boxes.

But mostly Eve was in Mrs. G's basement, working with her group of sewing ladies. René and Leon would go home with Mrs. G after class and end up waiting on her basement sofa, Mrs. G's little mop of a Pekingese right next to them, up on the cushions. They'd leaf through their schoolbooks as Eve shouted orders, ground her teeth, and ripped apart some poor woman's stitches for the third time.

"It's back-asswards, Bea."

She'd tear out the seam without even standing up.

"See? It can't go on that way. *This* end has to attach over *here*. Otherwise you can't get your arm in. Then *there's* your seam. Here. I'll pin it for you."

She'd hand the lady a pinned-up seam.

"Now all you gotta do is stitch it. Right here. And they all go the same way around. Just like that."

The woman would go away, disgusted not only with Eve's irritated tone but with the whole process, and Eve would turn back to her machine and work on the complicated mess beneath her own needle for only about a minute before there'd be another question or someone else's screwup to fix.

Winter came early, and they found themselves heading for *Nutcracker* rehearsals in below-zero temperatures, their Levi's, damp from the dryer, freezing stiff on their legs before they could even get to the car. There were a million things to learn and practice and perfect. They did everything over and over, straightening, refining. Catherine's blisters broke and started bleeding, so she wrapped each toe first in gauze, then in first-aid tape, while Leon leaned over her, making grimacing faces to sympathize. And as dress rehearsals approached, Mrs. G started saying she was going to tear her hair out.

On the staging side, Mrs. G had rallied some of the high school's drama club kids to make the sets, but their commitment was spotty, and things weren't turning out the way she'd imagined.

"We need a tree, Eve," she worried. "It has to start small, then get bigger, bigger right onstage, till it reaches all the way up to the catwalk. How in the *hell* are we going to do that?"

Eve glanced up from her hot glue gun and shrugged her shoulders. She was bending over a card table, putting the Snowflakes' headpieces together—pinning silver pipe cleaners onto a spray-painted base, then gluing them in place so that it looked like a small, icy crown. She glued, held the crown up to the light to check the positioning and angle, then glued again.

"I have no idea," she said through the straight pins she was holding between her teeth.

"Jesus Christ, Eve," Mrs. G said, pacing. "We have to figure this out. It's the most important part of the whole ballet."

Eve raised her eyes skeptically.

"Well," Mrs. G conceded, "it's certainly *one* of the most important parts. And with the way these kids are dancing," she continued, "it may well end up being the most *interesting* thing that happens." She laughed. "It's got to be extravagant, over-the-top." Then she came to a halt. "Good God, Eve," she said. "What have we gotten ourselves into?"

"Hell if I know," Eve said, still not stopping.

There was something disarming and unifying about the level of concentration suddenly permeating their house, as if the very walls and floorboards were taking on a new order, committing themselves to the virtues of proficiency and correct alignment.

Leon could be found at all hours in the front room, practicing his Russian steps. There was what Mrs. G called the "Cossack Hop" and "Around the World," and he had to be able to do both sharply, strongly, with precision and speed, Mrs. G said, just like he threw a fastball. And every evening after dinner, René would put on her toe shoes and practice bourréeing lightly back and forth across the dining room. But Mrs. G was right: the pounding of her feet against the floor sounded like gunshots; she was going to scare the audience to death; they were going to have to wear earplugs.

Eve's sewing corner was exploding with all colors of satins and ribbons, zippers and feathers, sequins and lace. There were parts of legs and arms and halves of bodices piled here and there, scattered all over the hallway. Eve would be on the phone with the other sewing moms night and day, explaining how one thing fit into another—"No, not *that* way, the other way!"—and how they shouldn't be afraid, they should just go ahead and sew it up.

Then late one afternoon, Mrs. G asked Eve to meet her at the high school, so René and Jayne tagged along.

"Go out and stand in the audience, Eve," Mrs. G said, as she directed the drama club kids to pull out the sets. "And move around. One side to the other. Tell me what you think."

Act One included a large painted fireplace, a big grandfather clock, and a Christmas tree on rollers with garlands and old-fashioned candle lights, all set against a screen painted to look like pink scroll wallpaper. There was a larger tree hidden behind a scrim. When Clara returned to cradle her beloved Nutcracker and the clock struck twelve, the scrim would lift and the bigger tree would be wheeled forward into the light, while the smaller one, pulled by an almost invisible tether, was rolled offstage on squeaky wheels.

"It's the best I could do," Mrs. G said, shaking her head in disgust. "Just about makes me sick."

"It's perfect," Eve said. "I think it's going to be just right."

"At least the snow's all set," Mrs. G said. The drama kids were going to be up on the catwalk, and on Mrs. G's cue, they'd sprinkle glittering white confetti down on the dancers at the end of Act One. "Good God, it's going to be slippery," she kept saying. "I just hope it doesn't kill somebody."

For Act Two, there were thrones for Clara and the Prince, tilting painted candy canes ten feet tall, and brightly colored, oversized gumdrops, lollipops, and licorices arranged across the back of the stage. And that was it.

"It looks marvelous, Helen," Eve said. "It'll be perfect."

"There's supposed to be a sleigh," Mrs. G said, coming up to the footlights, standing over the orchestra pit. "There's supposed to be a sleigh that floats right up in the air, carrying Clara and the Prince from the enchanted forest to the Land of the Sugar Plum Fairy, but that's beyond me." She sighed. "I think our Prince and Clara are just going to have to walk." She laughed, not happily. "Sounds just about like it, doesn't it, Eve?"

"Sounds just about like it," Eve echoed.

Then, with Thanksgiving drawing nearer, Mrs. G handed out packets of tickets and told all the kids to go door-to-door.

"People in this town don't know an arabesque from an out-house," she said. "You have to convince them. Tell them what we're going to do. Tell them we're going to give them a show they won't ever forget. You have to make them believe!"

So René and Leon divided up the map. He got on his bike and headed for the houses on the far side of Mount Rushmore Road, a wool scarf tied just under his eyes like he was a bank robber and large bundles of tickets bulging from his pockets, while René simply put on her mittens, grabbed some tickets from the stack on the countertop, and started ringing the doorbells close to home.

Eve had found a Nehru jacket pattern at the fabric store and sized it down for the Chinese costumes. They were bright green brocade with braided gold trim around the neck and off-center down the front. René and Catherine would wear black tights, black beanies, dyed black pointe shoes, and would have to practice shuffling and bowing in unison.

The Snowflake costumes were long white tutus with silver trim and shining silver crowns. Some of the girls in the back would wear long-sleeved white leotards and tights, with tinsel fringe sewn down their arms, across their chests, and down each leg. Mrs. G called them "Icicles," but René thought they looked more like snow-covered Indians.

René's doll costume was pastel green with a pink tulle underskirt. It had bright sequin flowers outlining the bodice top. Eve tied a wide satin ribbon around her waist, cinching a metallic-painted windup key made of heavy cardboard onto her back, and told her to bend, then stand, then jump. When the doll number started, René would have to be bent in half, as though she were a completely useless mechanical toy, until Drosselmeyer pretended to wind the key and she jerked up, up.

"That'll work," Eve said. "Thanks be to God."

Leon and Joey got fitted into their Russian costumes, which included big furry hats.

"Those are going to be fun under the lights," Mrs. G laughed. It was already dark outside. "I don't know if they're going to be able to wear those, Eve."

Eve shrugged. "Fine," she said. She took a deep breath and kept gathering and repinning the tulle to the fitted bodice on one of the older girls.

"You can try them," Mrs. G said to the boys. "See how it goes at dress rehearsal. Either way."

Eve and the sewing women had been tacking, stitching, taking up, letting out all day, and they each had a stack of costumes taller than they could carry to take home and fine-tune before the first dress rehearsal, which was just a week away.

Tickets were sold, sets finished, dances in various states of readiness, and now the costumes were nearly completed. A couple of dress rehearsals to iron out lighting cues and staging, and it would be *Nutcracker* time.

"Mrs. G looks like she's about to blow a gasket," Eve said on the drive home. "And when this is all over," she went on, "you kids can just check me into Yankton." Yankton was the insane asylum, and

Eve talked a lot about going there. "Looks like I'm going to be up late again," she said. "And there's no dinner. Good thing your dad isn't home."

"That's okay," Leon managed, holding his share of the costumes Eve still had to tweak. "I'm not hungry."

"I am," René said, letting three tutus fall to the floor. "Let's get pizza."

"Hawaiian pizza," Jayne said, her voice muffled by layers of netting and shiny, sequined polyester.

"Hawaiian pizza and Coke!" René said.

"Okay," Eve said. "We'll stop at Shakey's."

Jayne and René turned to each other in the backseat. If they hadn't been trapped under so much fabric, they might have jumped up and down.

Eve drove straight past the turnoff for their house and continued up Mount Rushmore Road, all the way to the top, where they sat with their elbows propped on plastic red-and-white checked table-cloths and listened to the mechanical cowboy band, Eve holding her head in her hands, taking deep breaths and sighing wearily at the day behind them as they waited for the beautiful ham-and-pineapple pizza and pitcher of Coke that were definitely in their future.

"Well, we've come a long way," Eve said, looking up, dark circles making full moons around her eyes.

Leon nodded.

"One—more—week!" René started to chant, and Jayne joined in, banging the table.

"Oh, Jesus," Eve said, smiling. "Stop. Good God. Don't remind me."

"Jeez," Leon said, laughing happily, shaking his head. "Give somebody a break, why don't you."

17

Similar, Reversed

At school, René did her work like she was punching a clock. Dancing the way she was dancing left no room for anything else. She didn't think about Al and Eve and how they'd scrap and brawl; she didn't think about Leon and his more and more alien appearance; she didn't think about the other girls or what they might be thinking about her. As she sat at her desk, as she walked home, as she fell asleep, she went through her steps. She ate breakfast reviewing point by point—arms, head, shoulders, hips—outlining what was required to do the pirouettes or manage the sautés. She worked her arches, taking her feet out of her shoes and rolling up to the pointe, down to the ball, strengthening her metatarsals as the teacher explained how to divide and multiply fractions, how to find a common denominator. And with her mind on only one thing, without being pulled away or taken prisoner by random intrusions coming at her from the edges, she discovered that where there was focus, there was also stillness, rest.

Then one day, warming up for a full rehearsal, she suddenly found it—that elusive, wondrous place Mrs. Gilbert was always talking about, where the fixed outline of the body met the ever-longed-for freedom from confinement, where she was unbound, unfettered, where she could throw off the shackles of gravity and flesh and really dance. She dove in headfirst, as if flying from a high cliff, through an expanse of open air, straight down into the glistening embrace of deep water.

Mrs. G took one look at her and stopped the class. She came over, stood splay-legged, leaning forward on her stick, and put her face right up to René's, her eyes bulging.

"And just what in God's name do you think you're doing?" she said quietly, not shouting, but with a deep rumble, a bowels-of-the-earth kind of trembling in her voice.

René had been demonstrating for Mrs. G's Saturday classes for almost a year. Once in a while, after they'd finished teaching, Mrs. G would take her out to Dairy Queen for something to eat. René would always order the same thing: a fish sandwich and a lime slush.

What did she think she was doing? Was this Mrs. G's way of congratulating her? After all, she was only manifesting the most magnificent form a human body could display—loose and open, free and all-encompassing. Hadn't she seen it? Was she kidding? René could feel the heat of Mrs. G's breath on her cheek, and she could sense her own face going white, her blood running cold as creek water.

After staring at her deeply, searching René for the place in herself where she was hiding, Mrs. G said—her voice still shaking, but now rising in a tremendous, uncontrolled crescendo—"*Never* in my life have I *ever* seen *anything* so sloppy, undisciplined, lazy, junky, trashy, lousy, and, besides that, *completely crappy*! *Never!*"

The whole studio turned to look, including all of the kids René helped teach.

"Now get it together!" Mrs. G screamed at her. "Pull up, place your hips. You know better! I don't want to see garbage like that from you ever again! Not ever! Do you understand me?" René nodded repeatedly as Mrs. G walked away mumbling, "What in the *hell*? What kind of *idiotic*—?" She struck her stick against the floor. *"Again!"* she cried.

She restarted the music, and René uncoiled the knots of panic in her joints and slowly, carefully went back to the steps as she'd always done them—guarded, controlled, managed, contained. And as she concentrated to hold all the pieces of herself in check, to not let a millimeter of movement creep in where it didn't belong, one thing became clear: this was not going to be about freedom. It wasn't going to be about letting loose, letting go, or getting what she wanted. It was going to be similar, but reversed. She was going to have to rewind, forget her yearnings; she was going to have to use her judgment and clarity, her supervision and control to create an outcome; she was going to have to build a direction by wrestling and conquering, by attending to the most minute detail, by controlling her body and mind beyond the realm of the ordinary. Extraordinary control. No surprises. If she was going to be transported by anything, she was going to have to transport *herself*—through discipline and technique. She was going to have to know the rules, perfect them, make them unquestionable, become them, so that she stood above reproach, above even the thought of being unworthy or at fault. Once she'd done that, it would be *her* arena, no one else's. So whatever happened from here on was going to be because of René. Whatever she did belonged to *her,* no one else. And her time would come. But for now, finding her place, making her way, was most certainly not going to be about freedom.

All through the second dress rehearsal, which was going much worse than the first, Mrs. G was yelling and stamping her feet.

"You know what they say," she told Eve when it was finally over. "Bad dress rehearsal, good performance." She let out a "Ha!" that was definitely not a laugh. She was beside herself. The first performance was scheduled for that evening, and there'd be four performances to get through before it was done.

"That was a bad one," Eve conceded.

Eve almost never said things like that to Mrs. G.

"What was so bad about it?" René asked when Mrs. G took off at a run after someone backstage.

"Good God, I think she's going to have a heart attack," Eve said. She started gathering her things. "Oh, the lights were all haywire, the Snow Queen was completely in the dark, and half the soldiers were on the wrong side. And the mice still can't see where they're going. They were all over the place," she said to Rene. They were collecting their coats from where they'd left them in the orchestra. "I almost went offstage without Jayne getting back under my skirt. Did you see?" She laughed. "Well, there's not much to do about it now," she said. "We're all doing the best we can."

There were just three hours before they had to be back at the auditorium. Mrs. G had told everyone to keep going over their steps again and again, and to return at five-thirty sharp because the curtain was going up at seven, ready or not.

Everyone was back on time, and the Friday night performance was a great success. Tutus sparkled, lights hit their marks, dancers executed steps in sync, mice miraculously found their way through the battle scene, and Mother Ginger got all her little ones under her skirt and off the stage in one piece. Everyone was thrilled.

"No celebrating yet," Mrs. G warned. "We've got three more performances, don't forget. No room to jinx ourselves." But she was shaking hands, carrying around bouquets, accepting congratulations like everybody else. Mostly she seemed pleased and relieved that the problems of the dress rehearsals had disappeared.

And the next two performances went just as well.

"One more time," Mrs. G said, coming down under the stage to the dressing room after the finale on Saturday night. There'd be a matinee on Sunday afternoon; then it would all be over. "Go home. Get a good rest. Tomorrow, eleven o'clock sharp."

Eve hung up her hoop skirt. René put her shoes under her chair and her headpieces on the counter. She placed her silver crown for the snow scene in the box with the others, as usual. Then they all bundled up against the cold and headed out, happy.

When they got home, Al was there, sitting at the kitchen table.

"Well," he said as they came trooping through the door at ten-thirty, "how was the performance?"

"Great!" René said.

Al laughed. "Well, my."

Leon took off for his room.

"Great job, Leon," Eve called up the stairs. "Oh, it was good," she said to Al, exhausted and invigorated at the same time. "I think it's all been pretty good, which is a shock."

"I'm not surprised," Al said, standing up to give her a kiss.

"I still have a little makeup."

"You've been working so hard, Eve," he continued. "I'm not surprised. Not one bit."

"When did you get in?" she said.

"Just drove up. Just this minute. From over east. Highmore."

"Run to bed," she told Jayne and René. "Another big day tomorrow." She turned to Al. "You coming?"

"You're coming?" René said, grabbing his arm.

"That's why I'm here," he said. "I couldn't miss it. Not after the way everybody around here's been working so hard—every day, day and night," he said, singsong. He laughed.

René gave him a hug. He was her dad—the one who'd danced her around on his cowboy boots, the one who'd helped her plant a peach pit in their garden in Philip and, after she'd watered and tended and watched it for weeks without so much as the tip of a shoot poking up through the dead dirt, had secretly gone inside, brought out an enormous cantaloupe, buried it, and told her to run get her trowel. He'd matched his astonishment with her own as she'd dug into the newly tamped earth. It had been confusing and led to endless discussions of the properties of seeds and their bewildering capacity to create an entirely different kind of fruit, but still. This was *her* dad. And now, he was being *her* dad to everyone.

"Whoa—!" he said, lifting her and Jayne off the floor as they swung from his arms. "Off to bed, like your mom said. See you in the morning."

They kissed him good night and skipped up the stairs for bed and sleep. Al was coming to *The Nutcracker*. He was going to see everything Eve and Jayne and Leon and René had been working on for so long.

In the morning, Eve gave Al his ticket and told him not to be late.

"René and Leon are both in the first scene, so you won't want to miss it," she said as they hustled to the car.

Al was sitting at the kitchen table, still in his pajamas. He looked at the ticket and nodded. "And after," he said, "I'm taking you all out to Daisy Dell for dinner."

"Right!" René hollered from the back door.

"We won't be dressed—" Eve started.

"You don't have to be dressed up," Al said. "It's just us."

"Well, all right," she said, grabbing her coat. "Let's go," she called to the kids. "Come on. The weather's really lousy. Let's hope people show up."

And they were out in the car in a freezing rain, skidding their way down, one more time, to the auditorium.

Eve sent Leon to peek out from the wings and make sure Al was in his seat before the curtain went up.

"He's here," Leon reported.

"Good," Eve said. "I know he'll be so proud of you. Just do what you always do, honey," she told him as he walked away. "Break a leg."

And the music started, and the curtain went up.

Everything went along without a hitch through the first scene. Then Clara went to caress her Nutcracker, and René dashed down to the dressing room, as usual, to get the doll makeup off her face and make a quick change into her Snowflake costume. She had to get back up into the wings and in line with the others before the music for Scene Two started and the snow began to fall. The box of silver pipe-cleaner crowns would be backstage, as always, so she'd just pin one into her hair before taking her place; then she'd enter stage right, at the front of the line of dancing Snowflakes, with light-as-air bourrées and floating ports de bras.

She changed into her white tutu, ran to get up into the wings, stopped at the crown box, and to her amazement, to her total stupefaction, it was empty. The other Snowflakes were all in line, each with a dazzling silver crown pinned in place. The crowns were to be put back in the same box after every performance so that everyone would have one. What had happened? Where was hers? She stopped everyone she could get her hands on.

"Where's my crown? It's supposed to be in here!"

No one knew anything. Eve and Mrs. G were nowhere in sight.

"There might be one on the other side," one of the drama club girls finally said.

"What?" But there was no time to argue. Eve's costume room was on the far side of the stage. Maybe there was an extra.

"You could go check," the girl said. "If you run through the hallway, you could go quick."

She couldn't go on without her crown; Mrs. G would have her hide. But, more than that, she couldn't miss her cue.

"Mrs. G is going to kill me," René said as she took off running in her Snowflake costume, out a side door, slipping on her toe shoes through the polished school hallways. She tore past the ticket booth and concession stand the drama kids had set up, and hightailed it to the other end of the stage, where Eve was sitting in the costume room. "My crown!" she yelled.

Eve jumped up and they dug around backstage until they found an errant silver crown lying on the floor, next to the box of long ribbons the girls used for the Candy Cane number.

"Some idiot must have dropped it back here last night," Eve said.

"Hurry, hurry," René pleaded, desperate.

So Eve was standing behind René in the wings on the wrong side of the stage, pinning the crown in place just as quickly as she could, as René missed her cue. The line of Snowflakes came out from the other side—without her.

René watched from across the stage in horror. And suddenly, there on the far side of that vast plain, on the other end of all those dazzling lights, past the long line of dancers who kept glancing across at her like, *What's going on?*, was the white-domed head of Mrs. Gilbert. She was clearly livid, motioning frantically to René from the other side of the stage.

Eve finally nudged her. "I think you'd better get out there," she said.

But René was wide-eyed, mute, stock-still.

"I think you're just going to have to run across," Eve said.

Mrs. G was signaling wildly: *Get over here*. You *get over here* right *now!*

So René took off, bourréeing as quickly as she could through the falling confetti-snow, from the wrong side of the stage to the very front of the line of Snowflakes, who were completing their series of turns. She got to her place and stepped into the dance. She only had to not let her eyes wander to the wings, stage right, where Mrs. G was leaning, crumpled against a post, her hands raised, hanging on to the hair on either side of her head as if it were the only thing keeping her from falling over.

Between the first and second acts, René got an earful. Mrs. G was trying not to yell, but luckily they were in the basement and the audience was presumably in the hallway René had just careened through, at the refreshment stand.

"Check, double-check, check, double-check!" Mrs. G kept saying. "*Your* job. *Your* responsibility. *Your* head. *Your* dance. No one else! *You* dancing out there." It went on and on. And the one thing René never said was *It wasn't my fault*.

But Mrs. G seemed to understand that, because she finally tilted her head and just grabbed René and gave her a hug. René was buried for a moment in Mrs. G's enormous, pillowy bosoms, and after that, it was all back to normal.

"That's crappy," Catherine said when Mrs. G left.

"It's okay," René said, because it was, because Mrs. G had been right. If René wanted this, if she wanted to do this, it was all on her, nobody else, no matter what. There was no room for uncertainty—no wondering or confusion or discussion about who deserved what or who'd caused what to happen. So she didn't mind. Really, it was one of the things she loved most about it.

René and Catherine got into their Chinese costumes, and when the music for Act Two started, they made their way upstairs. They stood in the wings and watched as Leon danced his Russian number, sailing across the stage in his leaps, executing his Around the World at full tilt, then dazzling the audience with his multiple tours and perfect, flashy Cossack Hops.

"What a show," Al said when they met him in the lobby. He'd had to wait as they all got changed and packed up their things. Everything had to come home.

"We'll have to make another trip tomorrow," Eve said. "To get the last of it."

"Very nice," Al said, patting René on the back. "Good job," he said, meaning all of them.

And Leon turned his head away and smiled.

They went to the Daisy Dell, which was a kind of fancy restaurant, with baby blue leatherette banquettes, hanging globe lights, and big menus.

René had deep-fried shrimp, iceberg lettuce with chunky blue-cheese dressing, and French fries. Eve and Al and Leon all had French dip, and Jayne had a cheeseburger. Then Eve got the mile-high lemon meringue pie, while the kids got hot fudge sundaes.

"To a job well done," Al said, raising his cup as they all started on dessert. They clinked their water glasses to his coffee mug.

"Thanks, Al," Eve said. "Thank you for coming."

"I wouldn't have missed it," he said, stealing a forkful of her lemon meringue. "Not for the world. You all did such a good job."

"Did you see me come in from the wrong side?" René said.

"Nope," he said, and everybody laughed.

"I have a feeling you haven't heard the end of that," Eve said. "But thank God it was the last performance. Maybe she'll just forget about it. I know she's relieved it's over."

"You better hope she forgets," Leon said.

But René was eating her way through homemade whipped cream with chopped nuts.

"She just might," Eve said, "considering what happened to the Snow Queen."

"I *did* see that one," Al said, laughing, his mouth full of pie.

After René's screwup in the beginning of the Snow Scene, the Snow Queen had made her big entrance—an enormous grand jeté to piqué arabesque, just like Mrs. G had promised—slipped on the confetti-covered stage, and landed flat on her butt.

"Poor thing," Eve said. "You have to give her credit. She just got up and kept going. Turns out she twisted her ankle. Helen thought maybe she'd broke it, but it seemed fine. She got through the whole second act."

"So maybe Mrs. G will forget about your big mistake," Leon teased.

"It wasn't my fault," René said. "Plus, she already yelled at me."

"My, oh my," Al said, shaking his head.

"All's well that ends well," Eve said.

René had to agree. Even if she had got in trouble for something that was totally not her fault, with Eve and Al and Leon and Jayne all happy and laughing together, it seemed like everything had turned out just right.

18

Overlapping Lines Converge

With the rush of *The Nutcracker* behind her, Eve started taking in alterations for a men's store downtown. Combining the income from that with what Mrs. G had started to pay her for teaching the little ones' Pre-Ballet class, she now had a bit of her own money. She kept it in a cardboard check-box in the kitchen. Al was constantly dipping into it when he wanted to go downtown for coffee, but Eve didn't mind. If she felt like buying herself a new pair of gloves, or one of the kids needed ballet slippers, or she wanted to get her hair done, she didn't have to ask him. And not having those conversations was a pleasure and a relief.

One day when Al was home and the kids were at school, Al asked if Eve would like to ride with him over to the Pine Ridge Reservation, where there were some cattle he'd been meaning to look at. Though there were still patches of snow on the ground, the sun was shining across the prairie and the sky was bright winter blue, end to end, so it was a nice day for a drive. They got in Al's Buick and off they went, through Scenic, past the boarded-up Longhorn Saloon—where Russell Means had shot a man point-blank in the back of the head in the men's room, or where he'd been held down on the pool table by a rival faction on the reservation and castrated, Eve had heard both—then on through the Badlands and down to Porcupine, about twenty minutes north of Wounded Knee. Eve had been to Wounded Knee. She'd seen the peeling crosses the Indians had planted willy-nilly in the dirt, as if to deny that there'd ever been any such thing as kidnapping, raping, scalping of the honest, hardworking folks who'd broken their backs to settle this land, as if what had happened in that place had blossomed out of thin air, out of simple meanness. Still, it was a shame things had to be like that.

Billy Little Horse was waiting as they pulled up to his pastel government shack, standing just next to the two old cars in his front yard, one with its windows busted out and its doors hanging open on broken hinges, the other with all its tires missing—one side up on blocks, the other melting into the earth, drowning in mud and icy slush. Both cars had their hoods up and auto parts strewn nearby, as though someone had been in the middle of repair work, maybe a decade ago, and simply walked away and never come back.

"Hi there, Billy," Al said, getting out from behind the wheel.

"Hey," Billy said.

Billy Little Horse wore a plaid shirt, buttons stressed against his paunch, and jeans belted low with a shiny rodeo buckle. He was dark, a full-blood Indian, with a tough, leathered look that came both from his people and from working outdoors in all weather. Al's dad had known Billy's father, traded cattle with him off and on, so though Al and Billy weren't friends, they weren't strangers.

Al had told Eve that Billy wasn't a drinker but that his son was. And now Eve could hear the TV going inside, could see in her mind three or four half-naked Indians sprawled on a dirty mattress on the floor, drinking Budweisers for breakfast, tossing empties into a corner already piled high.

"This here's my wife, Billy," Al said. "Eve."

"Hey," Billy said. And though Billy barely cracked his lips to speak, Eve could see he didn't have many of his teeth.

"Say there, Billy," Al started again, "I hear you've got some cattle you're looking to sell."

"Sure" was all Billy said. Then he silently led them down to the pasture where the cattle were grazing. The three of them walked the fence line.

"I think I can give you a good price for these, Billy," Al said after a while. "You've got some great-looking cattle there."

So Al and Billy came to an agreement, shook hands, and Al said he'd have the trucks at Billy's place in a day or two, to load them up.

"Nice doing business with you, Billy," Al said as they got back in the car.

Billy nodded and went inside.

This was going to be a good deal for Al, and he was giving Billy a fair price, about as good as he was going to get. And Eve was happy that it had all gone quickly so she hadn't had to use the off-angle outhouse she'd noticed in the weeds.

Al got two truckers from Pardo Transport lined up, and in a few days they were on the road again, in a caravan this time, back to Porcupine to pick up the cattle. When they pulled up to the pasture gate, Billy stepped out of his house. He started over to the fence to meet them as Al got out of his car.

"Say there, Billy," Al called. "What do you know? Another beautiful day." He motioned to the bright sun, the clear sky overhead, the jagged juts and drops of the cutaway buttes in the distance. "Looks like it's about time to settle up." He bent to get his checkbook from the center console.

When Al stood up, Billy was right there by the car door, hands in his pockets.

"No deal, Al," Billy said.

"What'd you say there, Billy?" Al thought maybe he'd misheard.

"No deal," Billy said again.

"Now, Billy," Al said. "I just left here not three days ago, and we'd agreed. We agreed, didn't we, Billy? We shook on it."

"Yeah," Billy said.

"So we got a deal, don't we, Billy. We made a deal. That's why I hired these big trucks, these two drivers. That didn't cost me nothing, Billy. That cost me something. But I did it 'cause we agreed, we had an agreement."

Billy Little Horse nodded. He wasn't talking.

"Now, Billy, I got my checkbook right here, and I'm ready to write you a check for the full amount. Right now." Billy had to need the money—for food, for beer, for glass to replace the boards and plastic sheeting covering his windows, for running water, an indoor toilet.

Eve could hear that there was trouble, and she'd just as soon stay in the car anyway. The only real menace on the reservation was Indian on Indian, she figured, with the whole place split into half-bloods versus full-bloods—which came down to nothing more than those for and against working with the whites—and with Dickie Wilson, the mixed-breed, white-appointed headman, and his so-called Guardians of the Oglala Nation goon squad shooting up the place, starting their own people's homes on fire in the middle of the night. Still, Indians were Indians. They didn't make any sense. The one thing you could depend on from an Indian was that you'd never know what he was going to do next.

"I'm going to write this out to you right now, Billy," Al was saying, opening the checkbook, filling in the date on a blank check.

"No deal, Al," Billy said. "No deal."

Al stopped writing and looked at Billy Little Horse for a good long time.

"No cattle. No deal," Billy repeated, shaking his head. He spit on the ground by his boot. Then he turned around, hands still stuck deep into his pockets, and went back in his house.

"Well, for crying out loud," Al said as he fell into the car.

"What in the world?" Eve said. "What happened?"

"I have no idea. Maybe somebody offered him more money."

"Maybe one of his relatives wanted them," Eve said.

Al paused, sick, shaking his lowered head. "Lord knows I'm still going to have to pay these guys." And he got out to talk to the truckers, to tell them to go ahead and turn their rigs around and head back to town, that he'd meet them at the trucking office.

So Al was baffled and disappointed.

"Only an Indian," he said as they pulled away from Billy Little Horse's place. "Only a godforsaken Indian."

Eve nodded. Only an Indian could change his mind like that and not even bother to let you know, then not feel any obligation to tell you why he'd backed out even when it had cost you time and money. Eve remembered the Indians that had come through her house when she was just a girl. With the Chicago Northwestern Railway in town, there'd been Indians, gypsies, hoboes, the lot. They'd walk right through the front door without even knocking, take whatever they wanted from the kitchen, and continue straight out the back without so much as a word. At first, her mother had stood quietly and let them go. But after a while, when the displaced Indians and gypsies and hoboes came through, she'd make them sandwiches. She'd stand in the kitchen and hand them whatever kind of sandwich she could manage—mostly just bread and butter with a sprinkle of sugar—until they'd all disappeared out the back door without a single "Thank you," as if not a one of them spoke any English. Eve could hear the train whistle from her front porch, but she never knew where the drifters had come from or where they were going. It seemed to her, as a child, that they appeared and vanished with the mist that rose around the river, like hungry ghosts.

"I feel sorry for them," Eve's mother would say, though she herself didn't have two dimes to rub together. And they all just got used to it, like it was nothing unusual.

"If he wanted more money, he could have asked me," Al was saying. "I probably wouldn't have given him any more, but if that's what he wanted, he could have said something."

"You'd think so," Eve said.

"I'm not doing any more business on the reservation, Eve."

"Well, maybe if you had him sign a contract instead of just depending on a handshake, you'd have something to hold him to and you wouldn't have all this trouble," Eve said, mixing her irritation over Billy Little Horse with the maddening long line of freeloaders crowding her mother's kitchen. "This isn't the olden days, Al," she added. "I've told you time and again. A handshake's just not good enough."

"I'm awfully glad to know you've got the answers to everything, Eve," Al snapped, stung.

Eve didn't respond. Wasn't it a shame he had to be like that, giving her a cruel, offhand put-down when she was just trying to help? And after all she'd done for him—like when she and Leon had fed the cattle he was keeping out by Ellsworth Air Base. They couldn't get out of town until Leon was done with school and dance class, so it would be dark, dead of winter, sometimes fifty below. Leon would freeze his hands chopping through the creek so that the cattle could get to some water. They'd swing and heave hundred-pound feed bags across snow-filled gullies, "One, two, three—!," then trudge through thigh-high snowdrifts in the dark of night to feed the poor steaming beasts, to try to keep them alive. A few had died, in spite of everything, frozen to death in the bitter cold, but that wasn't her fault, or Leon's, either. She'd never asked for so much as an acknowledgment for any of it, but she deserved respect. She'd earned the right to at least that much.

Still, they'd been getting along so well lately. If she wanted to keep it that way, she'd have to let it slide off this time. *Like water off the back of a duck,* she thought, turning her head away.

"You can take my word for it," Al was going on, "since I do happen to know a thing or two about it. It wouldn't do any good. Paper or no paper, doesn't matter. They can do what they like on the reservation. They make their own laws. It's a Wild West show out there."

Eve bit her tongue.

"Lord knows I can't make money hiring truckers for nothing," Al said, half-trying to pull her back to his side of the fence.

"True," Eve said, steely.

"Looks like I'm out nearly five hundred dollars today," he continued, with a desperation he hardly ever let her hear. "A couple more deals like this and we'll all be in the poorhouse." He let a puff of air escape his lips, like he was spitting.

"God forbid," Eve said, lighting a cigarette and cracking her window.

He had a point. Not that there was such a thing as the poorhouse anymore, but there were the possibilities of loans you could never repay, of losing your home, of losing everything. With Al self-employed—no paycheck, no sick days, no pension—there were always those possibilities.

Al dropped Eve off at the house, and she went in to start dinner, throwing open cupboards and banging pots and pans down onto the stove. The kids would be home from school any minute, and Al would be back from the trucking office soon enough, unhappy and looking for something to eat.

19

Spring

Spring was coming. Crocuses were pushing up through the frozen ground. You'd look down to find one blooming impossibly in a mound of melting snow, a magical circle of green and pale purple or yellow or white.

Leon was still pulling out his hair, and Eve was talking to him every day, as if to a wounded animal.

"Don't pull at it, Leon," she'd say calmly, gently running her hand over the top of his head. "Look," she'd say, "it's growing back. Just keep your hands off it and I'm sure it'll come back in no time."

But nothing was working. So, after nights filled with argument, counterargument, insistence, and refusal—all of which would invariably escalate into name-calling and accusation, door-slamming and tears—Al finally gave in, and the three of them went to see a psychiatrist.

"Quack, quack," Al said in protest as they pulled up to Dr. Harris's office. He laughed, even though neither Eve nor Leon joined him. "Anyone can hang a shingle, Eve," he pointed out.

"Be quiet, Al," Eve said. "Just shut your mouth." And she got out of the car, already thoroughly disgusted with him.

Inside, the doctor asked them to sit. After they'd chatted a few minutes, the doctor said, "And what is it you three would like to speak with me about today?"

"Well," Al started, seeming to feel it was his duty as head of the household, "we don't really have much to talk about. Eve here had some bridge buddies who thought you might be able to help Leon with a problem he's having."

The doctor looked to Leon. "Okay," he said. "And what seems to be the trouble, Leon?"

Leon shrugged, on the hot seat.

"He's pulled out all his eyelashes and eyebrows," Al continued, "which you can plainly see. And now he's pulling out the hair on his head. That's the problem."

"I'm sure," Eve immediately countered, "that's not the only problem, Dr. Harris. There are a lot of problems." She looked at Al and left it at that.

Al shifted uncomfortably and glared back at her. He knew better than to add their dirty laundry into the mix, and the one thing he had not expected when he'd agreed to all this nonsense was an ambush.

"Would you like to go on with that?" Dr. Harris asked.

"Well, of course we're seeking help for our son," Eve said, "but I'm not convinced that's the main point. Because, well, there can be a lot of friction at home. His father and I don't get along all that well, and to tell the truth, there can be a lot of uncalled-for derogatory remarks and put-downs. It could be that Leon's problem is just a part of all that. Plus, his father's gone all the time. I don't know."

"Oh, for heaven sakes, Eve, a man's got to make a living," Al said, grinning at the doctor, intending to gain a foothold by cementing their agreement on this.

"And Leon," the doctor said. "What's your idea about why you're here?"

"I don't know," Leon said, sitting on his hands. "Because of my h-hair?"

"But things may not always be as straightforward as they seem on the surface? Is that right?" the doctor said.

Leon nodded.

"So, are there other things you might want to talk about, too? Like what goes on at home? Is that a possibility?"

Leon gave a circular nod like a bobblehead, as though he couldn't imagine how he might answer a question like that.

And as Leon finally looked at the floor and Al once again shifted noisily in his chair, the doctor said, "I'm sure there's something we can do. We can talk things through, see what comes up. How does that sound? Eve, Al, I'd like to make an appointment with the two of you to start with, if that's all right. Then I'd like to spend some time one-on-one—"

"Now, Doc Harris," Al interrupted, clearing his throat. "That sounds like a terrific good plan, terrific, and I'm sure there's lots of things Eve would like to talk to you about. I have no doubt she could complain about me from sunup to sundown." Al chuckled, still leaning on the doctor's unproven collegiality. "But we can't be making one appointment after the next. What I mean here is, this is not within our means. It just is not. I'm sorry about that. Besides, we don't have any problems. Not really. Eve and I have our squabbles, I'll admit. But that's to be expected. Right, Doc?"

"Oh, Al. Stop it," Eve moaned. "Stop."

There was a pause.

"I'm sure we could come up with some kind of payment plan," Dr. Harris suggested.

"No, thank you, Doc," Al said, recovering himself. "Thanks all the same." He started to get up. "I think we understand each other. I imagine this hair business is just a bump—"

"Stop it, Al. Just be quiet!" Eve said finally. "We can afford it," she said to Dr. Harris. "*I'll* pay for it."

"*You'll* pay for it?" Al sat back down. "Why—!" And sensing the doctor's attention, he caught himself. "Sure. Why, sure," he said. "Why not?"

"Okay," Dr. Harris said. "Shall we go ahead and make an appointment for next week?"

"That'll be fine," Al said, his body suddenly gone tense and wiry, like a cornered animal's, his face lit up with humiliation.

So they set a date. Then Al drove Eve and Leon home in silence, dropped them off, and left town without even coming in for his suitcase. And when the appointed day rolled around, Al was still on the road. He was on the road for a long time after that.

Eve ended up going to Dr. Harris by herself, blubbering her way through the hour. Then Leon had an appointment the next week and the week after that, and Al still hadn't returned.

Leon saw Dr. Harris quite a few times before Al finally came home. It was a Saturday, full-on spring, and Leon, René, and Jayne were all in shorts and T-shirts, just home from ballet class, sitting down to the tuna salad Eve had made for lunch. Al had been gone for months, it seemed, and it was a shock to hear the ring of his cowboy boots coming through the dining room. As he stopped and stood, filling the kitchen doorway, they all went silent.

"You can sit down and have some lunch, if you like," Eve said, not looking up.

Al didn't answer. He seemed to have arrived from some unfathomable distance, as if maybe, instead of driving the highways, he'd been teleported, with pieces of himself yet to arrive.

"Hi, Dad," René called out.

"Well, hi there," Al said, finally looking at them, as though he'd suddenly remembered where he was and how he'd got there, as if they'd all, in that delayed instant, just come into focus.

Then he walked up to Leon and stood over him, examining his bald spot.

"Go ahead and sit down, Al," Eve insisted.

"You've been pulling out your hair again, Leon," Al said, obviously warming up to something. "I can see that."

Leon looked up.

"Sit down, Al," Eve said brusquely, bringing a cup of coffee and setting it at his place.

"I'll sit when I'm good and ready, and not one minute before," he said sharply, turning his head but keeping his eyes to the floor, refusing to look at her. "And I don't want to hear another word about it. Not from you."

He turned back to Leon. "Leon," he said, rough but steady, weirdly calm, yet clearly at the edge of something, "have you been pulling your hair?"

"No, Dad," Leon said. "I haven't. I swear."

Eve and Leon had just been talking about this before Al came in. Eve had been saying what good progress Leon was making, how his bald spot was filling in a little more each day, how she could see downy hairs nearly a quarter of an inch long, and how she was proud of him for leaving it alone.

"Don't lie to me, Leon," Al said.

"I swear, Dad," Leon said. "Honest. I haven't been pulling it."

"Oh, Al, for Chrissakes," Eve said impatiently. "He's not lying. Now sit down."

"You stay out of this, Eve," Al said fiercely, keeping his gaze on the far wall. "For once in your life, stay out of it!"

René and Jayne sat frozen, following the high-stakes back-and-forth that had suddenly erupted in their kitchen.

"You're lying to me, Leon," Al said. "I can see that much with my own two eyes." He paused and stepped back to look Leon in the face. "If there's one thing I will not abide in this house, it's a liar."

"Promise, Dad," Leon said. "I'm telling the truth." He was almost crying. "I swear I'm not lying. I swear it."

"Leon, you can swear and promise and give your word of honor, but I can see that bald spot is bigger than when I left here, and that means only one thing. You've been pulling out your hair. And now you're lying to me. You leave me no choice, Leon. No more choices. I've got to do what I should've done a long time ago, when all this nonsense first started!"

"You just cool down, Al!" Eve ordered, perfectly matching Al's expanding rage. "You come in here after disappearing for weeks on end and start yelling at everybody, causing all this trouble. You just cool down! He's not lying. *I've* been with him every day. *I've* been watching him."

"And no one in this house is going to spend one more dime at that goddamn psychiatrist. You hear me?" Al said, finally looking directly at her, his eyes watery, blazing. "I don't care where the money comes from!"

"That's not for you to say," Eve muttered.

"Well, *I'm* saying it," Al said, "and *everyone* around here's going to listen!"

Then he turned back to Leon.

"Stand up and come outside. I'm going to teach you to not pull out your own goddamn hair. That's right. *I'm* going to teach you a lesson you will not forget!" He looked at Eve. "Guaranteed!" he said. Then: "Now, Leon! Right now!" And Al walked straight on through the kitchen and out the back door, letting the screen door slam behind him.

They sat, each one trying to reel back the day, no one taking the slightest breath.

Then Leon started to get up.

"You sit down, Leon. You don't have to go out there," Eve said, adamant but still. "You just stay right here with me. I know you're telling the truth, and there's no need. None whatsoever."

Leon set his jaw and stood up. He took the time to push his chair back under the table.

"Leon, just sit down," Eve said. "You stay right here."

"I'm going out," Leon said.

"You are *not* going out there," Eve said again.

"I'm going out," Leon said, suddenly strangely resolute.

And Leon walked out, his legs loose-jointed, unsteady beneath him. He closed the screen door softly, carefully, then went into the small detached garage, where Al was waiting for him.

René jumped up and ran to the edge of the sink as Eve plunged her hands deep into the hot, soapy water and started furiously scrubbing dishes. Then Eve stopped and just stood there, leaning forward against the rim, letting the water soak her shirt. René stayed clinging to the sink as the cries went up, uncontrollable hot tears streaming down her face. She stared up at Eve, overcome and confused, gasping, heaving, trying to say, with her eyes, *Why are you standing here? Why don't you go out there? Why don't you do something?* But Eve kept her hands locked in the water and didn't move. She wasn't going to stop it. She was going to stay right where she was, motionless, turned to stone.

And when Eve finally looked down at her—as René continued to grip the sink, her eyes red and streaming, her face contorted and swollen—René could see that all the old inequities, all the injustices, all the favoritisms, all the things Eve figured René had incited from the very beginning that had allowed something like this to happen in the first place, were gathering, circling, as if Eve's myriad resentments against her were swarming in from all directions, assuming formation, firing on her from every angle.

Eve narrowed her eyes and glared at René as if to say, *You favored. You lucky. You spared, spoiled child.* Then she inhaled sharply.

"What's your problem?" she hissed. "It's not *you* out there."

René fell away from the sink and ran to her room. She collapsed beneath her open window and listened all alone to the beating as it went on and on.

"Please, please. No," Leon was crying, pleading, howling. "I didn't do it. I didn't do it," he screamed as the leather strap, or whatever Al was using, kept falling and falling, ringing through the bright afternoon.

Many years later, Leon would tell René that Al had beaten him with a wooden board fitted with nail-head studs. Though René couldn't imagine what this might have been or how Al could have come up with such an instrument, from the sounds filtering through her bedroom window that day—as she lay crumpled beneath the screen, weeping, sobbing, her two arms wrapped tightly around her middle as if to hold her in one piece—and from the pain and fear and heartbreak she could hear in each of Leon's desperate cries, she could believe it.

And Al was right about one thing: it wasn't something any of them was likely to forget anytime soon.

Part Three

20

How Things Get Broken

Chuck started following some Indians downtown. They'd rented a place up the hill but didn't have a car, so they'd walk to town every afternoon, "to do some drinking," Eve said. Chuck was so bored he'd been running bare circles in the grass around the two scraggly trees in the front yard, "chasing his own tail" was Eve's guess, "or worms." So one day when the Indians passed by the house, Chuck tagged along. After that, he was gone all the time. René would imagine him sitting at the corner of Main Street and Mount Rushmore Road, outside the Lucky Spur, neon signs lighting up his muzzle.

Then one night, when the neighbors were coming home later than usual, likely stumbling their way through the dark streets, Chuck was hit by a car. His rib cage was crushed. Eve got a call from the animal clinic, but by the time she and Leon arrived, Chuck was dead. They went in anyway, said goodbye to Chuck for the last time.

"No one took care of him anymore," Eve said when they got home that night. "I fed him, but no one paid any attention to him. He must have started following those Indians just to have some company."

Leon went up to his room without a word, but he hadn't been saying much lately. He might answer if you asked him something directly, but otherwise he was quiet.

"I know Leon feels bad about it," Eve said.

Leon has to feel bad about a lot of things, René thought.

At ballet, Mrs. G noticed something different about Leon. "It's like a light went out," she said, but Eve didn't offer any explanation. "Do you see it?"

Eve nodded.

"Kids," Mrs. G said. "Maybe it's just a phase. Right, Eve?"

"His dog died" was all Eve said.

"Oh," Mrs. G said. "Terrible." She dropped her head, and on the way into class that day, she put her arm around Leon's shoulders.

Al was gone all the time. He'd come home, change the clothes in his suitcase, and leave again.

No one said much about any of it.

"You should just divorce him," René said to Eve one day when they were out in the garage, unpacking some of Emma's old dishes for a yard sale.

"I can't divorce him," Eve said. "I have three kids to raise, for God sakes. And there's rent to pay and groceries to buy. Don't be silly."

"You could if you wanted. We'd get by."

"We would *not* get by. I don't even have a job, not one that counts, and who's going to pay me? To do what? Plus," she went on, "somebody's got to do the cooking and the cleaning and the driving and the shopping. Are *you* going to do it? Or am I supposed to hire someone? With all the money I'm making?"

"Well, nobody loves him," René said, upping the ante.

With Al gone, René and Eve had started fighting. As far as René was concerned, Eve had proven herself willing to sacrifice any of them just to hang on to the miserable life she'd happened to put together, a life she hated, a life she railed against continuously. And all of her excuses were cowardly, weak as fluff.

"Nobody loves him," René said again, insisting.

Eve didn't even look up.

"So, why not divorce him?"

"*I* love him," Eve said finally.

René was speechless. It was the most outrageous lie she'd ever heard.

"*I* do," Eve said again.

"You do not," René said, letting the plate she was holding fall onto the already unwrapped stack, chipping the rim.

But no matter how hard she tried, no matter how much she forced herself to remember what he'd done, she, too, still loved him. Every time he came through the door, she was happy and relieved to see him, as if, perhaps, he'd come back from someplace he might well have decided to stay. And, in an awkward contortion of logic, since Al was around only as a kind of gift, showing up now and again just as René was beginning to wonder if she'd ever see him again, it was Eve she hated for Leon's beating. She hated her because she'd stood there, listening to Leon being battered, and done nothing, because she'd stood there, renouncing her responsibility, breaking her bond without the slightest whimper of remorse, then had followed it up with a steady stream of vitriol just to shuck off any blame.

And René could see that, from her side, Eve now felt free to un- leash all of her resentment over what she saw as the blatant unfair- ness of things, how everything had been tilted in René's direction from the very beginning. As far as Eve was concerned, René had been favored, exempted, eager to take whatever she wanted as birthright, no matter the cost to anyone else. Who but René had displaced Leon in Emma's and Al's affections? Even now, tendrils of that early favoritism lived and breathed in everything. On Jayne's and Leon's birthdays, Emma sent extra presents for René, but was there a gift for Leon or Jayne on René's special day? Never. Only layers of presents, all for her. According to Eve, René was "spoiled rotten," happy to assume the royal privilege, demand what others could only silently wish for, all the while complaining and shouting orders like a princess doomed to suffer a rash of peasants. And more than that, Eve was right: it would *never* have been René out there.

"Careful, René!" Eve said, glaring at her in the half-light of the garage. "Be careful. And don't be ridiculous. Of course I love him." She turned to open another box. "Now go get the broom," she said harshly. "And hurry up. This garage has to be swept before we can do anything else."

Eve kept unpacking as René went inside. But by the time the screen door closed behind her, René had made up her mind; not only was she not going to hurry, she wasn't going back at all.

René started attending the Christ Evangelical Youth Ministry meetings at the church they sometimes went to on Sundays. There was something about the way God could love you, regardless— regardless of the anger and hatred growing, twisting inside you like a gnarled oak. She thought if only she prayed hard enough, that oak might shrink down instead of taking deeper root. That was the promise. God could do it. And a God who was powerful and true, who could heal and protect, keep her from evil, and would never step away or turn his back, was just what she was looking for.

When she thought of God, René didn't imagine Christ on the cross, crying out unanswered, left to suffer the agonies—nails pounded through bone and sinew; lance piercing the side; prolonged hanging from flesh that would support only by tearing away—but Christ risen, victorious, beloved of the Father.

The youth group took a field trip to see *The Cross and the Switchblade,* a movie about a gang member who became a preacher. It had everything they'd heard of but never seen: drug addicts, prostitutes, stabbings. Pat Boone, as Pastor Wilkerson, gripped his Bible and told the bad guys God loved them.

"God'll get you high," he said, "but he won't let you down." Which to René—trying to forget things she couldn't admit or explain to anyone, not even herself—was appealing.

A few weeks later, Wilkerson and his team came to town for a Youth Crusade, and the group went en masse to the high school gym, just down the hall from where René had danced *The Nutcracker.* The place was packed, folks lined up on folding chairs and filling the bleachers, spilling into the aisles. Wilkerson gave a talk, and there was a slide show. Then members of the audience, young and old, got up to witness, telling stories of being struck by heavenly glory—realizing the powerful presence, the wonder and love of God—while driving home from work, or playing cards, or just sitting at the kitchen table, gazing out at the falling snow. And as the night went on, the crowd began to sway, open palms waving in the air to testify to the depths of pain and the truth of healing, until the whole gymnasium looked like an undulating ocean floor.

Before long, anyone who wanted to accept Jesus Christ as Lord and Savior was invited to "answer God's call." Wilkerson himself would bless you and pray over you, plead with the Holy Spirit to enter your heart and heal your life.

René watched as people filed up to the stage. They knelt down, and Wilkerson bent over each one, laying on hands and bowing his head to pray. He was powerful and sure, and it seemed that God was raining down blessings on each of them, and on everyone, together. It was then—seeing the gentle touch, feeling the shared blessing in the welcome act of tenderness and caring—that René started to cry.

She wiped her eyes with her long sleeves and, in a flash like a tracer round, remembered lying in Grandma Emma's bed—how the colored lights had sparked and whirled in the three-dimensional darkness of her closed eyelids as she'd drifted off to sleep. It had been a magical fireworks show—reds, blues, yellows bursting, falling, shifting in infinite patterns—a profusion of ease, a warm blossoming of happiness. What had happened since then? Somehow the colors had drained, the lights gone out, and she'd fallen into an increasingly dense and frightening darkness.

"You want to go up?" An older girl, the daughter of their pastor at church, touched her shoulder.

"No," René sobbed, hyperventilating.

The girl sat with her and rubbed her back, which made it worse, but she didn't say anything, which was noticeably kind of her. And under the gentle influence of her calm, René regained her composure and reconsidered.

"Maybe I'll go up," she said.

"I can go with you," the girl said.

So, like a big sister, the girl held René's arm as they walked up the aisle. They stayed together until they got to the portable stage set up in the middle of the gymnasium like a raft in floodwaters. Then she let go.

"Jesus loves you," she said as René started up the steps. "And I'm proud of you." The girl smiled encouragement, and looking at her, René felt she was gazing across an unbridgeable chasm. *What could her life possibly be like*, René wondered, *filled with such strange tenderness?*

And she was onstage. She took her place in front of Wilkerson.

"My daughter," Wilkerson said, clutching his Bible and looking at her deeply, kindly. And with those two words of love and acceptance and caring, everything went right off a cliff. René started weeping.

"Do you accept Jesus Christ as your Lord and personal Savior? Do you renounce the sin and pain and confusion of this world, and will you follow our Lord Jesus Christ in every step of your life from this day forward?"

She was eleven. She nodded, letting the tears roll off her cheeks.

Wilkerson placed his hands on her head and prayed, and she felt the light and heat, the love and power and blessing. It was true. There was love and power, unending. There was a fountain of protection and forgiveness and renewal all around, showering everyone in light and color continuously, if only you knew how to close your eyes and see it.

Then Wilkerson put his hands on either side of her face, wiping her tears away with his open palms.

"You belong to Jesus," he said to her. "God loves you so much. No matter how hard you tried, you could never measure the depths of God's love."

From then on, René sat with the youth group in the very last pew, and when there was a call to testify, she stood and said she'd been saved at the Wilkerson Crusade, telling how since that day she just wanted to do everything for Jesus. Whenever Eve came to church, even from the back row René could sense her embarrassment as the other grown-ups turned to hear René witness and the preacher peppered whatever she had to say with "Praise Jesus" and "Praise the Lord for our young folks bound for glory."

"I'm happy for you, René," Eve said one day on their way home. "I was raised Catholic, and I guess we just weren't encouraged to make a show of it. But your father's side is full of preachers. They're Bible-thumpers from way back."

Eve talked about these "so-called Christian" relatives often enough. One of them had tried to French-kiss her in the kitchen while Al stood right outside in the driveway. She thought they were a bunch of hypocrites.

"Looks like you got the preacher gene," Eve said.

And more and more often, René found that the one thing she wanted to do for Jesus most of all was to turn off the vulgar pop music Eve liked listening to on the car radio. "I can't listen to that," she'd say, reaching up to switch it off. "I'm a Christian now."

Though Eve wouldn't protest, would simply crease her eyebrows and draw her lips into a thin line, the long, silent drives would be a trial unto themselves, edgy and complicated, unnerving.

When Al finally started coming home again, René would butter him up at the dinner table, telling jokes and stories about her day, debating with him about everything—school, government, Indians—as the rest of the family ate silently, not looking up from their plates.

"So, he says to me," Al was saying, telling a story about a man who'd been struck by lightning three times, speaking mainly to René because the others didn't seem the least interested. "He says, 'I must be the luckiest guy in the world.' Ha! Struck by lightning! Blown straight out of his boots! Three times!"

They both laughed.

"Luckiest guy in the world, you bet."

His stories were outrageous, involving high-stakes poker backed by nothing but lint, midnight falls into waist-high snowdrifts while trying to round up freezing livestock, and natural wonders like meteors streaking green and blue, chasing him as he drove through the darkest prairie nights. René loved them, and through the wide avenue of his joy in recounting them, she loved him.

Eve saw it differently. "He's a born cattle dealer," she'd say as soon as he was out of earshot. "He certainly knows how to shoot the shit."

And Leon would keep himself and his ever-growing bald spot as far out of the picture as possible, at every turn running outside or up to his room.

Then one day, when Eve and René were in the middle of one of their myriad skirmishes, Eve happened to say, "Oh, René, you're just like your dad," which meant not that she hated her, exactly, but that she found her repugnant, reprehensible, that René was selfish, superior, unfeeling, ungenerous, a liar.

After that, if Eve said it once, she said it a thousand times.

So, even though from all appearances it seemed she was mistaken, René didn't feel wrong in blaming Eve for what had happened. Whose job was it to protect them if not hers? She was the one. And as René watched Eve becoming more and more angry and distant—striking at whatever came within reach, turning to reveal the steely, slit eyes of a viper—she found herself firmly dug in with Al.

Still, some days it would seem that all the trouble between them was just a fluke, as if Eve and René had simply been out of step, listening to different music. Without being able to say why, they'd end up sharing goodbye kisses in the morning and fresh-baked cookies in the afternoon. It was unpredictable. Yet regardless of the seeming surface of the day, they both understood that there'd been a shift, a realignment of the planets that no amount of effort could put right, and they were each set, continuously, on their guards.

21

Twinkle Toes

Leon spent most of his time in his room with the door shut, his new PRIVATE! DO NOT ENTER! sign dominating the upstairs hallway. But when he wasn't home, René would go in and rummage around in his things.

Mrs. G had taken a trip to Florida and mailed them a Sugar Daddy caramel bar larger than their torsos. "Looks like she's giving what she'd like to get," Eve had said, opening the oversized package and holding up the enormous sucker in wonder. "What am I going to do with this?"

She'd put it high in Leon's closet, so that was one thing worth going in for. Plus, Leon had his records in there. There was Paul Revere and the Raiders, and *Whipped Cream* by the Tijuana Brass, the first album Leon had ever bought, which René guessed he'd chosen for the cover with the naked lady sitting in cream, finger in her mouth.

So René was busy going through his drawers one day when she found them—Marlboro Reds, in a flip-top, about half of them gone.

"Leon's smoking!" she called, charging down the stairs.

Eve smacked her dish towel against the counter just inches from where René had come to a stop.

"Don't be a tattletale," she said. "And stay out of his room."

"Okay, but he's smoking," René said, putting on what Eve liked to call her high-and-mighty voice, "so you probably want to know."

"Go on," Eve warned, "unless you want something to do." Which meant she had vacuuming or dusting if René was going to hang around. "Just leave the cigarettes."

When Leon got home, he was in trouble, and Eve didn't bother to hide the fact that René had told on him. She didn't do anything about it, really, just took away his cigarettes and told him not to smoke. Then Leon ran up to his room and slammed the door.

He stayed in there all night, coming out only just before bedtime to stand in the girls' doorway as René was reading a small-print Bible and Jayne was sniffing miniature Kiddle Kologne dolls in their perfume bottles.

"Stay out of my room, René," he said, towering over her, somehow inflating himself with righteousness. He was tall, and if she hadn't known how tender-hearted he was, she might have been intimidated. "Just keep out of my room," he said again when she didn't answer, his voice softening, almost pleading.

"Then don't smoke," she said, holding up her Bible. "God loves you, you know."

Leon shook his head and rolled his eyes at her like she didn't have one idea what she was talking about. But she'd also found an envelope in Leon's drawer addressed to "LeonRStoned" from one of his friends, a kid Al really didn't like—though, as Eve said, Al didn't like any of Leon's friends. She didn't know exactly what it meant, but she knew better than to tell anyone about it.

Leon continued taking ballet classes even after his junior high gym teacher called him "Twinkle Toes" in front of the whole school, at assembly.

"That's just idiotic," Eve said when Leon told her. "And inexcusable. I'm going to have a talk with your principal."

"Don't," Leon said. "I never should have told you. Just leave it alone. Just forget it. It was probably my fault 'cause I was late getting to the gym."

These were more words than Leon had put together in three months.

It wouldn't have mattered how many seasons René and Jayne had dragged back and forth from the bleachers to the concession stand for Lemonheads and rainbow taffy while Leon pitched shutouts, or how many times Leon had been selected for the all-star team, or that Eve had become so well acquainted with the rules of baseball that she'd been elected official league scorekeeper for the past three years. All anyone needed to know was that Leon studied ballet, which to ranchers and sons of ranchers, cattlemen and sons of cattlemen, farmers and sons of farmers—who'd grown up with an open horizon stretching before them, the smell of earth and grain and hard work filling their nostrils, and the firm belief that they knew what was what and weren't going to be bamboozled by some fancy, newfangled, citified way of thinking—meant only one thing: homo, freak, weirdo, faggot, queer, fairy, "Twinkle Toes." And coming up against that was like standing in front of a moving wall of water and asking it to turn around.

"I know he shouldn't have been late to assembly," Eve said to the principal over the phone the next day. "Still, that doesn't mean a teacher should be able to get away with purposely demeaning a student in front of the whole school. Honestly. My husband and I are going to want to discuss this with you and that P.E. instructor," she said. "I don't want this to just be forgotten."

"Of course," the principal said.

"First of all," Eve continued, "your teachers have no right to humiliate kids, especially with ridiculous, ignorant remarks like that. And second, for goodness sakes, the gym teacher, of all people, should know that ballet is very athletic. Even professional athletes take ballet class to develop strength and coordination. It's just asinine."

"It'd be good to hear all sides," the principal replied, obviously amused.

"Believe me," Eve shot back, enraged at his condescension, his attempt to turn this into something that looked like it had two sides, something less than a clear-cut violation of manners and trust, "I'll let you know when my husband's in town, and you make sure that P.E. teacher of yours is available. I have a few choice things I'd like to say to *him*. *Ignoramus* being number one!"

When Al got back home and Eve told him what had happened, he just looked at her. He just stood there and looked at her, blank.

"Well?" she said.

"Well?" he said back. "Well, what?"

"Well, what are you going to do about it, Al?" She was already wound up, already drowning in layers of prefigured rancor and indignation.

"Well," Al said. "To tell the truth, I'm certainly not going to make a federal case out of it." He turned away from her. He was just off the road after a long week and there was already steam coming out of her ears. All he wanted was something to eat. "You got anything a guy can have for dinner around here?"

"I've told that principal we're coming in for a meeting with that damn P.E. teacher," Eve said.

"Oh, Eve. For heaven sakes."

She'd gone out on a limb, walked the plank, and now he was going to say, *Go ahead. Jump.* She should have known. She should have known better.

"What in the hell do you mean by that, Al?"

"I mean, I guess you can go right ahead," Al said. "Feel free."

"So, you're not coming with me?"

"No. I'm not coming with you."

"And if it was René who'd been embarrassed like that, in front of the whole goddamn school, then would you come with me?"

"What in the sam hell are you talking about, Eve?"

"I'm talking about *you*!" Eve said, overcome, the familiar fury and despair welling into her eyes.

"Then it's the same old story," Al said. "No need repeating it." He was looking in the refrigerator, taking out the cottage cheese.

"Do you really mean to tell me you are not willing to go with me to talk to those idiots about what they did to Leon?"

"I think you've picked up the general gist," Al said. "Yes. That is exactly what I mean."

"Just like that. Just let your son be treated like a second-class citizen by anybody, by the whole goddamn world."

"I'm tired, Eve. I just walked in the door after driving five hundred miles today. I'm not going anywhere, and I'm not doing anything other than finding myself something to eat, apparently. And as far as I'm concerned, this whole ballet deal with Leon is your mess. It's what you wanted for him, and you got your way. So, if there's a problem, which I don't doubt there is—I do not doubt it, no sir—I trust you can handle it. To tell the truth, I don't know what else you expected. We don't live in some big city. Lord knows, I tried to tell you that way back. Way, way back."

"He's good at it," Eve said. "And it's good for him. You know that."

"Be that as it may," Al said. "It doesn't change the facts."

"I guess I'm not surprised. Why should I be surprised by you acting like nothing around here has anything to do with you?"

"Now you're talking," Al said.

And that was it.

Eve stomped off to her sewing machine, filled her mouth with straight pins, and muttered to herself as she lined up some of the alterations that needed doing. And Al sat by himself in the kitchen, eating whatever he could find in the fridge before going to bed and falling into a heavy, snoring sleep.

Neither of them mentioned it again except from time to time as years went by, generally deep in the middle of the night when they were lost in some bitter, screaming ramblings about what had gone wrong—or when, for René's benefit and edification, Eve would once again go over the litany of what a shame it was that Al had never stood up for Leon.

"He'd go in for *you*," she'd say to René, like a ricocheted bullet finding its home. "Sure. He'd be right there for you, but not for Leon. You think that might have made a difference?"

René could only nod.

"He was always right there for *you*," she'd repeat, shaking her head.

"Yes," René would say, suddenly introspective and cross, looking for both an easy exit and a rock she could use to defend herself, to deal her own blow. "He *certainly* was."

22

Revelations

Emma came to visit and spoke in René's ear about white slavery, about girls her age being taken, made to do unspeakable things. Emma shuddered to think of it. She was thrilled that René was now a "young person of the Lord," she said, though René was beginning to wonder. She wasn't turning out to be a natural Christian.

When someone in her youth ministry class had unveiled a LIFE, PASS IT ON! poster, René had been the one who'd giggled and poked the girl next to her, raising her eyebrows in the direction of the one cute boy. "Does that mean what I think it means?" she tried.

"Cut it out," the girl had growled at her. "That's not funny."

"Such a pretty thing," Emma whispered, tsking and shaking her head as if René's fate were sealed. "Don't trust anyone. Not anyone. You have to be so careful."

At school, René's class had been studying mythology, so Emma's warnings instantly brought to mind Persephone, who'd been kidnapped by Hades and forced to rule as Queen of the Dead. Each year, she'd be captive in the Underworld until spring, when her mother, the Goddess of Nature, would come to take her home. On Persephone's return, the sun would shine and green grasses lift their heads, because her mother was so overjoyed to see her again.

But with the way things were going, if René were to be carried off by the King of Hell, she doubted her mother would come for her. More likely, Eve would take her disappearance as a blessing.

Still, according to Emma, white slavery meant being kidnapped by someone far worse than the Lord of Death.

"You'll only *wish* you could die," Emma told her.

At night, while everyone else was downstairs watching *Gunsmoke,* Emma read to René from Revelation, stressing passages about the devil's horsemen, the coming earthquakes, the rain of fire, when smoke would rise from the Great Abyss to blot out the sun. The sun would turn to ash, the moon to blood, as stars rocketed from the sky. People would try to hide themselves in the mountains, praying for the rocks to fall and crush them. This was the Great Tribulation, when anyone not marked by the Seal of Christ would be tormented beyond imagining. Emma read and gasped.

To René, it all seemed somehow familiar. Like Prometheus, who'd stolen fire from the gods and ended up chained to a cliff, his liver endlessly pecked out by a circling eagle, or Pandora, who'd opened a forbidden box and accidentally filled the whole world with suffering—they were all in line to pay, she figured, one way or another. You just never knew how it was going to happen. You could be condemned and left behind to suffer the Tribulation because of a single thought you hadn't meant to think; opening the smallest gift, you could unwittingly unleash a horde of winged furies; off by yourself, picking flowers, you could wind up being taken straight to hell without having committed a single crime. You couldn't run from the devil's horsemen, just like you wouldn't win fighting a three-headed dog. And you'd never be able to recognize the Antichrist, no matter how hard you tried.

"He'll wear a blue turban," Emma told her. "You have to remember that. He'll be charming, famous, charismatic. No one will see that he's really a serpent!"

As Emma read from John's Revelation of the Apocalypse, René would gaze out her window at the silver moon suspended in the sky—its reflected light illuminating the shifting pines in eerie, dark relief. And for René, the moon became the touchstone of all the other prophecies, an outward sign she could depend on to let her know exactly when the coming dawn of horrors was upon them.

"The signs are coming together," Emma told her, closing the Bible. "Likely in your lifetime. But, oh my, that will be a challenging, difficult time."

Though she intended to shrug them off, René felt the revelations combine and compress in her, adding to an already persistent dread.

For now, God seemed to be granting a reprieve.

But it will happen, René thought, on the edge of sleep as Emma turned out the light. *One day I'll look to see my moon turned dark and dripping with blood.*

The next day, Emma took René shopping. Leon was nowhere to be found, and Emma refused to take Jayne because Jayne was constantly running off, exploring under racks and hiding in dressing rooms.

"She's too much for me. She's going to give me a heart attack," Emma explained to Eve, who simply pinched her lips together and turned her back.

So Emma and René headed downtown—Emma in her smart

navy pantsuit with the white piping around the collar and pockets, René in the sharp floral jumper Eve had made for her—and they went from one store to the next, attracting the attention of the salesladies as they uncovered a cornucopia of pretty things just René's size.

"I'll be lucky to get out of here with my teeth," Emma joked, and the salesgirls laughed.

They returned with their arms full of packages—entire matching outfits with new shoes to complete each one. And though Emma giggled like a naughty schoolgirl as they ran up the stairs, Eve just went on with her housework as if nothing at all out of the ordinary was happening.

That night, Emma explained to René that the moon would likely turn to blood because of things that happened here on earth.

"It'll be our final warning," she said, and René felt a compounding of the gravity of each moment, like the vacuum seal of a Mason jar taking hold. Would she be left behind in the Rapture? Would her selfishness cause Leon and Jayne to be left behind, too? Would they all end up ruled by the Beast, fooled into an eternity of damnation? And did she even believe in hell?

The next morning, René decided to put on her new green-apple-print shorts outfit with the matching braided headband and yellow patent-leather sandals and ask around.

Emma confirmed that she believed in hell. "For the most part. Maybe not real fire, but close."

Al just nodded a quick yes, then shook his head no, then laughed. He tapped René on top of her head and took off out the door.

"I believe we live our hell on earth," Eve said. "I don't see why anyone should have to suffer any more than we do right here, every day." Then René seemed to come into focus. "That's a cute outfit," Eve said. "I bet Jayne would like an outfit like that."

Night after night, Emma read from John's Revelation, holding René's hands or rubbing her legs as René dozed off. But then she went back to Fort Pierre, and René was once again on her own, gingerly selecting each foothold through the day. And at night, with the way the walls would shake and the windows rattle with "Your mother—!" and "So insulting—!" and "Goddamn right, I'm not going to take it anymore. Not for one more goddamn minute!," it began to seem that all of Emma's most hair-raising predictions were already coming for them, speeding straight down the pike, headed right for their front door.

René would wake from a dream of bad weather—tornadoes, hail, hurricanes, floods—then lie in bed listening to footsteps on the stairs in the dead of night, or cracks and pops from the hallway closet, or the long scrape of something against the boards just under her windows, sounds Eve dismissed as "the house settling."

"Stop being such a worrywart," Eve told her one morning when René was once again going through the list of unnerving noises.

But that night it was Jayne who woke up. René looked over to find her shivering, blankets pulled up to her eyeballs. Jayne slid silently out of bed, crawled from the room on all fours, then tore down the hall for Eve's room with René right on her heels, screaming like a banshee.

"There's a clown in my window," Jayne cried. Their bedroom was on the second floor, but Jayne had clearly seen a painted clown peering through their darkened window. "He had orange hair, sticking up," she moaned, "and he was knocking, trying to get in." She buried her face in her mother's shoulder.

Eve said it was nothing, but René could see that Jayne wasn't making it up.

"Maybe it was Satan," she said.

"That's what I thought!" Jayne cried.

"Oh, René," Eve scolded. "Just be quiet. Go back to bed. You're scaring her so much with your stories."

But René shook her head. She wasn't going anywhere. And she hadn't been telling Jayne stories, certainly not stories about clowns.

23

Matilda Stripes

Jayne dragged in every stray cat she could get her hands on. Some of them, Eve said, just couldn't get away from her fast enough to make it back home. But the day she came through the door with her umpteenth orange tabby kitten less than eight inches long, Eve just sighed and said, "Okay. All right. You win. But just this once."

Eve made it clear that the cat would be Jayne's responsibility, and Jayne was good to her word. She named her cat Matilda Stripes, and from that very first day, Matilda followed Jayne everywhere.

Jayne would lie on the floor in the kitchen with Matilda curled on her chest, fast asleep, purring against her neck, as Eve cooked supper.

"My goodness," Eve would say, "somebody really loves you." And Jayne would smile and scratch behind Matilda's ears.

"Maybe she wants some milk," Jayne would say, and she'd be up at the stove, heating milk, or "Maybe she'd like to play with some yarn," and she'd ask Matilda, "Would you like to play with some yarn?"

"Don't just go through my basket," Eve would call as the two of them started for Eve's sewing corner. "I've got some old yarn I'll get out for you."

If Jayne wasn't around, René would catch hold of Matilda and try to lie on the floor with her. But instead of settling in, Matilda would spring away and run into the other room.

"She hates me," René would say.

"I guess she knows who she belongs to," Eve would confirm.

Then Jayne would come in, and Matilda would trip over her own four feet to get to her, rubbing against her legs, reaching to be picked up. And Jayne would lift Matilda, throwing the cat over her shoulder like a dishrag, and carry her outside. "Let's go do something fun. You want to? You do? Me, too."

Sometimes René followed along and ended up accidentally chasing Matilda up a tree, which meant that Jayne would have to climb high into a tangle of branches, then shinny out onto a limb to rescue her little cat.

Matilda grew, but she never got very big.

"She must be the runt," Eve sighed.

"Naw." Jayne picked up Matilda and turned her belly up, cradling her like a baby. "She's a big, strong kitty. Aren't you, Mati? Yes, you are." Matilda's legs splayed and she arched her back as Jayne scratched her neck and chest.

When it was Jayne's turn to say the prayer at dinner, she started adding, "God bless Matilda and keep her safe," while the others just smiled at how crazy Jayne was about that silly little kitten.

So Jayne decided she wanted to be a veterinarian, and René decided she should probably give up trying to force Matilda to like her. Matilda was Jayne's cat, and it didn't look like anything was going to change that.

"What's in Mati's eye?" Jayne said, coming into the kitchen early one morning.

"Just get a Kleenex and wipe it out," Eve told her.

But the next day Matilda's eye was yellow-matted and crusted over worse than before. Jayne swabbed it with a little salt water, but by the time she got home from school that afternoon, it was filled with yellow-green pus all over again.

"Give it a few days," Eve said. "Animals know how to take care of these things."

So, though Jayne would wipe at it once in a while, mostly they all just forgot about it. Matilda had simply turned out to be a one-eyed cat.

"Looks like that cat's got a pretty bad eye infection," Al said when he got home.

"Well, I'm not paying good money to take some stray cat to the vet," Eve huffed. "Are you?"

"No. No, I'm not."

"Just give it some time. Who knows?"

They quieted when Jayne came through the kitchen, Matilda at her feet.

Al left town, but by the time he came home again, both of Matilda's eyes were glued shut. Jayne was at a neighbor's house, and Mati was lazing around inside, mewing, obviously uncomfortable, essentially blind.

"Only one thing to do, Eve," Al said. "Might be about time."

Eve nodded. She knew what happened when sick strays got sicker.

René was sitting at the table, so Al looked at her.

"Now," he started, "if Jayne asks what happened to that cat, you say it ran away."

"She," René corrected. "And why would she run away?"

"Never mind," he said.

"We'll just say she ran away," Eve said from where she was punching down dough for rolls.

Al opened a can of tuna fish, scooped out all but a spoonful, then took the open can and coaxed blind Matilda outside.

"Where're you going?" René said, getting up.

"You stay put."

But she followed after him, hanging a few paces behind. He went to his car and got his gun. She stayed with him as far as the end of the driveway, then stood and watched as he crossed the road, quickening his pace, calling, "Here, kitty, kitty, kitty," his shotgun slung over one shoulder, the tuna fish held low.

"What're you doing?" René called after him, raising her voice urgently as he reached the field and began to work his way through the brush.

"You stay up by the house," he hollered back. "Do as I say."

Then he disappeared into the woods, Matilda following briskly at his heels, craning up to get to the little bit of tuna fish.

René ran and sat on the front steps, gazing into the blank canvas of tree cover across the road. There was silence, a few long moments as she waited, puzzling, too many questions coming too quickly: Was he just going hunting across the street for some reason? Maybe there was a rabid skunk or raccoon that needed killing. But why bring Matilda? And why with such a special treat? Matilda wasn't really sick. Not really. She just needed eye cream, like Jayne when she got pinkeye.

Then there was the single gunshot.

Al came out of the woods with the tuna can, which he threw

into the garbage, and the gun, which he put back in his car. He went to the kitchen and washed his hands.

"That's it," he said to Eve.

"Too bad," Eve said, frowning, still fussing over her rolls. "Jayne really loved that cat."

"No lack of stray cats," Al said sadly. "She'll find another."

"No doubt."

René didn't say a word. She didn't hardly breathe. She'd been invited into the world of grown-ups, where you did what you had to do no matter how you felt about it. She wanted to show that she was up to the job, but she couldn't keep from wondering why they hadn't just taken Matilda to the vet and got her some medicine. It seemed so simple. What was she missing? It sounded like it was about money. But it was always about money. Anytime anyone needed anything at all, it was money. How could it always be money?

When Jayne got home, she went into the kitchen, where Eve's rolls were baking in the oven.

"Where's Matilda?" she asked.

"Haven't seen her," Eve said casually.

"Maybe she ran away," René said.

Jayne darkened, and Eve shot René a hard glance.

"She wouldn't run away," Jayne said, and she searched through the house, looking behind the furniture, lifting the drapes.

Eve rolled her eyes in dread. "Time for dinner!" she called.

"Where can she be?" Jayne fretted when they raised their heads from the blessing.

"Maybe she got out and tried to follow you up to the neighbor's," Eve suggested. "And she had that terrible eye infection, so who knows where she might have ended up?"

Jayne looked like she'd been struck.

"Don't worry, honey," Eve went on. "Wherever she is, I'm sure she's just fine. And if she doesn't show up, I bet you can find another kitty somewhere. Seems like you're always finding a new little cat that needs a good home, doesn't it?"

But Jayne wouldn't be soothed. She jumped up every few minutes to call out the screen door, until Al finally told her to sit down and sit still. After dinner, she went outside to search the neighborhood. She came in well after dark and ran upstairs. She threw herself on her bed next to where René was scanning the Psalms, searching for something that said something about cats, and she started to cry.

"I know she wouldn't run away," Jayne said. "I just know it."

"Maybe she got lost." René's throat constricted, the lie choking her as she pictured Jayne's dead cat, Matilda, right across the road, torn through, most likely exploded from the neck up and kicked into a pile of tangled underbrush.

"Why would she get lost?"

"Sometimes things get lost for no reason," René tried, feeling the hollowness of a liar. "She was lost when you found her." The words echoed in her chest like a BB fired into an empty rain barrel.

Jayne looked at her, distraught.

"You can never tell what's going to happen," René said, relieved to finally be saying at least one true thing.

"I know she wouldn't run away."

Tears dripped from Jayne's stained, red cheeks, splattering her pillowcase with dark polka dots.

"I know," René said.

"She loves me," Jayne said. "I know she does."

"I know she does, too," René said, nodding as Jayne melted into sobs.

They didn't say much after that. René just kept handing Jayne Kleenexes.

But in bed that night, as she tried to review the Ten Commandments, René kept getting mixed up: *Honor thy father and mother; Thou shalt not lie; Thou shalt not kill; But we can't afford to be taking some stray cat to the vet; Yet not one sparrow shall fall to the ground; But there's more where that came from; And all of the very hairs on your head are numbered; So we'll just say she ran away; And the greatest of these is love.*

Everything was running together; things were bleeding all over each other. René was never going to be able to untangle it or figure it out. And it seemed that God didn't really care much about any of it.

And it was that—even more than Matilda, and Chuck, and Leon, and Eve and Al, and now Jayne—that accounted for René lying awake long after the lights had been turned out, imagining herself following the railroad tracks straight out of town—away, away to anywhere else, anywhere else at all.

24

The Wide, Wide World

A rancher friend of Al's came by for a surprise visit. He was with his two sons, who were just a little older than Leon, and they all stopped in on their way home to Billings. They'd been visiting family in Pringle, they said, and the rancher couldn't pass through Rapid without seeing his old pal.

Al was tickled to welcome him. Eve took out the ham from last night's dinner and started making sandwiches. She put out potato chips and some of her homemade watermelon pickles. Then Eve asked Leon to sit with them at the table, and they all had a lovely kitchen picnic. There were even lemon bars dusted with powdered sugar that Eve had made the day before. She set them out on a plate for dessert, and the boys dug in. They were polite western boys, and they complimented and thanked her as Leon watched circumspectly, keeping his head down but raising his eyes, not saying a word. The other boys were quiet, too, attending to the grown-ups.

"Now my boy Pete here is taking care of the livestock these days, Al," the rancher said.

"Is that so," Al said, acknowledging Pete.

"Good for you," Eve said. "It's good to get in there and do things yourself, isn't it?"

"Yes, ma'am," Pete said. "I'm enjoying it."

"And James is taking over the harvesting this year, first time."

James nodded. "We'll be mowing and puttin' aside for the next three weeks or so," the boy said, smiling.

"Well, you've got some fine help there," Al said to the rancher. "Looks like you might be fixin' to retire."

They laughed.

"That I am," the rancher said. "Sooner the better. Right, Al?"

Al laughed. "You got that right," he said. "I say."

"Well, you got your boy there," the rancher said, indicating Leon. "No doubt he's getting ready to take over the trading business for you."

"God forbid!" Eve howled.

"Well, yes, sir. Yes, yes," Al said, looking to Leon, who kept his eyes on his plate and his hands in his pockets. "Get your hands out of your pockets, Leon," Al said.

Leon quickly withdrew his hands and set them in his lap. His eyebrows were puffs of bare flesh, his eyelashes were nonexistent, and the gleaming bald spot on top of his head was on full display, the beating clearly having made things worse instead of better.

"Leon's busy in school during the year," Eve said, recovering herself, "and this summer he's got lots of activities. Right, Leon?"

"Why, that's fine," the rancher said.

"Now, I hear you've been looking at buying some land out near

Kadoka," Al said, taking the conversation off in a different direction.

The men finished their coffee, then stood up from the table, and the boys rose, as well, the two rancher-boys holding their hats. The group was moving toward the front door, to say their goodbyes, when suddenly Al and the rancher started talking about something, their heads bent close together.

Al was saying, "Might be helpful, if you don't mind" and "If it's not too much trouble. Might be just the experience."

And the rancher said, "Not at all, Al. It'd be our pleasure. I know James would appreciate the help and the company."

"Why, yes, sir," James agreed from the front walk, where the two boys were waiting on their dad, matching white cowboy hats now low on their heads.

Leon was standing just behind Al, shifting foot to foot, hemming and hawing, trying to get a word in.

"All right, then." The rancher nodded.

Al turned to Leon. "You go up and get a bag packed. Make it quick."

Leon started, "But, Dad—"

Al gave him a look. "Go on, now."

And suddenly Leon was up the stairs, going through his drawers, throwing clothes into a duffel bag. He came down ready to go.

"Leon's going up to Billings for a few weeks to get some experience working with Pete and James here," Al said to Eve when she'd finished gathering the dishes from the table and was at the door.

She stopped, nearly knocked off her feet. "Well—" she said. "I—"

"It's all arranged," Al said to quiet her.

The rancher tipped his hat. "Thank you kindly, Eve. I'm going to have to report to Milly about those lemon bars. She just might be writing you for the recipe. And don't you worry. We'll take good care of him."

"Of course. Of course, you're welcome," Eve said.

She tried to catch Leon as he passed, his bag slung over his shoulder, but he just tore his arm from her grip and went to the car. He got in the backseat with the younger son and did not wave as they pulled away.

When Leon got home after six weeks on the ranch, he was deeply sunburned and his hands were torn and scarred, but he was "no worse for wear," Al said. Al had been on the road and gone up to Billings to see about some cattle. He'd picked Leon up on his way home.

"If there was one thing I never wanted to see you do," Eve said after Al had left town again, "it's farm work."

They were all at the table.

"For heaven sakes," she said, "I don't know how your dad managed to arrange all that on the fly and just kick you all the way up to Montana like he did."

The rancher in Billings had put Leon up in a side room in the barn. Leon had a cot to sleep on, just next to the horses, and a washroom with a plastic, rust-stained shower stall. In the mornings he'd have breakfast with the family; then James would order him out to the fields and disappear. Neither of those boys lifted a finger the whole time he was there, Leon said. Most days, Leon would be all by himself, mowing or raking in some distant pasture. By the time he got back to the house, his dinner would be cold. He'd eat alone on the front steps, then head back to the barn for the night.

Leon talked about how the ranch people would send him out to work in the fields all day with no hat, no water, no lunch, nothing. One particularly hot day it got so bad he thought he was going to die of heatstroke or dehydration, he said, so when he finally spotted a farmhouse on the far horizon, he turned his tractor and just kept driving in that general direction, through ditches and pastures, over two gravel roads, until he got to it. He knocked on the door to beg for a glass of water. The lady at the house gasped to see the state he was in. She ran to get him a cool drink, brought him a wet washcloth, and made him rest in the shade for half an hour before sending him off with an old straw hat and a canning jar full of lemonade. He said he thought that lady probably saved his life, that if she hadn't answered the door, he might have died that day.

"I don't see how they could treat you like that," Eve said. "They're such good friends of your dad's. I just don't understand it."

"They're business acquaintances. That's all," Leon said. "And I don't think it was supposed to be a sleepover party."

"Well, it wasn't supposed to be a concentration camp, either. How could your father do that to you?" Eve said. "How could he just send you off like that without even asking what you wanted, or what I thought about it?"

Leon started to get up. "He wanted me to experience real life. That's what he said on the way home." He shrugged.

"Real life, my ass," Eve said. "That's a load of crap. Real life doesn't mean farm work. There's a lot more interesting things to do than work a farm eighteen hours a day. God knows. You've got lots of options, Leon. It's a big, wide world out there. You can be anything you want to be, anything you set your mind to. Remember that."

Leon nodded and took a deep breath. "Okay," he said. "I'm going to Mike's."

Mike was the friend Al didn't like most of all, because of his "Geronimo" hair and overall "wild-man" appearance. He was also the one who'd written "LeonRStoned" on the envelope René had found in Leon's drawer.

"The world is your oyster, Leon!" Eve called after him. "You can do whatever you put your mind to. I mean it!"

But Leon was already out the door and on his bike. He was half-way down the block like a streak of lightning.

Through the years, Leon collected all kinds of "nearly died" stories.

In his twenties, he ended up by himself deep in the woods near Silver Mountain, clearing trees for the state. He'd just lifted his roaring chain saw high above his head to reach an entangled branch when the saw slipped from his grasp and fell onto the leg that was bracing him against the hillside. Still rotating, the blade cut straight through to the bone in a heartbeat. Leon ripped off his shirt, made a tourniquet to slow the bleeding, and dragged himself back to his truck, operating the clutch, gas, and brake with his one good leg until he'd got himself to the nearest gas station, twenty miles away, at which point he laid on the horn and promptly passed out. He got three layers of stitches, over a hundred and fifty in all, at the hospital. He'd missed the peroneal nerve by a fraction of a millimeter, the doctor said, shaking his head at how Leon had survived at all.

"He might never have walked right again," the doctor told Eve. "And that's the least of it."

"I think he's got nine lives," Eve said.

Then there was his story of dropping by to do a few lines of blow with some friends up in the hills above Keystone. He'd just stepped through the door when three speed freaks with semiautomatics busted in, eager to settle an unpaid debt.

"Luckily," Leon would say, "I'd somehow got myself an American Express card. Shit. They had us all lined up against the wall and I was waving that card around. Finally I got everybody to calm down enough so I could convince them to let me go to town and get them some cash." He'd get to laughing. "Hell, I could do a credit card commercial," he'd say, not missing the irony. He had unpaid bills all over town, had even spent time in jail for writing bad checks at every liquor store within fifty miles. Then, getting serious, he'd add, "But, Jesus, those guys were so high. And they weren't kidding around. We could of all died that day. Easy."

25

Chicken

"Mom's looking for you," Leon called, coming around the corner and finding René at the back door of the Congregational church, where she was hiding out, smoking cigarettes. He was driving their VW camper around the parking lot, working the stick shift. He'd be fifteen in a few months, ready to take the test for his driver's license. "You'd better get home," he said.

Since the Christ Evangelical Youth Ministry had begun to seem more and more prudish and dictatorial, and René was always on the wrong side of every topic—Indians, homosexuals, dancing— she'd slacked off and started hanging with some outliers from school. They'd meet behind the church across the street from her house and light up a cigarette, pass it around, then chew pine needles. There were three boys and two girls, so they'd come up with a lot of dare games, including one in which a boy stood behind a girl and inched his hands down into her pants until she screamed, "Chicken!" There were no winners or losers, but that didn't mean they weren't competitive. René never shied away from a challenge, and she and Tom held the kissing record, a timed two-minute full-tongues session in the makeshift "make-out" tent, a small pup tent one of the boys had managed to swipe from his older brother.

Luckily, when Leon came around the corner that day, they were all just sitting on the steps, smoking cigarettes.

"You're gonna be in so much trouble," Leon said, putting the VW in reverse, revving the engine and grinding the gears, then trying again and backing away like a pro.

"What's the matter with your brother?" Tom asked, referring to the eerie combination of Leon's denuded face and his perennial sullen glare.

"Nothing's the matter with my brother," René said bitterly. "What's the matter with your fat mom?"

"Jeez. Okay."

By the time René had chewed some needles and got back across the street, Eve was gone to the store.

"She's coming back," Leon said. "Just wait."

So she waited in the kitchen.

Eve finally came through the door, looking like she'd been dragged around behind the car. Her sweater was drooping off one shoulder, her hair was ratted and disheveled, and her face was pasty, bloated. She dropped the groceries onto the counter, then plucked out a carton of cigarettes and hurled it sideways as if skipping a rock. It skidded across the table, knocking René solidly in the chest.

"Smoke 'em!" she growled.

René figured Leon had told, but the punch of the cigarettes and the heat of Eve's stare took her breath away. She started to cry; then Eve started to cry, not mournfully but furiously.

"You're gonna smoke 'em," Eve said, coming to stand over her. "And you're not leaving this room until that whole carton is finished. You hear me?"

"I won't!" René screamed. "I'm not going to. Leave me alone!"

Eve raised a hand and slapped René across the face so hard that her jaw torqued and her ears rung. Though René understood that her mother harbored plenty against her, it was a violation of everything she imagined Eve felt about her deep down, all the love and pride she thought Eve kept secreted away, just for her. The solid, ancient hills and plains René counted on beneath her feet might as well have split apart, the ground opened up to swallow her.

"You will," Eve said, struggling to tear open the carton, ripping into a pack, shoving a cigarette into René's mouth, then lighting a match. "You think you can do whatever you want and you don't have to answer to anybody. Just like your dad. Well, I've had it! I'm going to stand right here and watch you smoke every last one of these goddamn cigarettes. Right now!"

Eve had sobered, so René was the only one crying.

"Inhale," Eve said.

"I did."

"You did not."

René inhaled and choked.

"That's right," Eve said. "Now keep going." She turned to put the groceries away as René smoked and cried, smoked and cried, lighting up one cigarette after the other.

Jayne and Leon had fled just after Eve pitched the carton at her, so René was on her own.

"Keep going," Eve said when René began to flag. "You're just getting started."

René lit up again and again, until she couldn't do any more. Her head was spinning, and whatever had been in her stomach was on its way up. She ran to the bathroom.

"That's right," Eve called after her. "Serves you right."

René came back dizzy, wiping her mouth.

"Sit down," Eve said. "You're not done yet."

René sat, but she didn't take another cigarette. She put her head on the table and didn't move.

"Go to your room," Eve said finally. "And don't come out until you can apologize. For smoking and whatever else you've been doing, sneaking around behind my back, lying to me. I've had enough of it. Now go."

So René climbed the stairs, doubled over, holding the rail, and fell onto her bed. Jayne came up to check on her. Leon, too.

"Sorry," he said.

"It's okay," she said, her mouth hanging open, spit dribbling onto her pillow.

"I didn't know she'd do that."

"No," she grunted.

When she felt up to it, René went back downstairs. She found Eve bent over her sewing machine.

"Sorry," she said, trying to sound sincere.

"Not good enough," Eve said, not even looking up.

"Sorry for sneaking around, smoking cigarettes," René tried.

"Is that all?"

"Yes."

Eve stopped and glared at her, skeptical.

"Promise," René said.

As far as René was concerned, the kissing games were personal and none of Eve's business. And René certainly wasn't going to tell her that she sometimes passed around the half-empty bottle of Bacardi Eve kept for company, not if she didn't already know.

"I don't want to hear about you smoking, not ever again," Eve said. "Come here."

Eve didn't get up, but she opened her arms, mechanically, almost against her will.

"Now get yourself something to eat, and go straight to bed." And René leaned in for a hug that felt mainly like a metal restraining device closing around her. "See you in the morning," Eve said.

Eve was working at a clothing store downtown in the afternoons, doing on-site alterations, and Jayne had started playing at a neighbor's up the street, so when René got home from school, there'd be no one around. She still met her friends behind the church, but it was a while before she felt like having another cigarette.

Then one of the boys told her that you could spray deodorant on your thumb and light it up without getting burned.

"You could do your whole body," he said, sounding dumbfounded by his own information. "Be, like, Fire Man."

"Yeah, but who wants to be a *fireman*?" René scoffed. "That's a dumb name."

"I do," Tom said.

"Figures." René laughed, and Tom started after her, chasing her through the tall grass until he finally caught her around the shoulders and rolled her to the ground, holding her in a steady embrace, tumbling her over and over.

The next afternoon, when she was home alone, she tried it on the kitchen counter. First, she sprayed a short, straight line of deodorant, then lit one end and watched the fire zip across the countertop. It was like a miniature Evel Knievel, and nothing got charred or even discolored. Then she tried it on the refrigerator, spraying a loop and lighting the beginning, watching the flame race its course. From there, she became more confident, lighting up the walls and cupboards, holding a match to one end of her latest design and

watching the flame ride and jump and spark as it faithfully followed the loop-de-loops and curlicues, the long, winding peaks
and valleys, the spirals, corkscrews, circular mazes.

There was never a mark, so no one ever seemed to know she'd
done it, but for a while there, after coming home from letting the
boys look down her shirt, René was lighting up that kitchen every
day.

Tom was short and strong, like a Russian sailor, and had scraggly
yellow hair, electric-blue eyes, and deep-set dimples. He and René
started riding his bike all over town—René on the back end of his
banana seat, arms around his waist, as he pedaled up and down the
inclines. Then one day, instead of meeting the others behind the
church, Tom stopped in her driveway, and they went up to her room.

"I'm making up dances," she told him when he picked up the
album she'd left on her bookcase. Mrs. G had given Eve a record
called *World's Greatest Ballet Hits,* and René had been playing it
over and over, making dust motes scramble in the dim light that
filtered through their living room windows as she choreographed.

"Cool," Tom said.

"I could teach you."

"No way," he laughed.

"You could put on Leon's tights," she said, unfazed, and they
snuck into Leon's room and got out a pair of his black tights.

Tom put them on and came out pulling down on his T-shirt,
stretching it nearly to his knees.

"What am I supposed to do in these?" he said, embarrassed,
hopping one foot to the other.

"You can be my partner," René said.

So they clasped hands and went downstairs. René made Tom
stand behind her and put his hands on her waist. They tried a few

simple steps, mostly getting caught up on each other's feet and tumbling into the furniture or lurching sideways to catch their balance, laughing. Then René put on some music and tried a spin. She fell into Tom's arms. And he caught her.

"You should take ballet," she told him.

"No chance."

But just like that, the very next week, Tom was in Mrs. G's Beginners class, and no need to say that Mrs. G was over the moon to have him. And after just a few weeks of him grinning through every exercise at the barre, then bounding wildly across the floor when Mrs. G gave a big jumping combination, Tom invited René to his birthday party.

René stayed by Tom's side as everyone had pizza and cake. After he'd opened his presents, she grabbed his arm and tilted her head toward a darkened room where his mother had put a stack of records on a turntable. "Let's dance," she said. "Come on."

They went into the other room, and Tom secured his hands around her waist as she linked her arms around the back of his neck, resting her head on his shoulder. They were used to being close to each other from their afternoons at René's house, but as they began to sway, René could see that the girls from her class were starting to pile up in the doorway, with some of the boys right behind them, on tiptoe. They were all leaning in, keeping their feet behind the threshold, the girls raising their hands to cover their gaping mouths.

"We should go steady," she said in Tom's ear. It was something Leon's friends had been doing—giving tokens to the girls they liked best—and René figured it was a sure thing for her and Tom.

When he didn't answer, she said it again. "I could be your girlfriend."

"What do you mean?" Tom said, pulling away, suddenly noticing the crowd.

"I bought a medallion," she said. She'd walked all the way downtown for that express purpose. "You could just give it to me."

"I don't want to," Tom said.

"Why not?"

Tom stopped. He didn't want to dance anymore.

"Maybe we could go steady later?" René tried as he stepped away, clearly ready to get back to the party.

"No," Tom said. "I don't want to at all."

Then Tom was out of the room, back with the others, and René was left standing alone with the music still going. And while the boys broke away and fell in with Tom, putting their arms around his shoulders and slapping him on the back, she could tell by the way the girls stayed glued together, grinning at each other and raising their eyebrows, that mainly, they were thrilled to see her left behind.

She followed Tom out, but the party wasn't the same. The girls were once again in a huddle, and Tom was off with the boys, so she went outside and sat on the steps by herself in the moonlight, feeling disembodied—as if the faintest breeze might cut right through her—until Eve showed up to take her home.

Kenny Bishop lived in one of the flat-topped underground houses René passed on her way to school. It was more like a basement for a house that would never be built. He was tall, loose-knit, and oafish, and sometimes out of the corner of her eye, René would catch him picking his nose. She invited him over and took him up to her room.

"Kenny," she said, getting right down to business, "do you want to be my boyfriend?"

He gazed at her wide-eyed, like she was his fairy godmother.

"Sure," he said, his body twitching as his voice caught.

"Take this medallion," she said. "And give it back to me. Then we're going steady."

"Okay," he said. He took the medallion, then handed it back.

Though Kenny's hands were dirty and his teeth looked many days' worth of unbrushed, she put the medallion around her neck.

"What do we do now?" Kenny said. "Do we kiss?"

"No," she said. "Nothing."

They walked to the edge of her driveway, and she sent him home.

The next day, Tom took one look at the medallion hanging from René's neck and Kenny Bishop hovering at her elbow, turned his back, and walked away.

René broke it off with Kenny that very afternoon. He walked her home without talking and came up to her room. She took off the medallion, handed it back to him.

"Why?" he said. "What did I do?"

"It's just a mistake."

"You're a bitch," he said, giving her back the medallion, since it was hers in the first place. "Everybody says so."

And she didn't have one word to defend herself. In fact, she thought maybe she agreed with him. It didn't matter. Either way, there was no reason to keep up the lie. She put the medallion in a drawer and just tried to forget about it.

But Tom didn't speak to her again, and after school he didn't meet the others behind the church anymore. If he saw her at school, he'd go the other way. And if she saw him coming out of the Beginners class at Mrs. G's, she'd nod, but they wouldn't talk. Then sometime before the year was over, he simply disappeared.

Mrs. G told Eve that Tom's family had moved out of town, that she should have known better than to think a kid like that might stick around, that having him in class had been too good to be true.

"Lord knows he'll have a better chance in North Carolina or wherever the hell else he ends up than he'd ever have here in South

Dakota. Right, Eve?" Which made René understand that Tom, having just weeks ago stepped out of Leon's bedroom, giggling and prancing idiotically in Leon's tights, was now going to have chances she'd never have, simply because he could pack up and move away.

At school, she pretended the whole thing didn't interest her, but her stomach was upset, and her face felt pinched. Still, whenever the other girls looked her way, smirking as though they could see the loss etched on her features, René would let her eyes slide right past them, trying to seem absorbed with something they couldn't discern, something glittering and full of promise, waiting just for her on the far horizon.

26

The Fates Allow

Mrs. G was selling her studio. She wanted Eve to take it over. The two of them had put on *Nutcracker* performances and spring recitals for the past three years. They'd taught all the classes, kept all the books, designed and made all the costumes. Now Mrs. G was ready to retire. She kept saying she was tired of the winters, she was moving south.

"I can't do it," Eve said for the umpteenth time. "I don't feel capable, Helen. I don't have the training."

"Well, if you really don't want it, then I'm going to have to find someone that does," Mrs. G said, finally giving up the campaign. "I guess we've done enough damage." She laughed.

"I'll miss it," Eve said. "I really will."

"There's no one better than you to run this place. I built it. I ought to know."

Eve shook her head. "And what would I do with the Advanced class, when it's me who should be taking lessons from them?"

"René and Leon could help you," Mrs. G suggested.

René glanced up, then quickly stuck her nose back in her book. She was going through Mrs. G's Cecchetti method manual on classical technique. She knew the eight body positions, but she saw there were also five Cecchetti arabesques.

"That'd go over like a lead balloon with the other kids," Eve was saying. "Not to mention the parents."

"What if you started your own little school somewhere else, like someplace up in the hills? Tried it out? It'd be all beginners," Mrs. G said. "And I'll be here for the next year or so anyway before the hubby's ready to leave. I could help you. We could give it a shot."

"That'd be interesting," Eve said. "And it certainly wouldn't hurt to be making some extra money."

"That's the spirit!" Mrs. G laughed. "I'll go ahead and get a photographer to take some pictures of this place so I can get it on the market. Who knows? Maybe someone'll move into town and solve all our problems. Right, Eve?"

René closed the book, put it back on the shelf.

"What're you doing with that all this time?" Mrs. G asked her.

"Memorizing arabesques."

Mrs. G raised her eyebrows at Eve. "Well, then," she said. "Let's see."

So René showed her, reciting as she executed each one. "First arabesque, second arabesque," she said, continuing up to five.

"Did you learn those just now?" Mrs. G asked. "Just looking at that book?"

René nodded. Was it a trick? Had she got one of them wrong?

"Looks like you've found your little helper," Mrs. G said to Eve, cackling.

René's face tightened. *Never,* she thought, grinning fiercely at her mother. *Not ever.*

"Good idea," Eve said, laughing along with Mrs. G as they all started out the door, René shivering with the cold, buttoning her coat high around her neck as Mrs. G locked up behind them.

Mrs. G found a photographer to take pictures of the Academy of Ballet. He offered his services to photograph some of the kids, so she told him she'd let him know if anyone was interested.

"I don't care, Eve," she said. "But he says he's not charging anything, so if you wanted to take Leon and René down to his studio, maybe you could get some good photos out of it. Maybe there'd be one to use for the new school."

Eve had taken Mrs. G's advice and signed rental papers on a church hall in Belle Fourche, South Dakota—a cattle-trucking outpost about an hour north of Rapid City, where *ballet* wasn't even a word yet. She and Mrs. G were already busy making preparations for her trial year of teaching there.

So Mrs. G made an appointment for them with the photographer, and when the day rolled around, Leon and René got their costumes together while Eve and Jayne waited in the car. Then they all drove downtown to the photographer's studio.

The photographer shook Eve's hand with both his hands. He was tall, with broad shoulders, dark, curly hair, and a thick mustache, and he was flirtatious and open, as if he thought just about anything was possible. He kept smiling and twinkling his eyes at Eve, which was causing her to brighten more every minute.

After giving them a short tour of his studio, the photographer showed them to a dressing room in the back with a large, lighted vanity.

"You can change in here," he said, lightly touching his hand to the small of Eve's back. "Just come out when you're ready."

Leon dressed in black tights and a white T-shirt, René put on her pink tutu, and they headed out to where the photographer was waiting.

The photographer took Leon by the shoulders and positioned him under the lights, telling René to stand with him, in the same spot. He was using a large-format camera on a tripod, he explained, so they had to be where he could get to them. He went back and forth, adjusting the camera, the lights, chatting with Eve as he set up his equipment.

"Ready," he said, finally. "Now just go ahead and do whatever you like, and I'll take pictures."

Leon supported René in various poses—arabesque and penchée, attitude en avant and derrière. They turned sideways and René faced Leon in passé, bending away from him. They did a fish dive, a shoulder lift, whatever they could think of.

Then the photographer wanted photos of Leon by himself. So Eve brought out one of Leon's costume tunic tops, and he changed where he stood, handing Eve the shirt he'd just taken off, leaving his smooth, bare chest exposed for an instant to the rich, hot lights of the studio.

"Just us boys," the photographer laughed, stepping out from behind his camera.

Leon posed on one knee, smiling. He put both hands on one hip, twisting his torso like a toreador. He did tours and leaps, then jumped straight up and split his legs in the air, touching his toes.

"Wonderful!" the photographer said. "Magnificent! Oh, your children are just terrific," he said to Eve, coming out to shake her hand, as if to congratulate her. "So talented."

"Why, thank you," she said, beaming, her face coloring. "I like to think so."

"Nice job, Leon." The photographer placed his large hands on Leon's shoulders, nearly encircling Leon's neck, and René was left to wonder why he didn't say the same to her and why he hadn't wanted pictures of her by herself.

"You kids want to look through the camera?"

The photographer set a box behind the tripod so they could all see through the eyepiece, and Eve stood in place against the backdrop, pretending to pose.

"Beautiful," the photographer called to her. "Now lift your leg."

"You're joking." She laughed.

"It'd be fun to be a photographer," Leon said.

"His dad's a cattle dealer," Eve explained. "He's out of town all the time."

"It is fun," the photographer said to Leon.

"It's a great job," Eve confirmed, still lifting her arms and tilting her head for the camera. "You could travel the world."

Leon nodded and smiled his bright, bashful smile, which none of them had seen in a very long time.

"I'm going to be developing this film tonight, Leon," the photographer said, "if you want to give me a hand, see how it's done? If it's okay with your mom, that is." He flashed Eve a smile.

"That's an awfully nice offer," Eve said, stepping away from the backdrop, rejoining the others.

"You've got some awfully nice kids here," the photographer answered. "And if Leon's interested in photography, there's no better way to learn than to get in there and do it himself. Get his hands dirty."

"That's what I always say. See, Leon? The world's a great big place. You want to learn photography? He says he's happy to teach you."

"It'd be a good introduction." The photographer slapped Leon on the back and, with an air of tremendous ease and well-being, went to snap the spent film from his camera. "Could be fun."

Leon nodded. "Sure," he said.

"Okay," the photographer said. "How about I stop by your house when I'm done here, around six-thirty, and we'll head over to the darkroom. Sound good?" He looked to Eve.

"Sounds fine," Eve said, happy and grateful to have finally found someone willing to step in for Leon, to fill the void left by his absent father. It was just what Leon needed—a grown man to take an interest, to pay some attention.

So Eve gave the photographer directions, and he pulled up to the house after dinner, tooting his horn. Al was out of town, as usual. Eve and Leon were waiting in the living room, watching for the photographer's car, straining to see through their darkened front window.

"That's for you," Eve said. "See? I told you, Leon. It's a big, wide world out there. You can be anything you want to be."

But Leon was already out the door.

"Bye, honey!" she called after him.

It was only as Eve watched the photographer's car pull away, his taillights disappearing down the street and around the corner, that she remembered he hadn't told her where they were going. When he'd given them the tour of his downtown studio, he'd made a point of telling her he had no space there for a darkroom. She could still hear him saying something about having to develop his film off-site, across town. There'd been no sign or business card at his place, and he hadn't offered her any information, so she didn't have a phone number or an address. She was stunned to realize that she didn't even know his name.

The car was long gone, melted into the darkness, and Mrs. G, who was the only one who knew who the guy was and how to get ahold of him, was out of town, visiting friends somewhere in Colorado.

Eve lit a cigarette and told herself to calm down. She hadn't just sent Leon off without asking him whether he wanted to go or not, as Al had done; she hadn't shipped him clear out of state without warning, not giving him a choice, hog-tying him in front of company so that he couldn't even speak up for himself. She'd never do that. She was broadening his horizons, giving him options, showing him that his choices were wide open. And no, it just wasn't accurate to say she'd let a total stranger carry her boy off into the night. She simply needed to calm down.

She sat for a long time, looking out the window, trying to see past the point where the photographer's taillights had vanished. She started to pace, then forced herself to sit back down. She smoked and figured. Where could the darkroom be? How long could it take to get there? How long to set up? How long to wait for each image to come to life? How long? How long? She knitted and smoked, made coffee and watched, trying not to panic. And as the hours crept by, she reminded herself that it took time to develop film, probably more time than she knew, that she had to be patient, that most likely everything was fine. Not having the man's number was simply an oversight, she told herself, as much her fault as his.

By ten-thirty Eve felt light-headed and feverish, damp with sweat. There was a phrase that kept coming back to her, ringing in her ears, something about *boys . . . boys . . . just boys. Just us boys.* That was it. That's what he'd said, she realized, when Leon had changed costumes under the lights. *Just us boys.* Then he'd laughed. She drew a shallow breath and pushed the haunting noise away from her, out of her mind, but still she could hear the edges of it, ringing in the distance—*Just us boys. Just us boys,* then laughter.

At ten forty-five, Eve vomited. She rinsed her mouth but felt her insides burning up. She was just picking up the phone to call the police when a car pulled into the driveway.

"Oh, God. Hallelujah," she cried when she saw Leon getting out. And when he came through the door, she thought she'd die of relief. Tears sprang to her eyes as she ran to greet him, to collect him.

"I was so worried," she blurted out, unable to help herself.

He pushed right past her.

"Everything okay, Leon?" she asked as he tore up to his room. "You all right, Leon?"

"Fine," he said, not looking back.

"I'm glad you're home," she called up the stairs. "I'm so glad you're home."

It was all okay, Eve told herself. After all that, it was just her worried mind getting the better of her. *The things I put myself through,* she thought. *Too much. Just too much.*

The next morning there was a bundle of three-by-five black-and-white photos, like a double deck of oversized playing cards, wedged inside the front screen door. Eve brought it into the kitchen, where they were all having cereal.

"Your pictures," she said, placing the packet on the table.

Leon shot up with his half-empty bowl and headed for the sink.

"Leon?" she said. "How was everything last night? Everything okay?"

"I'm going to Mike's."

"Wait. Tell me about it. What did you do?"

"Nothing," Leon said. "Leave me alone."

"We want to hear," Eve said.

"I don't want to talk about it." Leon started out the back door.

"You have ballet class tonight, don't forget," Eve called after him.

"I'm not going," he called back.

"What?" She was instantly up and following him.

"I'm not going," he said again. "I quit."

"You can't quit," she said. "What are you talking about? You're not quitting."

"I quit," he said. "I quit. I'm going to Mike's."

They were standing outside now, Leon in the driveway with one foot up on his bike pedal, Eve in her nightgown beside him.

"Don't quit, Leon. You don't want to quit."

"*I do* want to quit! *I do!*"

René and Jayne were watching out the kitchen window. Leon was suddenly wiping tears from the naked red rims of his eyes, shaking all over.

"I'm not going to ballet anymore, no matter what you say! I quit!"

Eve just looked at him, her body angled in confusion and despair.

"Mrs. G won't like it," she said. Then, quietly: "Is there something you want to tell me, Leon?"

"No," he said. "Just leave me alone. Please. Please. I just need to be left alone. I'm going to Mike's."

And he pushed down on his bike pedal and slowly curved out of the driveway and down the road, riding away, ambling on his bike in a way they'd never seen him do before, like an old man.

Eve took the photos along to ballet class, but Mrs. G wasn't impressed.

"Look at that extension," she said to René. "Phooey. You can do better than that." René grimaced, but Mrs. G just kept going. "There's nothing worth using, Eve. I don't know about that photographer," she added. "The pictures he took of the studio were no good, either."

Eve didn't say anything at first. Then she said, "I don't know a thing about him."

"Well, now you know one thing," Mrs. G said. "You know he can't take a picture worth a hoot!" She laughed, but Eve just shook her head. "Good thing he didn't charge you for those."

Eve humphed.

"Time for class," Mrs. G said. "Where's Leon?"

"He's not coming," Eve said. "He says he's quitting, he's not dancing anymore."

"What?" Mrs. G was flummoxed. "Why?"

"He didn't say why. He's just done with it. That's all. He won't talk to me."

"Boys," Mrs. G sighed. "It's a crying shame. It's a crime, really."

"He seems set on it. I guess he's been through enough."

"It's his decision. It's got to be. But you tell him *I* want him to come back. I'll miss him too much if he's not in class. He's my buddy. He's like the star of the show around here."

"I know it," Eve said. "I'll tell him, but I don't think it's going to make any difference."

"Tell him anyway," Mrs. G said. Then she took René by the hand. "Come on, René. Time to dance."

And just like that, René was dancing and Leon was not.

"We didn't develop any film," Leon said many decades later, well past anyone's idea of his prime, back pain confining him to life in an easy chair in front of the television. He scoffed at the idea. "He attacked me," Leon said. "But I fought him. Yeah. I fought him off. I don't want to talk about it."

It was clear enough. No one believed that, at fourteen, Leon could have dominated that grown man. And recently it had surfaced that, way back then, not long after the night Leon had disappeared with him, a group of men had banded together to threaten the photographer, to drive him out of town.

"If I'd known," Eve said pitifully, her once thick, auburn hair reduced to wisps of silver, "I never would have let you—"

"I don't want to talk about it, okay?" Leon said sharply, ending things. "Is that all right with you?"

So, though they knew for certain that something had happened to Leon that night, out of consideration, no one spoke of it. And they were each set adrift, left to imagine the possibilities.

And after something like that—something that changed everything—René could see that her childhood belief in John the Apostle's moon turning to blood was simply, criminally, understated and insufficient. Why hadn't it exploded or fallen from the sky? And the ancient story of Prometheus having his liver pecked away endlessly by a circling eagle, having it grow back daily in order that the torment could be experienced as continuous, seemed merely accurate, descriptive; while being turned into a pillar of salt, to be washed away in the next rain, felt like benevolence, like something one might wish for.

And since, even all those years later, the moon persisted in hanging, shimmering silver in the deep night sky, it seemed that only the miraculous end to the tale of Lazarus—who'd died because Jesus had tarried in coming to his aid but, after being dead for many days, had been revived by Jesus's tears and prayers, brought back to life complete and strong and whole—only the miracle, the restoration, the reigniting of flesh and spirit, remained alien to experience, taking its place outside of even hope, and could be finally understood as it was, exempt from the realm of things that might just come to pass.

Part Four

27

Means to an End

Leon turned fifteen, got his driver's license, and disappeared. When he wasn't cruising up and down Mount Rushmore Road in the VW bus, he'd be over at an unsupervised friend's house, drinking from the liquor cabinet, relaxing.

He'd come home to an empty house—with René at ballet, Jayne at a friend's, and Eve either at Mrs. G's, working on dance routines for the new school, or downtown doing alterations. Since there was no one around, he didn't have to worry about staggering or slurring his speech. He'd just lie on the couch with his shirt off, watching TV, drifting in and out of sleep, or stumble up to his room and close the door.

And in June, when Al announced that they'd all be going on a cross-country trip to visit their aunt in Seattle, Leon said he was staying home.

"Of course you're coming with us," Eve said.

"I'm not going," Leon said.

"Don't be silly."

"Suit yourself," Al said.

So there was a call to Emma, and arrangements were made.

"I just hope she can handle him," Eve said as they pulled out of the driveway, waving at the two of them.

They were standing on the front lawn—Emma calling out and blowing kisses, Leon towering over her, lifting a hand, expressionless.

"Not much to do about it," Eve sighed as they started down Clark Street.

"That's the ticket," Al said cheerily. "We're on the road now. Right, girls?"

So Leon stayed home as the rest of the family made their way west—stopping in Idaho to swim and eat smoked fish, buying huge, ripe cherries at roadside stands, building a fire and folding down the bed in the camper each night while Eve made hot dogs and beans on the Coleman stove, until finally, they pulled into their aunt's driveway. She had fondue waiting for them, a color-coded, enameled fondue fork for each person. René and Jayne chose their colors, then skewered and cooked raw beef slices in the hot pot, raising their eyebrows at each other, giddy. And the next morning they stood together on their aunt's terrace, taking in the view over Puget Sound, until they were all ready to drive downtown, to stand in line for the Space Needle—all but Leon.

Leon always said that from the very first time he took a drink of whiskey, he knew exactly what he wanted to do with the rest of his life. And though, in general, he was adept at making himself disappear in order to accomplish his goal, still he'd surface from time to time. The school would call: Leon was flunking all his classes, or Leon had been caught drilling a peephole into the girls' locker room, or Leon was smoking on school property. He'd be suspended. Or a new, older friend of his none of them had ever seen before would come over, not saying hello or taking off his muddy boots, and the two of them would head up to Leon's room for a minute. Then the friend would turn around and leave.

"What was that about?" Eve would say.

"Nothing. He has to go to work. I'm going to Phil's."

"No, you're not."

"We're working on a project," Leon would say over his shoulder on his way out the door. "I've gotta go or I won't get credit."

Eve would shake her head, then go back to straightening up the kitchen, or loading the washing machine, or practicing the new steps Mrs. G had just given her for her school in Belle Fourche.

And, of course, when Al came home, they'd go round and round.

"You make sure Leon gets a haircut," Al would start.

"I don't know what in the hell you think you're talking about," Eve would say. "Tell him yourself."

Because, though Leon had finally stopped pulling out his hair, now he was growing it long, and with hair past his shoulders and his perennially red, glassy eyes staring into some distance none of the rest of them could see, he was looking even less like himself than he had when his eyebrows and eyelashes were missing.

"Nobody wants to see you like that," Al would tell him. "It's disrespectful. To yourself and everyone else."

But that would be it. Leon was suddenly taller than Al and filling out. He had the broad chest and chiseled features of a movie star, and he was not getting a haircut.

"He looks like a goddamn hippie," Al would say.

"Why can't you say he looks nice? Just once," Eve would fume.

"I think he looks like Jesus," Emma would put in if she was visiting. "Jesus had long hair, you know, but that was the style of the time. He wasn't trying to be rebellious."

But nothing made any difference to Leon. He was gone. He was up in his room, or at a friend's house, or dozing on the couch, and when it came to trying to reach him, every attempt only reconfirmed the hopelessness of the idea.

"What in the world?" Al said. "Think he's been here all night?"

They'd got up to find Leon passed out on the couch in the family room, still in his jeans and T-shirt from the day before, his boots right up on the sofa cushions, the TV hot to the touch, running through the morning shows.

"How the hell should I know." Eve switched off the television.

Al shook him. "Get up, Leon."

Leon moaned.

"Maybe he's sick. Maybe he doesn't feel well. Ever think of that?" Eve said.

"He's going to get himself kicked out of school for good. I know that much."

Eve creased her eyebrows. "Come on, Leon," she pleaded, bending to jostle him. "Come on, honey."

"What?" Leon said, struggling up from what might as well have been somewhere deep underground.

"Time for school," Eve said.

"No," Leon groaned. "I'm not going. I don't feel good."

"Get up, Leon," Al said again.

Leon rolled his eyes and didn't answer.

"I said, *Get up!*" Al threatened, giving the sofa a hard kick, rattling the joints. "Right now!"

"Or what?" Leon muttered. "Just go ahead and do whatever

you're gonna do to me. I'm not getting up." And with that, he turned over, rearranged the sofa pillow under his head, and went back to sleep.

"Well, that's just right," Al said, looking at Eve. "I got a god-damn drunk Indian living in my house. That's just dandy." And he turned and left the room.

Then Eve found the baggie of pot in Leon's sock drawer and decided that was something she could never tell Al about, ever. She waited until he'd left town again before confronting Leon.

"It's not mine," Leon said. "Maybe Mike left it in there. Leave me alone. I have no idea whose it is. I've never seen it before."

"However it got there," Eve said, shaking the buds and seeds out of the plastic bag and into the toilet, "that's the end of it. You have to promise me that much."

"Okay," Leon said, "but I don't know what you're talking about 'cause it's not mine." And he went back into his room and shut the door.

So, since he was failing all of his tenth-grade classes and had been suspended so many times that he was in danger of expulsion, since he was never around and no one ever knew where he was or what he was doing, since he was stashing pot in his room and lying about it, and since he seemed to not care that he was throwing his life away, or give a good goddamn about what anyone else thought about anything anymore, they had to do something. And what they decided to do came from none other than Doc Jensen, who told Eve about a Catholic boarding school for boys in Colorado.

"More like a military school," Jensen said. "They'll teach him discipline, you can count on that. He'll graduate from high school even if they have to handcuff him to a desk." And Jensen laughed, which Eve found thoughtless and arrogant, cruel. "Don't worry," he said. "I was just like him."

It was meant as an apology, but Eve didn't find it comforting, especially since Jensen freely admitted to having spent a good deal of his life as a raving alcoholic and, if you could believe what you heard, had been kicked out of more practices than anyone who depended on him cared to count.

But Al agreed with the idea, and Eve didn't see any alternative, so before they could turn around twice, Leon had a ride with one of Al's cattleman friends to Denver. The Brothers of the Order of Saint Francis would pick him up at the other end. And just like that, just naturally, as if they'd all simply awakened one morning to a change they'd known was coming—like looking out to see the first snowfall, or to find winter suddenly breaking, snow melting away, water running whichever direction was downhill in little streams—just like that, Leon was packed up and loaded into a stranger's car. He rolled away one early morning without even saying goodbye.

28

Over Like Dominoes

Eve and Al had been looking for a home to buy so they wouldn't have to keep throwing their money away on rent, but it wasn't until after Leon had been sent off to Colorado that Al found the perfect one: a brick-and-stone Tudor on a corner lot of the wide, green expanse of Pine Boulevard, where the doctors and lawyers and orthodontists lived. The boulevard angled uphill from town, a large grassy median dividing one side of the street from the other, running the entire length, right up into the foothills. Though there were the occasional pines and elms, even a stand of paper birches here and there, for the most part it was lined with tall cottonwoods— the thick, knotty trunks seeming to contradict the aspirational, shimmering branches, which extended and spread, leaves sparkling in the air.

The house had high ceilings with decorative crown moldings,

built-in cabinets, oversized picture windows, a library, and two fire-
places. Jayne would have the bedroom looking out over the side
yard, where a weeping willow bobbed and rustled in the breeze.
René would have the tiny, fairy-tale room set into one of the eaves,
with the slanted ceiling and the gingerbread-cottage windows that
were so small and low she'd have to kneel down to see out past the
driveway to the manicured back lawn. There was the master bedroom for Eve and Al, plus an empty room that would have been
Leon's but that Eve set up as a guest room, with two twin beds.

They moved in, and in the unfamiliar darkness René began to
wander, woozy with sleep in the middle of the night, through the
wide upstairs hallway to the unoccupied guest room, where she'd
collapse onto one of the beds, puzzling about where Leon might be
and what it was, exactly, that went missing when someone went
away. Was it a look, a gesture, a simple inflection? How could
something so intricately entwined, so deeply intermixed in the ebb
and flow of every day that it didn't even bear notice, just up and
disappear?

Sometimes she'd linger in the dark near the wrought-iron rail,
where the upstairs landing fell away to the first floor, and hear
music suddenly rising through the stairwell. It seemed that someone was downstairs, playing Eve's organ, and René would quickly
turn to check that Eve was still in her bed, asleep. Confirming that,
she'd stand spellbound, sensing that the music was coming to her
from some imperceptible parallel realm, pouring out for her
through some tear in the normal fabric of things.

It made about as much sense as the pictures that flooded her
mind whenever she thought of Leon: Leon was a stump with flail-
ing arms, injured and immobile, his legs cut off at the knee; Leon
had been flayed alive, his skin flapping around him in sheets as he
faced into a merciless wind. Everything was too painful for Leon;
he seemed too tender to be alive. Even when he'd been living at

home, he hadn't really been there, his presence like a riddle: *How can someone not be there when he's standing right in front of you?* And now, shipped off to Saint Francis Boys' School, who-knows-where in the middle of Colorado, it was as if the leaving he'd been practicing for so long was finally complete. He was simply and utterly gone.

Without Leon around, René found herself more on her own, more adrift than ever. It was one thing to no longer have him in ballet class, to have lost his companionship in that, but to not have him in his room, or rummaging through the refrigerator late at night, or breezing out the door on his way to "no good"? And to know that he'd been sent away against his will, without a choice? There was something about the way Leon had been cast out that made the walls feel too close, as though they were holding her captive, just waiting for the right moment to come down on her.

The music would roll, crest up the stairwell, and seem to sing: *We are watching. We are here. We are with you. We are here.* And René would stand very still at the top of the stairs, tilt her head just so in the deep of the night, and listen, comforted that, even though it was coming from somewhere far away, from some incorporeal other world, something, somewhere, cared enough to send her this ethereal music, to fill the silence and keep her company.

Sometimes she'd lean over the upstairs railing to be closer to the source, and other times she'd keep her back pressed against the hall cupboard, repeatedly checking around the corner into Eve's room to make sure she was still there, afraid that someone had broken into the house and, in some *Twilight Zone* perversion, was actually downstairs, playing the organ.

Eve had rented the United Christian Fellowship Hall in Belle Fourche, South Dakota, a town that claimed—according to a plaque set high on a nearby barren hilltop—to be situated at "the geographical center of the U.S. of A." She'd typed up a schedule of classes, then hauled René and Jayne along to put dance school brochures under all the windshield wipers in the Belle Fourche Livestock Auction's dirt parking lot, to tape homemade posters into grimy downtown storefront windows, and to walk the few dusty residential blocks, sticking schedules and price lists into mailboxes.

Meanwhile, Mrs. G had found a buyer for the Academy of Ballet. Deanne Johnson had tap-danced on Ted Mack's *Original Amateur Hour,* so she seemed at least partially qualified. She was moving to Rapid City for her husband's work, and she was young and eager to have her own school.

"She'll be a lot stronger in tap than ballet, Eve," Mrs. G said, letting her head fall into her hands.

"Oh, Helen. Maybe you just have to stay."

"If I stay, I'll have to get a divorce."

"Sounds like a winner," Eve said, and they laughed.

Mrs. G asked Deanne to teach some of the Beginners classes, as a trial, and Miss Dea made it perfectly clear that she wouldn't be needing René to demonstrate, and that she was happy to go ahead and take over Eve's Pre-Ballet class right away.

"Tell her to have at it," Eve said.

Eve got busy remodeling the big room in her new basement, turning it into a practice studio so she'd have her own place to go through combinations, to get herself ready to stand up in front of a class and pretend to know what in the hell she was doing.

She used a trowel and wet plaster to resurface the ceiling and made two mirrored walls with stick-on tiles from the hardware store. Then Al drilled holes and put up the double barre Eve had sanded and finished by hand.

"The floor's the thing. You're never going to have the floor you need down here, Eve," Mrs. G told her. Mrs. G was a stickler for an elevated wood floor, but Eve's home studio was going to stay just like it was—linoleum over poured cement.

Mrs. G had come up with a name for the Belle Fourche school—Royal Arts Dance—and drawn a logo that looked like a medieval shield divided into thirds, because Eve would be teaching tap, jazz, and ballet.

"Theoretically," Eve said.

"Don't worry," Mrs. G said. "René will help you. Right, René?"

But René didn't answer. She just buttoned her lip and tore upstairs.

"Of course she will," Mrs. G said. "Too bad Leon's not here. He'd be so good at attracting boys."

"True," Eve said.

"What do you hear from him?"

"Nothing yet."

Mrs. G had come over to help Eve with a new section of floor combinations, but Eve couldn't locate her notes from the day before.

"Gaw!" she bellowed. "I give up." Then she said again, "Nothing. We haven't heard from him yet."

The boys at Saint Francis were allowed to call home only one Sunday a month, for fifteen minutes—a privilege granted after an initial two-month residency period. It would be another few weeks before they could expect a call from Leon.

"No news is good news," Mrs. G ventured.

"I hope so," Eve said, digging distractedly through her pile of notebooks in the corner. "I really do." Then she found what she was looking for. "Well, for crap's sake. How in the hell!" And they got started, going through an adagio, a pirouette, a waltz.

———

When Leon finally called, after the second month, he had only one thing to say: "I want to come home."

"Oh, Leon," Eve sighed. "You haven't even given it a chance."

"I want to come home," Leon said again. "Please. Just let me come home. I hate it here. Brother Mulligan beat up my roommate real bad for nothin'. No reason at all."

"Well, I'm sure there must've been something," Eve said. "Who knows? But you can't just give up, Leon. You have to try. Just try your best and I'm sure—"

"I want to come *home*," Leon said. "Please."

A letter from the school had warned about this, about boys who didn't like to follow the rules wanting to come back home. "Be patient and make a commitment to trust in the good works of The Lord," the letter had said.

"I know it's a big adjustment," Eve told him, trying to sound stoic.

"Please, Mom," Leon begged. "Please."

"We can't always have what we want in this life, Leon. Lord knows. Just hang in there, honey. You can do it. I have faith in you."

After the first few phone calls, Leon didn't mention wanting to come home anymore, but he also didn't use the full fifteen minutes of allotted phone time.

"Hi there, honey," Eve would say, trying to keep it upbeat. "How's it going?"

"Fine," Leon would answer, his voice a deep hollow.

"How you feeling?"

"Good."

"How's school going?"

"Okay."

"I'm so glad to hear that, Leon," Eve would say. "See? Look at you. You're making the most of it already. I'm so happy it's all working out."

And Leon would say, "Okay, Mom. I gotta go," and hang up.

Al came home with burr stickers lodged in the inside flesh of his eyelid. The wind had kicked up while he'd been branding and inoculating cattle and castrating bulls, he said, and the stickers had blown straight into his eye. He'd driven all the way from Wyoming trying to keep his eye closed, to stop the burrs from scratching up his cornea. When he walked through the door with a hand clasped over his bloodshot, swollen eye, Eve put a coat over her leotard, got him straight back into the car, and drove him to the hospital. By the time René got home from school that day, Al was in bed, covers up to his chin, a black eye patch strapped over one eye.

He had a table full of pills and ointments, which Eve made sure to give him on schedule. She changed his dressing, gently applying creams and drops, and brought him warm broths along with clear, bright-colored bowls of Jell-O.

"Quiet," she'd whisper to Jayne and René as she came out of Al's room. She was suddenly light and gay, proprietary, like a kid with a new puppy. "Your dad's sleeping."

Soon Al was propped up in bed reading *True Detective* with his good eye, and Eve was bringing him chicken dinners with mashed potatoes and intricate Jell-O salads, and ice cream sundaes with butterscotch sauce and chopped nuts for dessert.

"Thank you, Eve. Love you, dearie," Al would say, even when she'd brought him just a magazine or the mail. When she came upstairs, still in her leotard and tights, with a plate of freshly baked cookies or a warm slice of apple pie, he'd say, "You're too good to me, Eve. You know that?" And he'd give her a sad nod to show just how much he appreciated it.

"I can't guarantee how it turned out."

"Looks like it turned out just right," he'd laugh, digging in.

With Leon gone, they didn't fight anymore.

Sometimes Eve would even sit with him in bed. "I don't know, Al," she'd start, and Al would sense right off what she was talking about and reach to pat her leg. "Let's give it a chance," he'd tell her. And she'd lay her head on his shoulder.

Of course it's all fine by him, she might think, somewhere far off, in a quiet, dimmed corner of her mind. *He's wanted to be rid of Leon all along.* But she'd be still, holding her tongue, not letting even the slightest resentment come up for air. There was nowhere to go with it. Besides, she had more than enough to worry about with the Belle Fourche school just weeks from starting. She didn't need to be going through the same old song-and-dance routines with Al.

She'd head back down to the basement to find the music she'd been looking for, the track that was supposed to work with the combination Mrs. G had just given her. She was spending a lot of time digging around in her ballet music and dance notes, looking for instructions on steps and combinations that had been clear to her, or at least right in front of her, just a moment before.

"It's going to be the death of me," she groaned one night, dragging herself up the stairs, her hair on end from yet another long day in the basement. "Thank God you're going to be with me," she added when she saw René in the kitchen. "I don't know what I'd do without you."

Indeed, René thought, willing her mind blank but sensing something like a lasso tightening around her.

And likely due to the novelty of such an offering—an obscure and cultured activity for the girls, something that might lend them grace and poise—the Belle Fourche classes filled up.

Eve kept a notebook by the telephone for registration. She'd have about ten students in each class and hold classes every Saturday from nine in the morning until four-thirty. René would have to teach the so-called Intermediate and Advanced Intermediate classes "for the older girls," Eve said, and Eve would cover the Pre-Ballet and Beginners. They'd need to lug their record player with them, along with all their music, and leave Rapid early enough to have plenty of time for the hour-long drive to Belle Fourche, plus to get everything set up once they arrived.

"Saturdays are going to be big," Eve would say. "And we have to be professional. You ready?"

René didn't understand how she'd got signed up for all this in the first place, but at least she didn't have to prepare anything. She could manage the whole day without the least effort, she figured, without giving Eve so much as an inch. Eve would have to review her notes the night before, make the lunch, load up the car. René only had to teach. And since barre and center-floor work were the same to her as breathing, she wouldn't even have to give it a thought. When the time came, she could put the needle down on the record and come up with whatever steps she needed as quickly and easily as she could say her own name.

29

The Battle of Bear Butte

The Belle Fourche United Christian Fellowship Hall smelled of damp rot and box elder bugs, which swarmed the moldy crevasses on the kitchen countertops and piled themselves into corners in the decrepit bathroom. Eve and René had to clear away the remnants of a bingo marathon from the day before—carrying stained, half-empty coffee cups into the kitchen, then collapsing the folding tables and stacking them, along with all the chairs, against a far wall. René took her place at the desk near the door and got out the attendance book and tuition pouch while Eve changed for her first class. When the little kids started to file in with their parents, René checked off names, took money, and made out receipts.

After the initial commotion, it was boring. So as Eve gathered her first class into the middle of the room, René milled around—opening random cupboards in the stinky church kitchen, eating the sandwich Eve had packed for her, then coming back to sort and count the money they'd taken in so far, making slender stacks of fives, tens, ones, and quarters until Eve came over and told her not to do that in front of the parents.

In René's classes, most of the girls were two or three grades ahead of her, some of them already starting high school. They were heavy-set and had large, rounded shoulders and stocky middles, as if they'd been built specifically for milking cows and wearing home-made aprons as they rolled out dough on floured breadboards. She tucked their hips and straightened their spines. She gave them dif-ficult combinations, demonstrating each one, happy to flaunt her superior knowledge and form, to lay out for them what might have been possible, if only they'd been born less bulky and cloddish, more slender and musical, and to bask in their easy, gawking admi-ration.

When classes were finally over and everyone had gone, René and Eve gathered their stuff, repacked the car, and made a quick stop at Taco John's, where Eve handed René twenty-three dollars.

"A third of the take," she said, like they were outlaws.

René felt herself perk up. "Wow."

"Isn't that the truth?" Eve said, smiling. "It's nice to have some of your own money. That's for sure. Thanks for your help today, honey." She looked sincere and exhausted. "I mean it."

"Sure," René said, unexpectedly overcome with sympathy for Eve, with admiration for her courage and persistence. And just like putting on a new jacket, René took on the feeling of being a part-ner.

As they covered the miles for home, playing the radio and sing-ing along, René found herself thinking that this new alliance, forced as it was, might end up being not so bad, after all. Maybe this was a fine way to spend her Saturdays; maybe she would like being a ballet teacher; and maybe, just maybe, being sent away from home would help Leon make a fresh start. How could she know? It might be a brand-new beginning.

But soon every Saturday was the same: the long, early morning drive to Belle Fourche, followed by the grinding boredom of her classes, which René could quickly see were going nowhere, then Taco John's, where Eve would throw her a few welcome bucks before they began the grueling drive back home. No more meeting up with pals behind the church, no more riding bikes to DQ with Jayne, no more strolling downtown to see what her money could buy, no more nothing. Every Saturday, all day long, René was Eve's prisoner. And Eve couldn't do it without her, so René was stuck.

Week after week, they'd end up squabbling on the drive out— mainly about René's bad attitude—and on the way back, they'd turn up the radio and try not to talk.

"I can't stand it, not one more time," René started in one bitterly cold Saturday morning, flopping angrily into the passenger seat. She'd given up trying to hold her tongue. No more zipping it. From now on, if Eve was going to force René to do this, she was just going to have to take it. "This is such bullshit."

Eve ignored her, giving the car a long minute to warm up. Then she pulled out of the driveway. "You're making good money. I don't know what you could possibly have to complain about."

"This isn't even my job. It's your job."

Eve took a deep breath. It was going to be a long day, and René was already fraying her last nerve. She looked straight ahead and drove.

When they were finally on the highway, getting up to speed, Eve lit a cigarette.

"Most people have to work, René. I don't know where you got

the idea that you're going to be handed everything for free, like you're never going to have to work for anything. There aren't any kings and queens anymore, so you'd better plan on contributing. Just like everybody else. There's no such thing as a free lunch."

"What are you talking about?" René said. "Kids my age aren't even allowed to work. Jesus. It's illegal!"

"Guess you got lucky." Eve smiled. She was trying to tease, to lighten things up.

"Stop talking. Just stop talking! You never make any sense."

"Well, that's something to say to your own mother." Any teasing was suddenly finished. "You should be ashamed of yourself."

"You should be ashamed of *yourself*," René slammed right back at her. "Making this supposed ballet school that you don't even know how to teach for!"

"I think you've said enough."

"I *know* you've said enough."

"Aren't you just like your dad. Think you know everything about everything."

"If I didn't know a lot more than you do about dancing, I wouldn't be stuck in this miserable, boring car having this stupid, idiotic conversation."

"We'll see. We'll see how it turns out for you. My mother always warned me I'd have a daughter who was twice as smart-mouthed as I was, and she was right. Here you are."

"Someday—!" René threatened, suddenly storming as badly on the inside as it looked like it might do out her window.

They were just passing Bear Butte, Mato Paha, the legendary birthplace of Crazy Horse, a sacred power mountain where Indians still gathered to seek holy visions and make offerings to the Great Spirit. On the far horizon, against a backdrop of distant hills, the sky was dark and heavy with clouds. There was something like a solid black wall moving in their direction.

"Someday, what? What are you going to do?" Eve said, goading, sick to death of all the screaming and hollering.

"Someday I'm going to take a knife and I'm going to kill you," René said, rage lifting her, elevating her beyond the ordinary, dissolving even the most highly fortified boundaries. She stretched up and let the words sail, fully formed, right out of her mouth. "How about that?"

It wasn't that René had been nurturing the idea, keeping it locked away, waiting for an opportunity, but she also wasn't shocked to hear herself say it. It hadn't come out of nowhere. It was like a simple warrior, waiting quietly at the back for just the right moment, then stepping up, ready. And once she'd said it, there was no taking it back. There'd be no un-saying something like that.

After a long, strained moment, Eve said, "Well, that sounds about right. You and crazy Lizzie Borden."

"Leave me alone! Just leave me alone."

And the rest of the ride was silent.

There would be no apology. Not from René. Eve could pretend all she liked, but no matter how nicely she acted with friends and strangers, or how sweetly she answered the phone, René knew her. She was someone willing to stand by as her own child was beaten just outside her window; she was someone willing to wallop her kid in the face and just keep on truckin'; she was someone willing to send a child away if things didn't work out just right. She was willing to be rid of people. So what René had said came close enough to what she'd wanted to say for a long time.

They set up the church hall as the snow started to come down. It kept coming, falling harder and heavier through the Pre-Ballet class, the Beginners class, the Intermediate and Advanced Intermediate class. By the time they were finished, the car was buried and the roads were covered with a thick layer of white, maybe two feet deep.

They dug the car out and edged their way back to the highway, then—slowly, slowly—crawled up the on-ramp, into the enclosure of a blinding snowstorm.

"Open your door, René," Eve said harshly, going maybe three miles an hour. "See if you can find the line. I can't see a thing."

René opened her door. She could sometimes just make out the line marking the edge of the highway.

"Are we still on the road?" Eve said.

"We're still on the road."

It took four hours to get home. René spent the whole drive with her head hanging out her open car door, saying, "A little left, a little back, oh, watch out, go back."

Finally, they arrived like they'd started out, in the pitch black. Al and Jayne were standing in the breakfast nook, staring out the window at the falling snow.

"We were beginning to wonder about you two," Al said as they came through the door.

"Good God," Eve said, shaking the snow off her coat and stomping her boots. "It's terrible out there. Just terrible."

"I've got some goulash on the stove," Al said.

"Thanks, Al. I'm just pooped."

"I don't doubt that." Al came over and brushed the snow out of René's hair, then tickled her back. "Come on, Pumpkin Eater," he said. "Get yourself some good hot soup, why don't you."

"Okay," she said, shivering, and she could have cried and she could have hugged him, she was so happy to be home and finished with yet another exhausting, horrible, boring, wasted Saturday with Eve.

Mrs. G came through the back door unexpectedly one morning.

"Can you believe it, Eve?" she said, and as Eve set two places at the kitchen table, she went on to explain that Deanne Johnson had made it clear to her—just after Mrs. G had signed over the Academy of Ballet "lock, stock, and barrel"—that she shouldn't be coming around the studio anymore. "Before the ink even dried on the paper," Mrs. G said, dropping into a chair.

It was a shocker.

"'As long as you're around, I'll never have the respect of the students.' That's how she put it, Eve. Like I was keeping the kids from looking up to her. Well, maybe they don't look up to her because she's a big fat nobody, that's what I say." Mrs. G shook her head and ran a hand through her poof of white hair. "After all these years, wouldn't you think—"

"You deserve so much better, Helen," Eve said, pouring the coffee. "I hate to say it," she added, "but I had a feeling."

"Poor kids," Mrs. G groaned.

From then on, Mrs. G started having René come along to her house for Eve's "teacher's classes," where they'd work on René's extension.

"Well, that weighs a ton!" Mrs. G would say as René held on to the breakfast bar in Mrs. G's kitchen and extended her leg, settling her ankle on Mrs. G's shoulder. "Hold it up yourself, René. I'm not supposed to be carrying it for you." Then Mrs. G would take a step closer, forcing René's leg higher. "Pull up," she'd say, adjusting René's shoulders and hips, pausing to let her muscles stretch out.

They'd work that way to the front and side, but to the back, Mrs. G would simply take hold of René's leg at the knee and lean into it, pushing it up into penchée arabesque. When it came time for René to try it on her own, without assistance, she'd lose about a foot of extension and her whole body would tremble with the effort.

"You have to build your strength, René," Mrs. G said, just a few days before she was leaving town for good. "Strength and extension. Not either-or. You keep working on that while I'm away," she said, as if she were coming back. "Just because I'm not here doesn't mean you don't have to work your hardest," she continued, reading René's mind. "It means you have to work even harder!"

She took hold of René's hand, and René walked her back to her chair by the television, where she flopped down, breathless as the raggedy Pekingese on the floor beside her.

And not even a week later, Mrs. G moved away to Phoenix.

It should have been an easy transition, but René soon found that though her new teacher, Miss Dea, could take the class through the proper series of exercises, she couldn't make their bodies sing or their eyes light up with trying.

Mrs. G had made it clear from the very first day René had ever stood in her class that a correction was the highest form of a compliment. It meant that your teacher saw your potential and believed in you enough to help you try to reach it. But now Miss Dea walked right past her, even taking the trouble to make an arc away from René's place at the barre as though she'd encountered a reverse energy field. And if Miss Dea gave René a correction at all, it would be something vague about missing a beat or having a "stiff arm," something that didn't make any sense, hollered in a high-pitched twang from the far end of the studio.

Though René still went to dance class every day, Eve hadn't set foot in the studio since Miss Dea had made a point of telling her it would be better for everyone if parents simply waited outside in their cars.

"She's going to be a pill," Eve said on the drive home that night. "No doubt about it."

So, with Leon dispatched to parts unknown, with Mrs. G moved to Phoenix and Eve barred entry, the mantle of improving oneself, of reaching one's potential, of attaining some increasingly mysterious lofty height settled solely on René's shoulders. And devoid of any company or advocate or guide, the whole thing began to feel like a long-deserted party—abandoned, wrinkly balloons littering the floor, the air slowly seeping out of them.

30

Brothers of the Order

After one full calendar year "of lockdown," as he put it, Leon got kicked out of the military Catholic school, and all of a sudden he was back at home. He set up a room for himself, dragging one of the twin beds from the guest room down to the basement, to the furnace room off Eve's dance studio. He put up posters of rock bands—Black Sabbath, Jethro Tull, Deep Purple with the band members' heads on Mount Rushmore—and bought a black light. He commandeered an old record player and set an ashtray right next to his bed, and no one said a word about it. He kept the window above his head cracked, wedged open with a paint stick.

He'd been kicked out for marijuana. They'd found a stash in his dorm room, under his bed.

"It wasn't mine," he said.

But the dismissal letter said it was his second violation.

"I don't even know what happened," he said. "Some kid went running past and threw this bag in the door, and it slid right under my bed. Then Mulligan came in with a whip and started beating me. Even though I kept telling him it wasn't mine."

"What about the other kid," Eve asked. "Did they catch him?"

"I have no idea," Leon said. "I didn't even know him."

"Well, at least he completed the school year," Eve said to Mrs. G on the phone, long-distance. "Just one more to go. Lord knows it's bound to be an uphill slog."

And not long after that, Leon's friend Husky—so called because he was skinnier than a toothpick—got kicked out of his house.

"He's got no place to stay," Leon said to Eve. "He's been sleeping in his pickup for a week. He's only asking if he can park it in the driveway."

"All right," Eve said. "But he's not sleeping in the driveway, for crying out loud. He'll have to share your room in the basement. And just until he can straighten things out with his folks."

So Leon and Husky dragged the other twin bed down to the basement, and like comrades at a bar bonding over a winning team, they'd come up the stairs laughing and slapping each other on the back. They were inseparable, sharing a single, secretive sense of humor, holding a common outlook, a unified perspective on the world around them. Nothing could be better than whatever they were doing down there, they seemed to say. Everyone else was simply missing out.

Sometimes when they were gone, René would go down and play darts on the dartboard they'd hung on an exposed pillar. She'd turn off all the lights, switch on the black light, and bask in the heady glow of their posters, then rifle through their albums.

She never found anything but renegade high-school-boy stuff, but many decades later, when Leon was living on disability in an old pull-behind trailer down by Rapid Creek, he told her that he'd started mainlining back when Husky lived with them. They'd tie off when no one was home, Leon said, then shoot heroin or speedballs, take black beauties, drop acid on top of it.

By the time Leon ended up parked down by the creek, he'd long ago traded his wild days for a simpler blend of prescription painkillers, coffee, and cigarettes. The pills were from his doctor, for the chronic pain in his back and legs. He'd had his sciatic nerves deadened with an electric needle, but it hadn't helped. Though he was barely middle-aged, he walked like an old man, bent over, legs splayed unnaturally wide. Years of opiate use had caused the cushioning between his vertebrae to soften and dissolve, and though he needed the pills to get through the day, they were becoming a sort of slow-motion death sentence, closing the deal on his liver failure.

He'd sit in his recliner in front of the TV, feet up to help ease the swelling. But soon, his feet and ankles would begin to turn black from the pooling blood, the loss of circulation.

It also came out around that time, when he didn't have much to do other than reminisce, that there'd been some big partyers in the Colorado chapter of the Brothers of the Order of Saint Francis. Leon said the brothers would come to the dorms in the middle of the night and drag him and some of the other boys from their beds, then walk them down the hall, like inmates, to the monks' quarters, where they'd include the boys in drinking wine and smoking weed.

"And those monks didn't mind getting touchy-feely," Leon said. "No kidding." He shook his head like a dog shaking off pond water.

Sometimes the monks would do things to the boys, and sometimes they'd make the boys do things to them, or to each other. Some of the brothers had to ease themselves into it, but others were comfortable taking a direct approach, simply beating a boy with a doubled-up belt or letting him drink himself nearly unconscious, then helping him take down his pants. It would be early morning by the time the boys were allowed to return to their beds. Looking back, Leon couldn't imagine that he hadn't failed all of his classes that year, especially since he'd been one of the regulars on the brothers' night-scene roster.

"They must've just passed us," he said, considering, taking a deep drag on his cigarette. "Course, they didn't do it to everybody," he went on. "They had favorites. Yeah. Sons-a-bitches. And Mulligan was head of the pack. That guy was a real sadist. He was something else," he said, mostly to himself, eyes adrift in painkillers and memory.

So when Leon finally got home, there was Husky, and Husky had not just weed but quaaludes, cocaine, hash, black beauties, mushrooms, acid, heroin—a banquet.

Leon said that one night he and Husky shot up, dropped acid, then decided to drive to Deadwood, to check in with the prostitutes who were always happy to accept the fish they'd caught that day as payment.

"So, first we had to go fishing," Leon laughed. "Yeah," he said.

He took a minute to glance at the TV, which was droning perpetually in the corner of his trailer.

"So we drove out to Deadwood," Leon went on, "and after the cathouse—excuse me for saying—we were walking down the middle of Main Street in the dark, with no cars and nobody around, and it was like I could see right over the tops of all the buildings, like I was towering over all the rooftops. I was looking down on all the chimneys and fire escapes and everything. Hell, I could see all the way out to the end of town, past the gold mine, almost all the way back to Rapid, like I was King Kong or Godzilla or something. I wonder how that happens. How can anybody see over buildings and shit like that? Jeez."

He paused as if René might have an answer, but her only acid trip had been a bad one. Everyone around her had started shrinking. "I'm right here, I'm right here," her boyfriend had said, holding on to her. "No you're not, no you're not," she'd wept.

"Yeah," Leon said, lost in the memory of towering over buildings. "That was pretty cool."

René didn't say anything. She didn't know if she believed him about the brothers. Not that many years earlier—as an excuse to have the long weekend off from work so he could get high without interruption—Leon had told his boss that Jayne had died in a head-on collision with an eighteen-wheeler just south of Worthington, Minnesota. His account had been frighteningly specific. René had unwittingly called his office that day, spoken with the receptionist, and ended up collapsed, knocked to her hands and knees, weeping over Jayne, who was actually fine, just not answering her phone because it was out of batteries. So now Leon was sick, but that didn't mean she was ready to believe him.

She also didn't know that this would be the last time she'd see him. Just a few weeks later, he'd be admitted to the hospital. That same night, an orderly would find him splayed next to his bed, having not pulled the emergency cord or rung for the nurse. Gone.

The autopsy revealed no sign of trauma, except that his stomach was filled with blood. The doctors couldn't say for sure, but it seemed likely that one of his esophageal veins—damaged from a lifetime of drinking—had burst, and he'd just quietly bled to death inside himself.

"We're getting older, René," he'd said, out of the blue, that very last day they'd been together, which René had thought was ridiculous.

She wasn't even forty, and he was just forty-two.

By that point, Leon had told her too many times that he didn't have anyone to blame but himself. But that was all talk. Because René did. She knew just where to start.

The next spring, after Leon returned home from Colorado, he graduated from high school in a flowing, light blue gown, laughing and throwing his mortarboard in the air, whooping it up with the others while Eve sat beside him in a madras plaid dress, her hair curled, a familiar exhausted smile on her face.

"Hallelujah!" Eve said over the phone to Mrs. G. "Praise the Lord and let the saints rejoice!"

And just after the ceremony, Leon hightailed it up to Hill City with Husky. According to Leon, Husky had found them logging work. Leon would drive a skidder, and Husky would work a chain saw. They'd live with about twelve other guys in one house, and they'd be making money.

"Lots of it," Leon laughed.

He stuffed his clothes into plastic garbage bags, jumped into Husky's truck, and they tore away from the house, smiling and waving, "happy as clams," as Eve said whenever she recounted Leon's departure.

So Leon was hidden away up in the hills somewhere near Hill City, with no phone, no mailing address, and no way to reach him. Eve spent a whole day driving around up there. It was a small mountain town, and she figured she could certainly find him by asking at the gas station or lumberyard, if not the market or the liquor store. And though folks said they'd seen him and took the time to point her down the road to various mile markers and rock formations, she ended up spending most of the day getting lost on the scenic loops and accidentally winding her way through Custer State Park and Keystone, repeatedly passing the Needles and Horse Thief Lake, endlessly disheartened by once again catching sight of Mount Rushmore out her passenger-side window—a paper bag full of sandwiches and chips for all the boys in the backseat.

She got home after dark having seen neither hide nor hair.

"As if I didn't have anything better to do than drive around in circles all day," she said, breaking open one of the bags of chips, then unpacking the sandwiches, putting a few of them out on dinner plates so that the "whole goddamn day" might not seem like such a complete waste.

31

Zipping Stones into Pockets

Just after Mrs. G had left town, Miss Dea decided that though she would continue putting on *The Nutcracker,* she wanted to give someone else a chance to dance the Doll and the Candy Canes, so René was replaced in these, her usual roles. Miss Dea also asked Joey to recruit some of his friends from school to dance the boys' parts, but they showed up in dirty jeans and T-shirts, refusing to put on tights, then huddled in a group at the back corner of the studio, giggling.

"Lackluster!" Eve started saying to anyone who'd listen. "It's just not the same as when Helen was doing it. Of course, Helen was such a professional. She had *years* of experience, and *that* makes a difference."

Eve still danced the part of Mother Ginger, but with Dea's husband backstage, working the curtain, she was made to feel like "somebody's idiot cousin," she said. Every time she exited in her hoop skirt, Mr. D had to hold the curtain for her to pass, and he never failed to give her a look like he'd just whiffed a bucket of rotting fish.

"No one seems to have any memory of how much Helen and I put into this production. People seem to think it just sprung up out of nowhere. But I can tell you that if it wasn't for Helen Gilbert—" Eve would break off only to resume: "Without Helen here to keep it alive, it's nothing but a rattletrap piece of junk. It's heartbreaking to see it falling to pieces like it is."

Eve had no beef with Miss Dea, she said, but neither could she bear to see things done "half-assed." What good was there in taking something so meticulously and carefully conceived, brought to life from nothing, tended and nurtured with so much effort and love, and "flushing it straight down the shitter"?

"Taking something like that and letting it crash into a heap just because you can't be bothered or don't know how to pay attention to it is worse than never bringing it up in the first place. It's a loss. It's a tragedy. And I'll be damned if I'm going to sit idly by and just keep my mouth shut. There's no excuse for it. None."

The next fall, when Eve called to sign René up for classes, Miss Dea had a different idea.

"There's no room for René in this school," she said plainly.

"Now, wait just a damn minute, Deanne," Eve started. "Your classes can't be full already."

"No," Deanne said. And she must have given it some serious thought, because her answer came without the slightest hesitation: "Classes aren't full. René just isn't welcome here anymore."

Eve hung up without shouting or arguing, without slamming the receiver, just pensive, still.

"What's going on?" René was in the kitchen with Eve, sitting at the table.

"Sounds like you're not going to be taking any ballet classes this

year," Eve told her. "Dea says you're *not* welcome to come back."
Eve deepened the furrow between her brows. "Did something happen with you two?"

René had taken Miss Dea's summer workshop that year. They'd done mostly country-western line dancing. "What the heck," Dea had drawled, putting the needle down on the latest Merle Haggard record. "Ain't it summertime?" But nothing had happened.

"How can she do that?" René said.

"It's her school. She can do what she likes."

René was dumbstruck.

"No classes this year," Eve kept repeating, mulling it over. Then she called Mrs. G.

"She's trying to get back at us, Eve," Mrs. G said. "For giving her a run for her money."

"What we gave her was the world on a string," Eve countered. "Still," she admitted, "it's probably my fault. I tell you, Helen, it's just a fiasco without you. It's a great big mess. But I should've kept my mouth shut. Maybe something I said got back to her."

"If she can't do the job, she deserves to hear the criticism. That's for damn sure."

They went round and round about what was going to happen next.

"No more reason to hold back on opening your Royal Arts school there in Rapid," Mrs. G said.

"And a good reason *to* start one." Eve laughed.

"She'll be sorry, Eve," Mrs. G said. "It's a terrible thing she's done."

After Eve had hung up—as she was trying to tell René about the possibility of expanding Royal Arts Dance into Rapid City, about maybe putting out some advertising and organizing a class schedule—René started furiously running through her all-too-familiar protests about helping Eve teach.

"It's going to be your dance school one day," Eve insisted.

"Not me. Not ever."

"Never say never. I'm building this business for you, you know. You might be happy to have it one day when you need the income."

"If I ever have to make a living like that, I'd rather die. I'd rather kill myself."

"How can you say that?"

Eve glowered at her, wondering how René could not have a single thought about how hard Eve had worked to get this school going, or how Eve had started from nothing, hadn't had even one of the advantages René took for granted.

"I'd rather hang myself from the railing or throw myself off a cliff," René was saying, going through her usual gyrations. "I'd rather find a river and drown myself!"

"Try to think positive, why don't you," Eve barked. "Just try. It'd be good for you." Eve had been reading Norman Vincent Peale. She thought he had just the right approach. "It works, René. It does. It makes everything better for everybody."

"Like it works for you?" René mocked. "Like it makes everything better around here?"

Eve stood up and left the room, pointedly whistling a happy tune. She headed straight downstairs to the pile of alterations that was crowding her sewing machine, proud of her decision to walk away from such negative-mindedness and her determination to make something worthwhile of her day regardless of everything going to hell in a handbasket around her.

As far back as René could remember, it had seemed like she'd been riding a stormy, disordered team of horses—Eve and Al, Leon and Jayne, school and ballet—standing astride as many saddles as her legs could manage, clutching a fistful of tangled reins, balancing in jerks and starts like an untrained circus performer. Achievement and focus were the only answers she'd ever known to the question of how to keep upright, how to stay above the continual rumble. Just as exaggerated hygiene might be a way to endure living in squalor, pushing herself, succeeding, came to seem like the only solution to the problem of everything always falling to pieces.

And considering the way things had been going at Miss Dea's, René was all in favor of some time off from ballet. Though she figured she'd never get out of her indentured Saturdays with Eve, at least on weekdays she could do regular things. She could focus on school with a singular purpose, a unified vision. With *The Nutcracker* fallen away, with Leon graduated and gone, with Eve and Al settled into mostly muzzled hostilities, things would be simpler. Without everything pulling her from one direction to the next, threatening to topple her entirely, she might just be able to let go of the reins and, for once, keep her balance.

So she settled on a year of normal life. And just like an actor sorting out a new role, on the first day of school, she tended to the details. She pulled back her hair, strapped her books and notebooks to the carrier on her bike, put her foot up on the pedal, and took off, sailing across town to General Custer Junior High.

She attended cheerleading tryouts, executing a front walkover to a full split, dazzling the panel of judges, and was unanimously elected head cheerleader. Though she'd been playing the flute since sixth grade, she now spent time practicing and captured first chair in the band. She continued her piano lessons with Mrs. White, who was finally not unhappy with her, since, for the first time ever, René didn't have to lie about going over her pieces at home. She started taking guitar lessons and begged her band teacher to instruct her on the oboe. When it came time to choose the ninth-grade student government, René was voted secretary. And that fall, when the Custer Long Hair Marching Band was scheduled to perform at halftime for the high school homecoming football game, René won the coveted role of band majorette. On the night of the big game, she exploded from the ranks with a dazzling scissor kick and a loud scream of her whistle. Then she led the band onto the field, taking her place at the front, holding down the beat with her baton.

It was a good start to the year.

She read Shirley Jackson's "The Lottery" in English class and thought it was sad and disturbing and totally unnecessary. Plus, it made no sense. No one deserved that.

In home ec she sat next to Carly, called Carl, a heavy-set Indian girl who either hated her guts or was in love with her. It was impossible to tell. Carly was constantly bending over her, challenging René in smoky whispers either to fight her or to kiss her, and when René refused both, Carly would say—always loudly enough for everyone to hear—that René was a conceited cunt.

And though she didn't have friends, exactly, as the year went on, it seemed that everyone knew her. Kids she didn't know would call her name. She understood that it didn't mean they liked her. In fact, since she didn't know their names, it was a problem.

René was the one who'd danced in every *Nutcracker,* been elected head cheerleader, led the marching band. She was the one who'd be called on in history class to make a run to A&W, to get the teacher a root beer and onion rings, with one of the boys assigned to drive her. They'd get sodas and spend time cruising the neighborhoods before coming back to catch some final tidbits about the French Revolution or the Enlightenment, never anything that wasn't in the textbook. So she was the one who cut class with impunity and still got good grades. She was the one who won the home ec sewing contest and got a ten-dollar gift certificate for the skill displayed in her patterned full-length, zipper-front jumpsuit. She was the one who danced the Sugar Plum Fairy in the talent show and performed the Mexican Hat Dance in the middle of the gym for International Day. She was the one who introduced all the songs the band played for its Christmas concert, and she was not only selected for All-County Orchestra but was the youngest-ever student to win a spot in All-State Band. She was the only one who could do a chest roll, a cartwheel, and splits on the balance beam during Gymnastics Showdown Week in P.E., and she had a floor routine that all the teachers and administrators left their desks to see because it was known to "knock your socks off." Amazingly, she even won the school-wide Ping-Pong tournament that year. All in all, she was an uncontrolled explosion, like a firecracker going off in your hand.

So, though some vague idea of having friends stayed with her, the situation remained pretty much the same as it had been since grade school. She knew the drill. She didn't expect to have friends. She simply turned her mind away, taking that place inside herself that felt like loneliness and setting it aside, like zipping a little stone into a pocket.

That winter, Leon left Hill City and moved, first to Lead, then to Spearfish, to live in a friend's trailer. In general, he didn't come home at all, except when he showed up to fall onto the couch and sleep for a few days. Still, there were phone calls for him—Leon owed someone money, or some "old friend" they'd never heard of was looking for him. Eve didn't give out any information.

But if Al was home, or even if he just caught wind of some trouble regarding Leon, the arguments would resume full blast from a not-forgotten midpoint—as though opposing warriors had suddenly been jolted from a deep, unconscious slumber and found themselves aching to get back to business.

First, Al would rail at either Leon or the impression he'd left on the couch; then Eve would square off with Al about his never having been there for Leon in the first place; then Al would forbid Jayne to do something, and Jayne would cry; then Eve would scream at Al that he had no right to tell any of them what to do; then Al would slam the door and roll away in his car, and René would swear at Eve, and Eve would slap her; then René would scream and run up the stairs as Eve called after her, threatening to wash her mouth out with soap. And just as abruptly as everything had started, things would quiet down, and they'd all gather, smoldering, to sit in front of the television.

So, even with Leon mostly miles away, sleeping on a cot in someone's trailer in Spearfish, or lounging on an old mattress in the basement of a friend's place in Lead, and even with Eve and Al generally keeping to their own corners, what René came to think of as the Black Bird of Anger continued to reside with them. It would alight on one of them after the other. And though, after stirring up blinding outbursts and deafening rages, the bird would finally lift, René began to realize that it wasn't going anywhere. It was staying. It was simply perching somewhere out of the way, biding its time. And while for the rest of them the days were passing, slipping quietly through their fingers, that bird seemed to have eternity on its side.

Then one day in spring, when the grass was finally coming up in Technicolor, the daffodils and tulips blooming, lilacs just beginning to bud, Eve went out to her garden shed to get a watering can and trowel, to put in her annuals. She opened the door, which she'd found strangely ajar, jumped back with a start, as though she'd seen a rattlesnake coiled atop the stacked chair cushions, then quickly reversed herself once again and lunged forward.

"Leon!" she cried. "Leon!"

He didn't respond, and she thought for a second that he might have come home just to die there in that shed.

"Leon!" She shook him, taking his face in her hands, turning his head back and forth until he finally opened his eyes. "My God," she said.

"What?" Leon said.

"For Chrissakes, Leon," Eve shouted. "What in God's name are you doing in here?" She stamped her foot at him. "Get up! Get in the house!"

And Leon got up, and she shuffled him inside, putting away all her plans for the morning. She sat him at the table and poured him some coffee. Then she sat down with him.

"Leon!" she said when his eyes began to close, his head bending inevitably toward the table. "What's happened to you? What were you doing out in the shed, for God sakes?"

"The door was locked," Leon mumbled, "so I laid down in there 'cause it was cold out. That's all."

"The door was not locked," Eve scolded.

"I tried it," Leon said half-heartedly.

Eve shook her head. It was no use arguing with him in this condition—whatever condition this was, drunk or stoned, Eve didn't know. Just thank God Al wasn't home.

"Go upstairs and take a shower," Eve said, "then get into bed. We'll talk about it when you get up."

So Leon did those things, and he slept all that day and all that night and all the next day, getting up once for a bowl of cereal and a big drink of water, then falling straight back into bed. Eve checked on him from time to time just to make sure he was still alive, but she figured that if he was that worn out, he might as well just keep sleeping. When he woke up, he'd feel better, and they'd have a chance to talk.

But Leon must have felt better in the middle of the night, because when Eve got up the next morning, the guest room was empty and his car was gone. He'd taken the clean clothes she'd laid out for him, left the dirty ones behind, and disappeared.

A few days later, there was a call from the county courthouse. Leon had been a no-show on a series of DUIs. They were looking for him. They had a warrant.

Eve gave the officer the address where she thought Leon was living, but the officer said they'd already checked that location and there'd been no one around.

"Then I don't know," Eve said. "I don't have any idea."

"If you see him," the officer said, "or if he happens to come by—"

"I'll have him come right down," Eve said.

"Just give us a call," the officer said.

But Leon didn't come back to the house, and Al was still on the road, so Eve was left to worry it out on her own. She called a few of Leon's high school friends, but none of them had heard from Leon in a long time.

"He'll turn up," she said to herself, digging out in the garden, finally putting in her petunias and marigolds. "Seems like he's got nine lives." She put down her trowel, carefully shook a young flower from its casing, and placed it evenly, steadily in the ground, watering around the exposed roots. "He'll show up one of these days when we're least expecting it," she muttered to herself, on her knees in the cool sunlight. "Then what'll we do?"

Eve finished her planting and went inside. She hung her gardening hat on a hook and sat at the breakfast table with a cup of coffee and a cigarette. She just sat there, smoking and looking out the bay window, watching the road. She sat for a long time before she finally said to herself, "Well, Eve, if you're going to accomplish anything today, you'd better get going." She ground out her cigarette and stood up, and just then Al's car pulled into the driveway. He walked through the back door and came into the kitchen.

"Hi there, Eve," Al said. And, seeing her carrying her cup to the sink, he asked, "What you got there?"

"You hungry?" She was suddenly tense, newly irritated.

"Famished. Just about starving."

"Well, sit down," she said, "and I'll get you something."

"Okay." And picking up a section from the stack of old papers on the table, he said, "Anything new around here?"

"Nothing new, Al," Eve said, disgusted, and she cooked up some bacon and put it together with ripe tomato, crisp iceberg lettuce, and plenty of mayonnaise on toast while Al looked over the last week's worth of newspapers.

"Oh, that's just dandy. Thank you," Al said when she set the sandwich in front of him.

"I've got things to do," Eve told him. "Seems I've gotten behind in everything."

Al nodded, not even looking at her. He was happy with his sandwich and coffee and newspaper, happy to be home, happy to not be driving anymore and to not have to sleep in a motel for the next few days. So Eve turned and took herself down to the basement, to her sewing corner in the utility area, to be by herself, so she could think, and so she could finally get to all the fixing and mending she'd left undone for far too long.

32

Breaking into the
All of Everything

When the cheerleading squad wanted to switch from gold to green tennis shoes late in the school year, Eve was against the idea, saying that it was "simply outrageous" for those girls to be demanding yet another pair of tennis shoes when the ones they had were still perfectly good. She went on from there with things like "For God sakes, you've barely used the first pair you made us buy" and "You girls should know better" and "Isn't it the end of the season? It doesn't make any sense." So René figured they might as well stick with the gold shoes they already had and avoid all the trouble.

No one agreed.

"You're the captain," Eve insisted. "You should have the say. Why not just tell them they shouldn't be so happy to spend their folks' hard-earned money?"

At the next meeting, René made her arguments. Then they voted. Everyone still wanted new green tennis shoes.

"Well, I'm captain," she said, in spite of the five-to-one majority, "and we're keeping the gold ones."

"You can't do that." The girls were indignant, nodding.

"You guys shouldn't be so demanding."

"We're not *demanding*," one of the girls said, mocking her. "We voted."

"Well," René said. "Either way. We're not getting new shoes."

At the next game, the squad showed up in new green tennis shoes.

"Mrs. Deacon said that since we voted, it was all decided."

Mrs. Deacon was their cheerleading adviser.

"It's not a dictatorship," one of the girls put in, obviously quoting Mrs. Deacon as she took out her pom-poms.

"If that's how you want it, then fine. I'll just be wearing these," René said, indicating her shiny, suddenly wrong-colored sneakers.

When she worried at home about her off-color shoes, Eve just smiled and said, "That way everyone will know that *you're* the captain and *they're* the crew."

René cheered for two more games before she got called into Mrs. Deacon's homeroom. "The girls said you took a vote," Mrs. Deacon noted and proceeded to give her an elementary lecture on democracy.

"I'm captain," René said, trying to explain that a good performance had nothing to do with democracy. It had to do with leadership. If people couldn't follow a leader, the whole performance would suffer, which was what was happening now, with their tennis shoes. "And it doesn't seem fair to ask our parents to buy us new shoes at the end of the year," she added.

"The parents don't seem to mind," Mrs. Deacon pointed out.

"They can do what they like," René countered. "We just won't match. That's the price."

Mrs. Deacon sent a letter home explaining that René had been suspended indefinitely from cheerleading for her inability to work with others.

"Fine with me," René said.

"You give those girls too much as it is," Eve agreed. "I've seen you. They wouldn't know their asses from their elbows if it weren't for you. I bet you made up almost all those cheers yourself, right?"

So the last games happened without her. Then cheerleading was finished for the year. But something about getting kicked off the squad changed the chemistry, made René vulnerable to things she hadn't even known were brewing. Suddenly, with the visible breach in her defenses, kids who'd said hi to her all year were silently passing her in the hallways, then turning to whisper to a friend, and boys were sneaking up behind her and yanking her hair or snapping her bra.

René lost her first-chair flute challenge, and Tami, who'd been fighting her for it all year long, took her seat. René recaptured it the next week but walked out of class to find, written across her locker in huge, red script, RENÉ SUCKS DICK, with a graphic of a long-haired girl on her knees, as described. She got a bucket of soapy water from the janitor and cleaned it off, but the halls had been filled with kids changing classes, all of them glancing sideways at her as her face went crimson, her knees and bladder weak, a mysterious, thin stream of pee surprising her, glistening down her leg as she squatted to cover herself, pressing her thighs together.

The next morning, someone in the trumpet section tapped René on the shoulder and handed her a piece of paper folded into a square. It was a petition, a form they'd been reviewing in social studies. There'd been petitions about protecting the whales and eliminating the death penalty, and René had signed them all. This one already had three full columns of signatures, single-spaced, on each side.

> *We, the students of General Custer Junior High, think that René shouldn't get to do everything she wants all the time. She never lets anyone else have a chance. There's lots of kids who want to do the things René gets to do, but there's no way because René takes everything for herself. René isn't better than anyone else, she's just conceited and stuck up because she always gets to do everything she wants. Also, René does too many activities, so she isn't doing a good job at any of them. There's lots of kids who could do a better job than René if only we got a chance. Everyone who thinks it's not fair that René gets to do so many things, sign below.*

She looked at the list of names, front and back. Everyone had signed it: the boy she liked had signed it; Tami, the second-chair flute, had signed it; the kids in the trumpet section had signed it; the glockenspiel player had signed it; even the one girl who sometimes sat with her at lunch had signed it.

When René finally looked up, the band teacher was pointedly holding out his hand, intending to collect the note that had been passed in his class. She handed it up to him and watched as he read. He got a strange, tired expression on his face and looked at René, tilting his head in sympathy. He sighed as he folded the petition neatly on its creases and wedged it under the sheet of music they were just about to play. Then he wearily lifted his baton.

After class, he called René into his office. And as the other kids shuffled out, peering back over their shoulders, he closed the door.

"You'll need to speak with your parents about this," he said,

handing her the petition. "They'll want to talk to the principal."
His face settled into a gloomy, well-worn frown. "I'm sorry this
happened."

She nodded, pale.

"Sometimes there's a lot of jealousy." He stopped. "You okay?"

René nodded in a so-so way.

"All right." He sighed. He was tired. He'd been a band teacher
for twice as long as René had been alive. "If you want to go home,
I can write you a note."

"I'm all right," she said.

"Good. Off you go to your next class. And be sure to show that
to your parents."

She left his office, securing the petition in her notebook, and
took off for algebra knowing there wasn't a kid in the building who
didn't hold something against her. That was just the way it was.
And no one could tell her that it was just some nagging paranoia
about nobody liking her or some resurrected, unrestrained yearning for friendship poking its head out from underground. She had
proof.

When Al came home, Eve handed him the note. "I'm calling the
principal," she said. "I want you to come with me."

"You bet," Al said.

So Eve and Al went to the school and demanded to know how
something like this could have happened, but there were no answers for a question like that.

"You can imagine," the principal sighed. "There are things we
can control and things we can't. Kids will be kids."

"That's nonsense," Al said, "and you know it. Believe me." He
lowered his voice and leaned forward. "If you're entrusted with

educating these kids, how they treat each other is one of the things parents are counting on you to manage. If you can't do that, you're not doing your job. It's as simple as that. It's inexcusable."

"I'm sorry this happened," the principal said finally. "I truly am."

"That's fine. I appreciate that. I do. Only problem is, what's René supposed to do now? Go through high school with this same bunch of numbskulls?"

The meeting ended in a stalemate, since there was nothing to be done about any of it.

"Thank you for that, Al," Eve said on the drive home.

"Thanks for nothing, you mean. Nothing's going to come from that meeting. Not one thing."

"But I couldn't have done it on my own. They wouldn't have taken me seriously. I'd have been just another upset mom."

"They get away with too much," Al said. "That's for sure."

Eve nodded. "I only wish you could have been there when it was Leon."

Al didn't say anything.

"I don't mean to be starting something," Eve said.

"This is a totally different deal."

"It's not different but that it's René. They treated him worse. It was the teachers, themselves, coming after him. And no one even bothered to stand up for him."

"I don't want to go over it," Al said. "We've been through it."

"Don't I know it."

Eve shut up. She cracked her window and lit a cigarette.

"Just so you know," she said, "I don't think Leon's doing so well."

"Leon hasn't been *doing so well* for a long time now, Eve," Al said, parroting her. "And I don't know what to do about it. Do you?"

"No."

"If I knew what to do, I'd have done it," Al said. "He's got himself in a fix—living down in his buddy's trailer like a drunken freeloader. I have no idea. I'm fresh out of ideas. I am."

"I just wish it could have been easier for him, earlier, when he was younger."

"I know you blame me," Al said. "But I've done what I can for him, and you've done more."

They drove in silence.

"It's already been a long day," Al said.

Eve nodded. But when Al pulled into the driveway and turned off the engine, she jumped out and slammed her door. Al sat for a minute. Then he got out and stood leaning against the car, and he took the time to have a cigarette before he went inside.

René kept a stiff upper lip at school, artfully shunning anyone who dared come near, but at home, she was crying all the time, tears falling like water from a busted dam. She'd stand in Eve's walk-in closet, raking through Eve's jewelry tray, and cry. She'd watch TV and cry. Right in the middle of a game of King's Corner with Jayne, she'd have to get up for Kleenexes. Sometimes she'd cry during dinner and have to leave the table, and every night she'd weep herself to sleep, then wake up in the dead of night to the sound of footsteps creaking up the stairs. She'd listen, counting, imagining some pockmarked cowboy with a rope to strangle her, a hook to tear her to bits, an ax to chop her to pieces. When she'd gathered enough courage, she'd slip out from under her blankets and dash across the hall, to Eve's room.

"Mom," she'd whisper, waking her.

Eve would open her eyes and lift her covers, and René would crawl into Eve's bed, where she'd sleep, cuddled in, until morning.

It was starting to happen every night. Though she was nearly fifteen, every night heavy footfalls echoed on the stairs, and every night she'd run to sleep with her mother, and every night Eve would open her covers and scoot over, and every morning René would be surprised to wake up still alive.

Even after their biggest fight—one night when René and Eve had just got home from yet another tedious Saturday in Belle Fourche, drawn and tired from the long drive and the endless, disheartening day of teaching, and after René had leveled her best at Eve as they'd stood in the kitchen, continuing their enraged altercation until René finally brought the whole thing to a close with the rousing finale of calling Eve a *Bitch!*, and even after Eve had flown across the tile floor and slapped René hard across her mouth and René had thought, *That's it! That's the very last time!* and cocked her arm and hit Eve back across the face as hard as she could and, bent from the sting of it, Eve had said, "You should be ashamed of yourself," and René had fired back, "You should be ashamed of *your*self!," not even crying—even then, even that night, René came on her knees, trembling and afraid, to where Eve slept, and Eve lifted her covers and moved over to make room.

René was reduced by the darkness. She couldn't navigate what she couldn't see. She'd been blind, mistaken, ill-advised and caught off guard. No one had told her that instead of making her admirable and praiseworthy, her will to excel, her determination and unyielding forward advance, would place her directly in the crosshairs.

"Striving for excellence," as Mrs. G had called it, had brought her a whirlwind of resentment and the sharp point of vengeance from those who felt themselves undervalued and overlooked, unappreciated and forgotten. Contrary to the years of Sunday school lessons, along with Mrs. G's lengthy orations on applying oneself with dedication and purpose, in an instant they'd made her understand that she'd better step back, that she'd better start hiding her light under a bushel basket. Or else.

She must have done the same to Leon as she'd done to her classmates—just like Eve had always said: eclipsed and overstepped him without even bothering to look. But the world wasn't tender-hearted or willing to hit the dirt, as her older brother had been. It wasn't the least bit interested in protecting her feelings or giving way. As it turned out, the world was upright and eager to hit back.

Now she was afraid of the slightest shadow on the wall, just like a baby. And Eve was there, ready—even after all they'd been through, and even though René held so much against her, had forged and hammered the heaviest armor in place around her heart just for her—ready to catch her and hold her close, keep her safe through the night like she'd done since the day René was born. Eve was there, always, every night, opening her arms when there was nowhere else to turn.

In the last weeks of Eve's life—many years after Al had passed away, and long after Leon had been found dead on the floor of the hospital, and after Eve had sold her big, empty house on Pine Boulevard and moved into her elder-community condo—René would come to visit, and the two of them would sit together in Eve's living room, Eve confined to her chair, watching *Bonanza* reruns, her hands and feet twisted in a crippling neuropathy, as René tried to keep busy by rummaging through Eve's pile of old papers, reading funnies and outdated shopping flyers. In general, Eve would sleep a lot and not speak much, but sometimes she'd stare at René so devotedly that, feeling the pressure of her gaze, René would look up and turn to her.

"Do you need something, Mom?" she'd say, finding her mother rapt, her eyes moist and lighted from within.

"No. I just want to look at you," Eve would say quietly, tentatively, conserving breath. And she'd continue, unashamed, letting a slight, mysterious smile overtake her as she gazed at René steadily, taking her in as though she were something brightly colored, sunlit, singular, and miraculous.

René would be older—her own children grown and gone, each living in a different far-off city—and still the depth of feeling, the force of Eve's love and longing, would come as a shock. How many times had those same eyes turned on her as sharply as blades, hard and accusing? How many times had they held a rain of judgment, or a curse meant just for her? But now, as Eve's powers waned, all the long-held grudges and resentments were dissolving, scattering, leaving only the essential seed—the sweetness and purity and shining love—burning bright, suddenly wholly visible and gleaming.

She must have looked at me that same way when I was a newborn in her arms, René would think. *Imagine.*

Imagine that it would all come around to this—from uncertain beginning to uncertain end—all the love she'd been looking for all her life, hidden away right in front of her, just like sweet, golden kernels of corn beneath a husk.

And her chest would constrict, as if heartbreak were just like it sounded—something physical and audible, something that left a mark.

All through the last, long weeks of the remaining school year, René's tears flowed without ceasing. She had to get back to ballet. She couldn't live without dancing. Suddenly everything depended on that one missing piece.

Eve and Mrs. G were on the phone day and night, and soon Mrs. G began to visit every studio within a twenty-mile radius of her new home in Arizona. She found Kelly Boyle and the Phoenix

School of Ballet, and sent Eve a newspaper clipping with a black-and-white photo of Kelly and his daughter in rehearsal. She'd marked it up in red pen, with arrows to note different necessary corrections: "She's got her weight too far back and her foot is over-arched," she'd written, "but they did a fine job."

The ballet school had just put on a performance of *Les Sylphides*. Now there'd be an intensive summer workshop. René would enroll. She'd fly down and spend the summer at Mrs. G's. Then Eve, Al, and Jayne would drive to Arizona at the end of July for a visit and to pick her up.

"You can give it a try," Al said when Eve went over the plan with him for the tenth time. "But no need going from the frying pan into the fire."

"Maybe you could even stay down in Phoenix for the school year," Eve started saying to René. "Wouldn't that be something?"

And René would stand motionless in front of her.

"But how are you ever going to sleep at night?" Eve would go on, musing, shaking her head as she bent to untangle her latest sewing project. "I simply do not know."

René didn't have any answers. She'd be fifteen in a few months, the same age as Leon when he'd first left home. Who knew what would happen from here? All the questions were going to have to wait until after the summer. For now, the only thing that was clear was that René was going to have to take this step; she was going to have to move forward on her own. She was ready. She was going to close her eyes and hold her breath—and go.

33

How Do You Solve
a Problem Like

Kelly Boyle had been a soloist with American Ballet Theatre, then gone out to Hollywood to dance in the movies—*Seven Brides for Seven Brothers, Daddy Long Legs, Oklahoma!* At the Phoenix School of Ballet, he suited up for every class and demonstrated combinations with focus and visible intention. He was elegant and handsome, powerful and sure, and for some reason René would never know, he took her to heart, welcoming her like a long-lost child.

As well as being beautiful, disciplined, and sweet-natured—which is not to say they weren't cutthroat—his students were thin. And though it was easy to tell that his Advanced class was deeply cemented, firmly enclosed within a sanctuary of uniformity and cliquishness, René could also see a sliver of light coming through a crack in the door, where Mr. Boyle himself was leaning in, forcing the door open for her with his own body weight. There was going to be a place for her. Mr. B was making that clear to everyone.

He included René as an equal in all the corrections, taking the time to show the class he was serious about her. He'd stop the music and stand behind her, using his toe to turn her heel to the front as he lifted her spine and tucked her rib cage, molding her body into a single, long line as the others stood, watching attentively. Or he'd interrupt the center-floor adagio to have René extend her leg. "A little higher," he'd say, gently lifting and turning her heel while at the same time adjusting her chin with purposeful, light fingers. "Just a tilt," he'd say. "That's it. Like that." And he'd step away.

"Beautiful," he'd say. "Yes."

René took classes from morning to night and started eating only protein and fat burners—celery, grapefruit, lettuce leaves—because, although she was thin, she could see that if she wanted to be an equal, if she wanted to be a real contender, she was going to have to be thinner. Dripping sweat during a break, she'd have a bite of tuna in water and a sip from the cooler in the waiting room. Then she'd head back into the studio, not even bothering to think about where she was or how she'd got there. Mostly she had work to do to make up for the year she'd lost and for the years before that when she hadn't got the training Mr. Boyle's girls had been getting. Everything needed rebuilding—her technique, her muscle tone, her flexibility and alignment.

So, day after day, she went to class and fought—pushing harder, stretching farther, concentrating with what began to feel like a beam of light at the center of her forehead—knowing that to fail would cost her more than any of Mr. B's girls could possibly understand, more than she could bear.

Helen Gilbert wasn't used to having a teenager in her house, upsetting her television schedule, giving her extra cooking and shopping, extra laundry, plus what she liked to call, after her favorite TV game show, the "daily double": having to change out of her pajamas and slippers for a twice-every-day round-trip to the studio, to drop René off and pick her up. Also, she was gaining weight. The heat didn't agree with her, and retirement was "for the birds," she said. She'd gotten so big she'd had to have her bed tilted, higher at the head, so she didn't suffocate in her sleep, and her legs were constantly swollen, road-mapped with bulging veins. She set the air conditioner to fifty-eight degrees and ate Baskin-Robbins in front of the television. And, since the house was about the temperature of a penguin exhibit, René would open her bedroom window to let in some heat, which was another problem.

The few letters that arrived from home were filled with weather reports: it was a beautiful day, nice enough to hang some bedding on the line; it was raining hard, but the moisture was badly needed, since everything had been so dry; it had been a bright, clear afternoon until hail, the size of softballs, started dropping from the sky, breaking out people's windshields, but not to worry. They were all okay.

Mostly René would stay in her room, assuaging her growling stomach with carrot and celery sticks, while Mrs. G sat with her little dog in the living room, where she preferred to be alone. Mrs. G's husband was always on the road, selling hearing aids for Sonotone, and her elderly sister, who was so frail and infirm that Mrs. G had to waddle in to help her to "the lavatory," was planted in the bedroom across the hall from René. Sometimes at night, René would knock gently on Mrs. G's sister's door and venture in to sit on the floor beside her bed, nibbling lettuce leaves and watching whatever was on the television on top of the dresser, telling herself that the poor crippled old lady probably appreciated the company, since she, too, was always all by herself. They wouldn't talk, but Mrs. G's sister didn't seem to mind René being there.

"Try not to get in the way," Eve told René over the phone. "Remember. Helen isn't used to having kids around."

And René had been doing that. But then a boy from home started calling. René had hung out with him just before she'd left town. He was homely, tow-headed and short, and he'd invited her to go along with some of his friends to a baseball game, then to Big Boy's for hamburgers and milkshakes. Now he was calling Mrs. G's every day.

"How'd you get this number?" René asked him when Mrs. G first handed her the telephone. But her surprise and anxiety must have sounded like something completely different over the phone line, because from then on, he just kept telling her not to worry, that his family was taking a trip to Arizona, that he'd be there before she knew it. He really wanted to see her again, he said.

René had never laid eyes on his parents, but she knew they lived in one of the broken-down trailers nestled in the gully between the K-Mart loading docks and the railroad yard, so she didn't think there was any chance they'd actually show up.

The night she opened Mrs. G's front door to find the boy standing there, ragged and breathless, overcome with the heat, panting like a stray dog, she was as surprised as anyone else. He'd hitchhiked from Rapid City to Phoenix all by himself, he told her. When she asked him where he was planning to stay, he just said, "I came to see you, silly. Like I said I would."

So she had no choice. She let him in.

"Can I use your bathroom?" He lifted his pale eyebrows at her, attempting to flirt. "I'm so dirty."

René got him a towel. And just as he was getting into the shower, Mrs. G happened down the hallway.

"René!" she cried. "Who the *hell's* in the shower?"

René couldn't get everything explained before Mrs. G flew into a spin. And once again—just like when René had accidentally left a bloody stain on Mrs. G's dupioni silk bedspread—there was a call to Eve.

"Well, you won't believe what's happened *now*!" Mrs. G hollered into the phone.

Then René had to get on the line and swear to Eve that she hadn't invited him, that she hadn't known a thing about it.

"He said he was maybe going to stop by with his family. I don't really even know him," she whispered, cupping her hand over the receiver.

"Well, Helen is very upset," Eve said. "Just try to keep her calm, and I'll see if I can contact his folks. Put Helen back on."

So René handed the phone back to Mrs. G, who was hovering just next to her.

"I'll try, Eve," Mrs. G said, "but I can't be responsible for some kid who's run away from home for God knows what reason. That's too much. It's too much to ask."

And as Mrs. G blanched, René turned to find the boy standing in the hallway, naked from the waist up, wrapped only in a towel, his dusty road clothes bundled under his arm, his colorless hair wet and dripping.

"Hey," he said, smirking at Mrs. G, raising his hand in a peace sign. "You got a washer?"

"Good God, René." Mrs. G fell onto one of the tall stools at her breakfast counter. "What are we going to do about this?"

And as René felt herself turning to dust, the boy just smiled.

"Hey, lady," he said. "It's cool."

Eve got ahold of the boy's parents, and though they hadn't known he was missing, thinking he was staying with a friend, they were relieved and grateful that he'd been recovered. They bought him a bus ticket home. Mrs. G would have to take him to the station early in the morning.

"He's going to need to spend the night, I'm sorry to say," Eve told her.

"Good God, Eve. I don't think I can take it."

"Don't worry. Just get an extra blanket and set him up on the couch."

"I'm not going to get a wink of sleep. I can see that."

"Probably not. But he'll be gone in the morning. All done."

"If you say so."

After dinner, René and the boy sat together at the edge of Mrs. G's pool, dangling their legs in the water. Stars came out and the boy leaned into her, placing a hand behind her hips. Then he whispered into her ear, "I brought a condom."

"What?" She pulled away from him, edging along the poolside. So he repeated it.

"I'm not doing that."

"Well, we can if you want," he said, bending to push his shoulder hard into hers.

"I don't," she said, alarmed at this strange, ugly boy who'd traveled so far and was now here, way too close beside her.

"That's not what you sounded like on the phone," the boy said.

He was instantly testy, accusatory, even though nothing of the sort had ever once come up in their conversations.

"You don't think I came all the way down here for nothing, do you?"

And from out of nowhere, all the solitary nights when René had kept him on the phone—talking with him even though she didn't like him, just to help ease her loneliness—were suddenly right in front of her, demanding their price.

"I'm going inside," René said, standing, thinking how everything she did made a problem, even just talking to this gruesome boy she hardly knew from a thousand miles away. The boy grabbed her arm as she stood, holding tight around her wrist.

"Let go of me!" she said, her strong legs suddenly braced, ready. And he must have thought better of it, because he let go, and he got up, too.

They went inside and sat at opposite corners of the living room, pretending to watch television as Mrs. G ground her teeth.

"I'm going to bed," René said after a few minutes. "I have class tomorrow."

Mrs. G looked at her hysterically, then struggled to her feet.

"You'd better settle in, too, mister," she said sternly to the boy. "Your bus leaves first thing in the morning. You ready?"

"Sure, I'm ready," the boy said, narrowing his eyes. He stared pointedly at René. "Let's stay up a little," he tried, waggling his eyebrows at her, this time right in front of Mrs. G.

"I can't," she said.

"She can't," Mrs. G confirmed. "You need anything before I switch the lights out?"

He shook his head at her. He was disappointed with the whole business.

Mrs. G and René walked down the hall, and when they got to René's room, Mrs. G leaned close.

"Lock it," she said.

René nodded. She went in and turned the little button on the doorknob.

By the time René got up the next morning, the boy was gone. Mrs. G came back from the bus station just in time to drive her to ballet class, but she was in no mood. She dropped René off at the studio, wrenched her car into reverse, and said she was going home to take a nap.

René danced all day, and that evening she went straight to her bedroom and closed the door. She didn't have any dinner—not even a hard-boiled egg. She didn't want any. She wanted to be left alone, she wanted to stay out of the way, and she wanted to go home. Even though everyone but Leon would be arriving in Phoenix in just one more week, she wanted to go home. One more week seemed like an eternity.

The next day there was a package from Jayne—chocolate-chip cookies and a note: "We'll be there soon! We're packing everything already." There was a line of *x*'s, a line of *o*'s, and a line of hearts. "But first we have to clean house." Then a frowny face.

René could imagine they'd all been having a peaceful summer. Eve would have been gardening, Al would have been traveling, then stopping home to rest and read the paper, Jayne would have been playing with her neighbor friends out in the sunshine. No doubt, by the time they arrived, Jayne would be "browner than an Indian," as Eve said, especially next to René's ghostly ballet-studio pallor.

Leon had vanished and wasn't likely to be coming home anytime soon, since Eve had warned him of the outstanding DUIs.

"If you come around, I'm going to have to call the sheriff," she'd told him. "I won't have any choice."

And now, with René gone too, Eve and Al would be getting along. They'd be happy. Jayne was easy-going, content to ride bikes, climb trees, go swimming, so there'd be nothing to fight about. Jayne would be baking cookies, playing hopscotch, setting up lemonade stands with the neighbors. There was no place for René in a pretty picture like that, not without marring it, without changing it from crisp, happy colors to a hazy wash of blacks and grays, not without everything grinding back into the same grim overlays of need and anger, ending in violent rages, quiet grudges, righteous swells of indignation.

"There's nothing for me here! Nothing. I can't stand it here any-more!" she could remember screaming at Eve just weeks before, during what Eve had begun to refer to as her "Reign of Tears."

And she'd got her way.

But given an inch, René "wanted a mile," as Eve always said. Even now, even so far from home, doing exactly what she'd insisted on, she was overflowing with wanting. Away from home for the summer, with the possibility of staying away for the entire year looming in front of her, René found that *home* was taking on the airy, spun-sugar consistency of a fairy tale. She could see it shimmering in the distance, a chimera—like nothing she'd ever known, like nothing on this planet—a far-off place of love and nurturing, of mutual sustenance and caring, a place of refuge where people knew and accepted you, where faithfulness and affection combined to blaze like a beacon.

Leaving home for the summer wasn't the same as leaving home for good, but somehow, in going away at all, René had wound up on the brink of her own permanent departure, with a great tide swelling behind her. What if it all came together? What if everything worked out so that she could stay in Phoenix for the whole year? What reason could she give for simply turning around and going home? Even if she'd wanted to, she couldn't change course now—not without upending everyone's expectations, without abandoning everything she'd said she wanted, everything everyone had spent good money on and worked hard for. "*Sacrificed* for," she could hear Eve adding.

And after rolling it around endlessly, like spinning rocks in a tumbler, she always ended up in the same place—doubled back on herself, doubting herself—because what was there, after all, for her to go home to? She knew well enough.

The ground was shifting, unsteady. Whichever way she turned, the landscape in every direction turned with her, so that whatever she'd been dreaming of didn't wind up in front of her. Whatever René was truly yearning for, she couldn't find it, couldn't get her hands on it; it wouldn't hold still. Just as a meteor streaking brilliant green across the blackest prairie night finally touches down to earth, becomes no more than simple, jagged rock, it seemed that the moment René got whatever it was she'd wanted was the moment her heart's desire metamorphosed from sublime to ordinary, from shining dream to dreary workaday.

There was only one direction. Forward.

She threw herself into training her body, controlling her appetite, silencing her loneliness, and strangling her fear. She tried to remember that she was at the beginning of "a great opportunity," as Eve had called it. And alone in her room at night, counting the days until Eve and Al and Jayne arrived, she closed up her heart, put it away just like shelving a book, and she tried not to cry.

34

In Spite of Behind,
In Spite of Ahead

As she finished the waltz step across the floor and looked up to see their three excited faces peering around the corner, looking for her, René felt like going not just across the room but right out the door and into their arms. She glanced at Mr. Boyle, who put two and two together and nodded permission, so she ran to give each of them a long, sweaty hug.

"You're here!" she whispered, hoping that the other girls wouldn't notice Eve's homemade plaid seersucker vest, Al's thin western cowboy shirt over his old-fashioned muscle tee.

"We couldn't wait to see you," Eve said.

"Well, well," Al kept repeating, laughing softly.

And Jayne just held on with her arms doubled all the way around René's waist.

"Go ahead," Eve said. "We'll be right here."

So René went back into the studio, finished the final combination, then took off for the dressing room as Mrs. G introduced Eve and Al and Jayne to Mr. Boyle.

René could hear Mr. B through the walls of the changing room saying how talented and full of promise she was, how she was going to make them proud someday, and how happy he was to have her in class. "Privileged," he said, as René scrambled into her clothes.

"Why, thank you," Al said. "We feel that way, too."

"Mrs. Gilbert and I have been discussing it," Mr. B ventured, "and I'm hoping there might be a way to have René stay on here for the year."

"Yes. Well, yes, we'll have to see about that."

"Come on back tomorrow," Mr. Boyle was saying, and René was out of the dressing room, standing with them, ready to go.

The next day Eve and Al came along to the studio while Jayne stayed at the house with Mrs. G to swim and watch television. After observing the first class, they wandered to the strip mall across the street. They came back after the next class, Al holding out a big, greasy cheeseburger wrapped in brown paper.

"I can't eat that," René said, pushing his hand away, getting her usual sip of water from the cooler.

"You've got to try it," Al said. "Best cheeseburger I ever ate! This one's got your name on it."

His eyes were twinkling at her. She thought maybe she'd never seen him so happy about anything. She smiled, gulping water, shaking her head.

"One bite," he pleaded.

"René!" Mr. Boyle called as the music for the Advanced class started. "Get in here!"

"Just one," Al said. "Quick!"

René leaned forward and took a slim bite of the burger Al had been hurriedly unwrapping for her. She gasped at the explosion of meat, cheese, grease. "Oh my God! That's delicious!"

"See? Didn't I tell you? I told you."

"René!" Mr. B called again, and she turned and ran into the studio, jumping into the first combination like a fish jumping into water.

When the final week of classes was over, Eve, Al, and Mrs. G met with Mr. Boyle at a coffee shop. They returned with the news that Mr. B was offering René a full scholarship, that she could attend the same Catholic school a number of his students attended, and that he'd found a family willing to house her for the year. It was all settled. Only Al was still unconvinced.

The three grown-ups lingered around Mrs. G's breakfast counter late into the afternoon before finally calling René in to join them.

"Your mother and Mrs. Gilbert here think this might be a once-in-a-lifetime opportunity for you," Al started, swiveling around to face her.

René nodded.

"And Mr. Boyle believes you have the talent to do something with your dancing," he added, looking drawn.

"If nothing else, you could always teach," Eve interjected.

René grimaced, and Al took a deep breath.

"I guess my question is this—" Al was proceeding slowly, weighing his words, stepping carefully, as though picking his way through a minefield, a place where he could lose everything all at once. "Are you sure this is what you want to do? It's a big commitment, and you're still young."

"Not young for dancing," Mrs. G put in sharply. "If another year goes by without any training, she'll be out of luck."

"I guess everyone else is pretty certain." Al sounded more and more like every step was taking him closer to something he knew he wasn't going to like. "I guess I'm the one that's not quite persuaded."

René nodded, feeling unsure, feeling like a mirror reflecting something she couldn't comprehend.

"Is this what you want to do, René?" he said again.

René looked from one grown-up to the next. "Yes," she said, trying it out loud, hoping that something in the sound of her voice would give her a clue about whether or not she meant it. She had to envision her legs as two steel rods to try to still the sudden trembling. "Yes," she said again.

Al turned to Eve and Mrs. G, who were both grinning like they'd just pulled the handle on a jackpot.

"All right, then," Al said, as though he'd sensed his weight lowering, felt the trigger, heard the click, and knew a little something about what came next. "That's that."

He looked back to René.

"You're going to have to be tough. There's no way around it. You're going to have to be a fighter."

"She's tough," Eve said, still smiling, resting a hand on René's shoulder. "She's the toughest." And she and Mrs. G laughed as Al just looked at René with pride and sadness.

"I'm going to miss you," he said. "That's my big problem."

"We all will," Eve said casually, dismissively. "But you'll come home for vacations, so we'll get to see you," she said to René.

"You couldn't have hoped for better," Mrs. G said, clearly grateful that her part in this was over. "Thank God Deanne kicked her out! Right, Eve?"

"Right," Eve said, suddenly sounding less certain. "I'm sure she's going to do just great." And she put her arm around René for real, pulling her close, claiming her.

Mr. Boyle's summer workshop was finished, so after a few days of touring the desert, Eve, Al, Jayne, and René piled into their VW bus and headed home. René would have only three weeks to get everything organized and be back in Phoenix, moved in with her new "family," and ready for her first day of classes at Mother Mary Ignatius High.

If she'd had the power to glimpse even a few short months into the future, René would have seen herself walking the back alleyways of Phoenix to the ballet studio every day after school, then waiting on the curb until Mr. Boyle's car pulled up and she followed him inside. She'd take the Adult class, Stretch class, Advanced class, Pointe class, everything Mr. B taught, before catching a ride "home" with the family of one of his ballet students, a family that had agreed—reluctantly, she'd come to learn, finally caving to his insistent pleas—to house her for the school year.

And sometimes during that early fall, as she stood beside him while he unlocked the studio door, Mr. Boyle would say to her, "When people ask who trained you—"

René would look at him doubtfully.

"They will," he'd say, "they'll ask you. You tell them it was Helen Gilbert. She taught you. She deserves the credit. Remember I told you that. Now take some B-12. It'll help with your energy. And eat! Like I told you. Come on."

She'd follow him around the studio like an orphan as he turned on the lights.

"You have to eat. You have work to do. You have to keep your strength up," he'd say to her. "Don't worry about your weight right now. And don't worry about those other girls!"

René would be starving herself as if in penance, trying to make her body match the bodies of the girls in Mr. B's Advanced class, girls who'd been training with him since they were five or six, girls who knew they were on their way to one of the big companies in New York City and had never found a reason to doubt it. She'd be limiting herself to five hundred calories a day, including gum and breath mints. She'd be losing weight, getting thinner, ranking up with the best of them, but she'd end up making herself so anemic that her periods would stop. By Thanksgiving, she wouldn't have the strength to drag herself up a flight of stairs, but she'd still dance every class, every day, from four-thirty in the afternoon to nine at night.

"You can worry about all that calorie-counting nonsense later," Mr. B would tell her. "It's not important now. Now, work. Work hard. Get your technique. And be patient. Don't be impatient!"

And sometimes that fall, when Mr. B pulled up and René was sitting on the curb in front of the ballet studio, waiting for him, he'd tell her to get in the car, and he'd take her out for ice cream. He'd order a double dip and wouldn't stop hounding her until she did, too. She'd lick around the edges, pretending, as the ice cream melted and dripped down her arm. Then, when Mr. B was done, he'd throw his napkin in the garbage, and she'd throw in her cone.

"Oh, you're useless," Mr. B would tell her, smiling, putting a hand on her shoulder and shaking his head. "Well. Let's go, Cinderella. Time for class."

Back when Mrs. G had first visited Kelly Boyle's studio, he'd treated her like a queen, setting a chair for her against the mirrors and bringing her a cool glass of water. She'd been to ballet schools all over town, but after she'd visited his, she'd called Eve first thing.

"Eve, I've found it. René has got to get down here. We've got to find a way."

So, long after the high heat of summer had passed—after Mrs.

G had gone back to her quiet life at home with her sister and her little dog; after Eve, Al, Leon, and even Jayne had been left far behind—René would be in Phoenix.

And Mr. B would be watching out for her. More than that, he'd be offering her the enormous kindness of seeing her as she wanted to see herself.

"Eat!" he'd say. "Eat!"

There are people in this world who really know what they're talking about, and if René could have forgiven herself for leaving everyone behind, if she could have let go of the pain and guilt of Leon's departure as well as her own, if she could have found the confidence to rein in her headlong drive, she would have followed Mr. Boyle's advice, and eaten. Though not eating seemed like a mark of her seriousness—a way to overtake her peers, a way to take charge and change herself, improve herself, a way to finally make herself into the person she needed to be—if she could have seen into the future, she'd have known that by Christmas vacation that first year, she'd be exhausted. She'd have transformed her body, carved it into glorious lines, yet she'd be nearly hollow, her energy seeping away with every breath. Though she'd continue to fight her way forward, like someone with a broken umbrella trudging on through a hurricane, she'd have whittled herself down to little more than thin strips of muscle over clattering bones.

35

Home Again

They said their goodbyes to Mrs. G, and on the drive home from Phoenix that summer they stopped at both the Grand Canyon and the Continental Divide.

"Highest highs and lowest lows," Al pointed out to no one in particular.

And as they pulled into their driveway, René leaned over the front seat and asked if Leon had been around at all while she'd been gone. Eve looked to Al, but no one answered.

"Does anyone know where he is?" René said.

"Somewhere nursing a case of beer, I imagine." Al laughed.

Eve glared at him. "Lord only knows," she said. "Maybe still out in Spearfish. He called from there just before we left."

"For crying out loud, Eve, I hope you didn't send him any money."

Al was more than ready to get into it, but Eve didn't answer.

"Home again, home again," she said, singsong. "Come on. Let's get this thing unpacked."

But before they could even get inside, the phone was ringing. It turned out the sheriff's office had caught up with Leon. He'd been in a holding cell for the last three days. The judge was willing to be lenient, they said, but a parent or guardian would have to come pick him up. Otherwise, he'd be going to jail.

With everything still in the car, Eve took the keys from Al and backed out of the driveway as Al just stood, lighting up a cigarette and staring into the planter by the steps.

Eve didn't return until well after dark, with Leon dragging behind her.

"Go to bed," she told him, pointing up the stairs. "And hand over your keys. You're not going anywhere for a while."

When she went into the kitchen, she found Al sitting at the table, chain-smoking in the dark. She turned on the light. Al shielded his eyes but didn't say a word.

"Well," Eve said. "I had to sign my life away."

"I don't doubt that," Al said.

"His car's in the impound lot. We'll have to pick it up tomorrow."

Al humphed. "Sounds right," he said. "And who's going to pay for that?"

"Not him," Eve said. "We can be sure of that much."

For the next couple of weeks, Leon slept. He slept all night in his bed, and he slept all day on the couch. He slept like Rip Van Winkle, days passing without the slightest intrusion of consciousness. He'd rouse himself only to turn over, so that eventually he came to be a fixture—a lifeless, three-dimensional outline they all simply passed on their way from one room to another. No one disturbed him and no one tried to bring him around, as if none of them knew how to meet him at such a depth, as if merely touching him could hurt him, as if—like with an electric current—by reaching out for him, they might accidentally end up included in the surge, carried away by whatever was holding him under.

But as soon as he could stand, Leon was ready to get back up into the hills. A job working at a lumberyard near Keystone had surfaced. It was just what he'd been looking for, he said. He'd be able to build a life around a job like that.

Since he was finally sober and seemed to be thinking straight, Eve didn't feel she could stand in his way. Maybe this would be just the thing to get him back on his feet. Maybe he'd even meet someone up there in the pines, some nice young girl who'd make him want to keep his nose clean and live up to things.

So Leon left.

But as far as any of them ever knew, Leon never met anyone up there. Even by then, love and physical desire must have been a complicated equation for Leon, and however he might have managed it over the years, he never had a date or a girlfriend. All of a sudden, he'd simply be living with an alcoholic woman a decade or two older than he was who already had at least three or four kids, all by different men.

"Where in the hell does he find them?" Eve would say. "It's uncanny how he can come up with one after the next."

He'd happily bounce other men's babies on his knee, buy their diapers, read them bedtime stories. He'd discipline other men's teenagers, giving them lectures of lived experience right on the spot. But always short-term, temporary. Because without fail, one day Leon would be gone, either kicked out for some unknown reason—"Lord knows, I wouldn't let the groceries walk out that easily, not if I had four kids to raise by myself!" Eve would say, defending him—or simply by disappearing, first into the dream state of long days on the couch, then straight out the door.

"You have to help me," René said to Eve just a week before she was scheduled to leave for school in Phoenix.

Being home, even for just this short time, had brought a firestorm of dangers—hams crusted with brown sugar and dotted with pineapples and cherries, morning waffles smothered in butter and thick maple syrup, hot casseroles of fat noodles and hamburger swimming in cream. She could lose everything here. She could be finished before she even got out the door.

"Please, please, don't let me eat anything."

Eve sighed. She was tired—overburdened by Leon's shaky departure and now having to take on René's demands along with everything else.

"All right," she said. "But I'm going to make whatever I'm making, so don't you get mad at me about it."

That same afternoon Eve mixed a batch of snickerdoodles and the whole house lit up with the smell of cinnamon and sugar dough baking in the oven. When the timer sounded, René went straight for the cookie sheet, broke off a minuscule corner of one of the soft, warm cookies for a taste, then lingered, trying to convince herself to leave the room, to turn around and not look back. She washed her hands at the sink just to keep them busy.

"Feel free to do the dishes while you're standing there," Eve said, unloading a new batch of cookies onto the cooling rack. Then she added, out of the blue, "I hope I'm not going to have to reread you *The Little Red Hen* before you leave," referring to one of René's favorite books as a young child, about a bunch of barnyard animals refusing to help grow the wheat but still wanting to eat the bread.

"Jeez," René said, blindsided, stung.

"It wouldn't kill you to help out a little, René. That's all I'm saying. And stay away from these cookies," Eve warned.

"You can just leave me alone," René told her.

"I'm only doing what you asked. Don't you dare start after me."

René grabbed a hot cookie, then turned on her heels and went to play a round of double solitaire with Jayne. But soon enough she was back in the kitchen with a napkin, taking three more.

"You put those down. I mean it," Eve barked.

"Leave me alone. Stop it," René shot back.

"Then why in the hell do you bother asking me in the first place?" Eve scolded, banging her hot baking sheet onto the stovetop. "That's what I'd like to know."

"What good are you anyway," René pointed out, "making cookies just when I need you to help me? Thanks a lot for *nothing*."

"You are the most ungrateful—"

"Never mind," René interrupted, hurrying out of the kitchen. "Just forget it!"

"Then don't ask me! Don't you ever ask me again!"

René stomped outside, letting the screen door slam behind her. There were good reasons for going away, she told herself, plenty of them. She just had to keep that in mind.

The days passed quickly, and the night before René was supposed to depart for her new home in Phoenix, she went to sit with Eve in her sewing room in the basement. She scooted a chair close, and they sat silently side by side as Eve buzzed alterations through her machine.

Then René said quietly, "I don't want to go."

Eve didn't miss a stitch.

"You can always change your mind, just stay home."

There was silence, then buzzing, then silence.

"It's your decision, René. You have to decide."

There was more buzzing, then a long silence as Eve unpinned a new seam.

"Once you're gone, I don't imagine you'll ever come back," Eve said, a sudden wash of sadness draining her features. "If you leave, you'll likely be gone for good."

"I'll come home. Of course I will."

"For visits," Eve said, "but not to stay."

She got up from her sewing machine and went over to the washer to switch the loads. René stayed in her chair, watching Eve work as she'd watched her work since as far back as she could remember.

"There's nothing to do about it," Eve said. "Unless you just decide you want to stay home."

"I do want to stay."

"I can call Mr. Boyle. That's easy enough."

"No. I'm going."

"I thought so," Eve said. "Don't worry. We'll see you at Christmas, and you can call us collect. It'll be expensive, so we can talk every other Sunday. Call person-to-person and ask for Mary. Since there's no Mary here, they can't charge you for that. Then we'll know to call you back, so it won't cost so much. Every *other* weekend," she repeated, coming back to her sewing machine. "It's going to be costly enough as it is." She sighed. "God knows."

"Okay," René said. "Sure. I can ask for Mary."

"We're going to miss you, René." Eve dropped her hands into her lap like a defeated boxer or someone who'd failed a test. "I can't begin to tell you how much."

"Me, too," René said, tears beginning to well in her eyes.

She stood up.

Wasn't there something she could say? Was this not her mother? Had René never been sick? Had her mother never stayed up late into the night to nurse her through a fever? Hadn't she brought her warm broths and lozenges to ease a sore throat, rubbed Vicks on her neck and back, pinning her into a flannel to loosen a cough? Hadn't she taught her to read, brushed and braided her hair, made her meals, washed her clothes, cleaned her dishes?

"Well," René said, trying to laugh, trying to shake it off.

"Oh, my," Eve said, picking up her sewing and blinking back the tears to see.

And René went up to her room, rearranged her suitcase one more time, then came downstairs and sat limp in a chair across from Al, joining him in staring blankly at a public television program about the Second World War, which the narrator kept calling "the good war."

36

Coda: Wherever It Was
They All Needed to Go

The next morning they loaded René's suitcase into the car and drove to the airport. After they'd checked her in for the flight, René and Jayne milled around the gift shop, quietly fingering plastic tomahawks, fake arrowheads, chunks of fool's gold, while Eve and Al smoked in the café, looking out the windows at the single airplane that was sitting on the runway. When it came time to board, they all met up in the hallway.

René gave Al a silent hug. His cheeks were hollow, picking up the pale shadow of his white Stetson, his dress hat, and he seemed to be moving in slow motion, barely able to lift his arms to put them around her, then barely able to let her go. Then there was Jayne, now officially an only child. Tears rained down her cheeks. She was being left behind without anyone to share in whatever might happen from here on, and she seemed to know that she was losing something important, that whatever hole this left in her heart was never really going to heal. Then, Eve. René and Eve were almost the same height, but now there'd be no chance for René to grow up and out of the fighting and complaining and name-calling; there'd be no time to make amends or come to a new, heartfelt understanding. René was going. And Eve was right: she wouldn't be coming back.

René handed in her boarding pass, carrying the afghan Eve had knitted as a surprise for her under her arm.

"You might not need it," Eve had said that morning after breakfast when she'd handed René the gift, suddenly almost shy.

It was constructed in bands of vibrant pastels, like a rainbow, and had small braided tags of horseshoe decorations, like Lucky Charms, tacked to one side. René couldn't imagine she'd use it. But if she'd only had a crystal ball, she'd have known that it was going to be cold at night in the desert, that over the years, she'd wear that delicate, loosely woven blanket to tatters.

René crossed the tarmac, climbed the stairs, and took her seat by the window. She could see the three of them back in the café—Al lighting a cigarette, Eve digging around in her purse, handing crumpled Kleenexes to Jayne. She waved and waved, then smiled, trying to see past her own reflection, as they spotted her and waved back.

And as the plane lifted off, up over the vastness of the prairie where she'd been born, over the ridges and outcroppings and gullies, over the flatlands and the rising Black Hills, up, up into the clouds, and she found herself on her own, hurtling through space with only the name of her new "family" scribbled on a piece of paper in her pocket, René suddenly understood that there were whole worlds, whole galaxies of unseen things ahead of her, things she couldn't even begin to guess.

How could she have imagined that—starting that very night—she'd be sleeping in the far corner of a big room on a broken-down army cot with an old door leveled on its frame to keep the center from sinking to the floor? And how could she have conceived that for the foreseeable future her tender bones would be cushioned by only a blanket-thin pad, while the girl whose family she was trying her best to belong to all the more gleefully occupied her overstuffed mattress in the center of the room, piled high with snow-white pillows and a lofty down comforter? How could she have possibly known that, while she'd be lying on the floor beside her cot every night, doing strengthening and stretching exercises, the girl whose room she shared would be glancing down at her with pity and disdain? Or that, no matter what she did, her new "family" would never conquer their impulse to look at her out of the corners of their eyes and go silent whenever she came into a room?

How could she have predicted that she'd be sitting all alone in the library every day after school, browsing food magazines, reading carefully through the details of each recipe, trying to taste the flavors vividly enough with her imagination to satisfy her very real hunger? Or that, confining herself to starvation rations, she'd grow too weak to face a flight of stairs, yet, in spite of her frailty, would keep going, keep pushing herself?

And there was no way she could have anticipated that she'd be chosen to dance *Swan Lake* right along with the rest of Mr. Boyle's Advanced class at the end of that first year, as a "full performing member" of the newly formed Arizona Ballet Theatre. So the idea that she'd be in a final dress rehearsal when the back doors of the auditorium opened, and that she'd instantly recognize her—silhouetted as she was against the light that was suddenly pouring into the darkness—simply didn't occur to her. Her mother! Eve. It had been too many months to count since René had seen her last.

When they finished rehearsal, she'd want to run and fall into her arms but could only squat near the footlights, in costume and full makeup, and reach down to take her hands. They'd stay, the two of them, squeezing hands for just a moment before René would be called backstage. And that night, for the inaugural performance, there Eve would be, all by herself, in her highest beehive hairdo and nicest new Butterick outfit, watching in awe from the fourth row of the orchestra, trying in vain to pick René out from the line of unearthly swans.

And she couldn't have even begun to hope that, before too long, she'd be living on the Upper West Side of Manhattan, in a one-bedroom apartment with five other young dancers and an overly bold population of cockroaches, sharing the one mattress—which they'd hauled in from the curb—on a "first come, first served" basis, or that she'd be in morning class with her idols, dancing alongside Gelsey Kirkland, Leslie Browne, sometimes even Baryshnikov, going across the floor, blending in with the others, yet still striving, still pushing herself to make herself worthy, even if only to fill out the ranks of the royal court in *Sleeping Beauty*, or to someday bring a willowy shade to life in *Giselle*. She'd be ready; she'd be almost there.

And it never once crossed René's mind that, even many years later—well after it seemed to her that, during her short visits home, Al had likely introduced her to every cattleman across the great state of South Dakota, each of whom had reached to shake her hand as though she were some kind of celebrity, telling her that her dad did nothing but talk about her, about how she was living in the "Big Apple," about how rigorous and demanding her ballet regimen was—that all those many years later, Al would start to fall. And though she might have rightly predicted that it would be Eve who'd care for him, running through the house in her worn slippers, wearing herself out to keep him clean and comfortable, in a

million years she never would have guessed that it would be Leon—
once again living at home, trying to make yet another "brand-new
start"—it would be Leon, of all people, who'd be there to lift Al up
off the bathroom floor and settle him into his chair.

As a grown woman with children of her own, René would end
up visiting Al in a hospital in Oklahoma, where he'd go in a fruit-
less, last-ditch effort to find treatment for his brain cancer. But she
couldn't have known—as she'd stand there behind him, having
driven the occupational therapist from the room by suggesting
that, perhaps, since Al was being belligerent and uncooperative
this morning, he could practice combing his hair at a later time—
that he'd ask her name, then look up to find her in the mirror and
say, "That's my name."

"That's not your name," she'd tell him, amused. The tumor had
made him sentimental. He'd been calling everyone in the family
every day to profess his love. "Your name's Al."

"No. No. That's my *daughter's* name," he'd correct himself.
"That's my daughter *René's* name."

"It's me, Dad," she'd say, suddenly realizing that he hadn't rec-
ognized her.

In spite of two craniotomies, he would remain fairly lucid.

"It's *me*," she'd say again. "I'm right here."

"Oh!" And he'd open his eyes wide and really look. "Is it you? Is
it really you? How old are you now? Are you sixteen? Seventeen?
Oh, René, where've you been? Where've you been all these years?"

And though she couldn't have known it, she'd place her hands
on his shoulders, let them fall around his neck as he'd go on, raising his sad eyes, tilting his sutured head to and fro in a great weight
of heartache and yearning and loss. And tears, unannounced,
would spring to her eyes, blinding her.

"No, Dad. I'm older now," she'd manage.

"Oh, I've missed you, missed you, missed you. Just want to hold you," he'd say, rocking himself side to side. "Just want to hold you again."

And the hospital room would swim with sadness, and the therapist would come back with her supervisor, angry at having been interrupted in her duties and sent away.

And even years later, long after both Al and Leon had passed away, though the young hospice nurse would be happy that René had arrived ahead of schedule, Eve would already be unconscious, so René would miss the part where they got to say goodbye. She'd run her hand across Eve's pale cheek, kiss her cool forehead, double the blankets around her icy feet, carefully, as though she might accidentally wake her.

The nurse would recap, telling her that Eve was "failing." Then she'd take Eve by the shoulders. "Eve!" she'd call, as if across an alpine chasm. "René is here. Do you see René?"

And Eve would struggle up, heroically, blinking just once before her eyes rolled and she succumbed to the grip of the higher power, helplessly heaving and moaning and falling away again. Then suddenly her mouth would warp, her face contort into a classic bas-relief of crying, and a single tear, gathering weight, would quiver and fall from the corner of her eye. And though the click-and-gasp of her breathing continued, violent and steady as the beating of wings, she wouldn't reach to take René's hand but, instead, would unlock her crippled fist so that René could hold on to her this one last time.

And within just a few days, René and Jayne, the only ones remaining, would be driving the length of the state, watching out their windows at the passing golden hills, the lopsided barns, the clean black cattle, readying themselves to transfer accounts, sell off real estate, and finalize all the necessary arrangements.

But René couldn't have foreseen any of this as she was climbing to thirty thousand feet, just barely fifteen, heading into the life that was waiting for her, the life she would, one way or the other, have to call her own.

"Don't be afraid," she told herself as the plane lifted higher and the hills and plains, the Badlands, the Needles, the great grasslands, even the wide Missouri River disappeared beneath her. "Don't be afraid."

She kept her eyes open. And she prayed that angels would come and fly beneath their wings, would lift and carry each one of them forward, delivering them safely to wherever it was they all needed to go.

Acknowledgments

I'd like to thank my editor at Random House, Andrea Walker, for her consistently thoughtful and focused guidance, her kindness and generosity, and for always approaching this work—from the very beginning—with an ear to hear it. I'd also like to thank everyone there who helped this project along, including Susan Kamil, Evan Camfield, Bonnie Thompson, Chelsea Cardinal, Melanie DeNardo, Avideh Bashirrad, Jess Bonet, Leigh Marchant, Emma Caruso, Dana Leigh Blanchette, and especially the singular Andy Ward, whose early advice helped me find the book I wanted to write.

My heartfelt thanks, as well, to the best-ever agents, Esther Newberg and Zoe Sandler at ICM, for their kind and enthusiastic support. I love you guys.

I'd also like to extend my enduring gratitude to my teachers and mentors over the years, those who have helped me along the way: Helen Griffiths, Kelly Brown, David Howard, Tobias Wolff, Douglas Unger, and especially Toni Morrison, without whose support and encouragement this book would not exist. To each and every one, my deepest thanks.

THE

Distance Home

Paula Saunders

A Reader's Guide

Reading Group Questions and
Topics for Discussion

1. What does this book show about the American family? How is it similar to and different from other iterations in literature?

2. Discuss the role of violence (both subtle and not so subtle) in the novel. Is the violence justifiable? Is it avoidable? How does it shape your interpretations of the characters?

3. How do René and Leon differ in the way they approach the tensions in the family? Whom do you relate to more, and why?

4. Discuss the role of landscape and setting in the novel. How do they contribute to the story and its themes?

5. How have your own family experiences shaped your interpretation of this particular family's experiences?

6. What makes this a uniquely American novel?

7. Why do you think the author chose ballet as the central passion of this novel? How would the story have changed if the author had chosen some other form of artistic expression?

8. What does this novel make you think about the idea of family in general and how, for good or ill, family members are knitted together throughout their lives? Does it change anything about the way you feel about your own family?

9. How does the author's inclusion of tensions between Native Americans and whites serve the novel's larger artistic concerns? In your experience, is this representation an accurate portrait of how we, individually and collectively, tend to response to difference?

An interview with Paula Saunders
on *The Distance Home*

This interview was conducted by Steven Wingate and originally published in Fiction Writers Review.

SW: *The Distance Home*, with its basis in your own personal history, is a classic Bildungsroman. You wrote on *Literary Hub* that "the material took a long time to brew and settle, and the book took me a long time to write." Looking back, what accounts for your hesitation—and what benefits do you see from taking your time?

PS: There were some hesitations, mostly because I was concerned with protecting my family. I didn't want to hurt anyone's feelings just by saying what I had to say, from my own point of view.

But there are other reasons for the lapse of time. My husband and I had two children very soon after graduating from the creative writing program at Syracuse University, and—with no extended family nearby and no money—one of us had to make a living and one of us had to watch the children. So moving away from my writing and this book happened by necessity. I didn't really have the space and time to pursue the lines of thought and deeper insight I needed.

There were years when I turned to other things—things I needed to help me develop my ability to be in a family, to be a better partner and parent—including Buddhist meditation practice. So these were very important years for me.

And the great benefit of taking my time and allowing things to flow somewhat naturally from the necessities of daily life was that I had the opportunity to really contemplate the relationships that had always troubled me and the situation of each individual in my childhood family without so much anger and resentment—with a little more empathy and open space. And this gave me a chance to approach this material with more open-mindedness and understanding. I do believe this book couldn't have been written without that element coming into play. That attempt at understanding is, to me, the essential heart of the book.

SW: I noticed that, unlike so much fiction set in the recent past, you use very few markers of the era in this novel—pop culture references, national events of the day, and the like. For me that served to accentuate South Dakota's relative isolation from the rest of America. Was this on your mind, or did you have other aesthetic reasons not to "stitch us in" to the times?

PS: This question is really funny, especially because my husband always says I'm like someone from Russia or the Ukraine—I just don't seem to hold any of the normal cultural references.

I didn't intentionally exclude any cultural references; it's just that for me, they didn't much exist, or weren't integral to what was necessary to survive growing up. Whether that had to do with the regional isolation of South Dakota, or with being caught up in my physical training as a dancer, or with the general stress of daily family life—where I felt I had to pay close and constant attention to what was going on in my immediate surroundings—I couldn't say. It seems that each of these may have contributed to my being generally unaware of the goings-on in the larger world. But my overall feeling is that it likely took a lot of energy just to keep track of what was happening around me at home—to make sure everyone was okay and the day wasn't going to veer off into territory that felt fraught and unstable.

SW: When people talk about South Dakota they almost always talk about the landscape, which is admittedly spectacular—at least west of the Missouri, with the Black Hills and the Badlands. But what about the South Dakota *mindscape*? What are its most salient features, and which did you want to make absolutely sure came across in the world your novel creates in the reader's imagination?

PS: I'm not sure that I can separate the mindset of South Dakotans from that of other Americans. To me the book is an attempt to look at our general cultural "mindscape" and the way it affects all of us—in rural America, suburban America, and urban America.

It seems that we as Americans have an idea of the primacy of personal success; there's something we're all trying to catch, and it's generally entwined with the competition and hustle of the marketplace, which leads us inevitably to an outsize aggression in everything we do and an underdeveloped sense of empathy and caring for each other. I saw the seeds of this in my own family, which is what led me to write *The Distance Home*—to try to look at where these ideas come from, where this aggression might be first planted in us and encouraged to grow.

There seems to be a need in the American psyche to "get ahead," to do the things we have in mind, which of course is not bad in itself. But when this need becomes determinative to the point of turning the main focus of our lives into outdoing each other, besting each other, even when that means stepping over those who need us most, those who can't get by without our help and attention, it's a problem. Because we're all made unhappy by it.

And I think the seeds that allow us to accept and participate in this aggression and striving are planted in our families—in the ways we interact with each other and the things we expect of each other, in what's rewarded and what's punished. Because most often we're acknowledged and rewarded for our strength/success and ignored or punished for our weakness/failure. So this dichotomy seems to be a big part of the problem.

SW: There's another line from your piece in *Literary Hub* that stuck with me: "If you're able to absorb and live this primacy of self—this narrative of vanquishing, conquest, victory, acquisition—you will survive, you will blossom; but if you are unable to learn this kind of lesson . . . you will suffer at the hands of those who can." Everyone in *The Distance Home* struggles with this. You wrote about it as a quintessential American problem, but I'm curious to hear about the specific ways the novel's landscape (and mindscape) make it manifest.

PS: I think it manifests mainly through the juxtaposition of René and Leon. René is naturally aggressive. She wants the spotlight, the attention, and she has enough approval and support in the family to get it. But when she finds that having the spotlight doesn't really help her, that she's just as unhappy seeing her brother suffer as she would be if she herself were suffering, she struggles to find a way out.

Leon, on the other hand, ends up seeming both unlucky and naturally despondent. He's unable to catch his breath between one reeling trauma and the next, and he's always ready to throw in the towel. He's not naturally self-protective. He seems to absorb too much of the pain the world throws at him, unwilling or unable to turn the tables.

Does this remind us of something, this tendency toward constant tenderness regardless of personal cost? For me, this is the most salient feature of our professed Christianity—this kind of losing.

So it seems that in this upside-down world—where strength and achievement are valued over tenderness—people who are not naturally self-protective or who refuse to participate in the aggression will always suffer. And without the protection and guidance of the wider society—as there is really no built-in incentive to care for others—it becomes hard for them to navigate the narrower passages of the resulting despondency and isolation.

All too often the answer for someone in our culture who ends up despondent and isolated is only more isolation and despondency through at-the-ready, self-soothing addictions to drugs and alcohol, which is what we see in the character of Leon, and which is how he loses *all* of his relationships, including his relationship with his sister and his family. He loses the life he might have made for himself, eventually losing his own life, literally, so early, to the effects of what he had hoped would ease his suffering—alcohol consumption and drug addiction.

SW: Leon is an incredibly poignant character, and he is punished for his unwillingness to perform the particular kind of restrained masculinity that is promoted and clung to on the Great Plains. He is a casualty of a particular kind of machismo that is fundamentally American but has a specific set of rules in the world of your novel. What, if anything, has changed about that performance of masculinity since Leon's youth?

PS: I had been thinking that our preconceived cultural ideas and prejudices were easing and that we as a society were becoming more inclusive and accepting of individuality and difference. But then came the current political climate, in which blatant aggression and the notion of "winning" at all costs have become so prevalent that it now seems any and all human values can be sacrificed in their name.

So I have to admit that I'm discouraged. I'm hoping what we see on the world stage is just a kind of swan song—the death of an era—and that most of us are softening around the edges when it comes to things like defined gender roles. I'm hoping that as the younger generation takes over, things will change. But for now, we seem to be taking giant steps in exactly the wrong direction— toward more overt aggression, more abuse of power, more turning away from humanity and our most basic human values, including love and caring, helpfulness, and the ability to listen to and respect each other, especially those who are not like ourselves.

I am lately hit head-on with the idea that where there has been progress there can just as easily, maybe more easily, be degeneration.

SW: René experiences a different kind of punishment: She's flattened, "taken down a peg" by her peers and even teachers for being ambitious and smart. She's quite capable of living the "primacy of self" and of meting out punishment to those who can't. To quote your *Literary Hub* piece again, she exhibits an "inherited habit of aggression [that] seemed to fester in the midwestern American psyche, turning endlessly to find a target, anything that seemed not quite right, not 'up to snuff.'" And yet she too is punished by her community. Could you talk a moment about the ways and means of her punishment?

PS: This is a really interesting question. It is my contention in the book that we all suffer from the aggression that is baked into our culture. So those who *do not* succeed, *do not* find a way forward, will suffer; and those who *do* succeed, who *do* find a way forward, often at the expense of others, will suffer as well. René can't be happy, peaceful, content because Leon is not happy, peaceful, content. Because of the harm brought on Leon, René has to find a way to leave her home. There is no peace for her there. So our lives—success or failure aside—are intertwined. We can't win without everyone winning. If the person standing beside us loses, we also lose. Because we cannot be happy while others are suffering. It isn't possible.

But the story of René has another aspect as well, which is that everybody is in the same fight and on some level everyone knows it. Winning and losing is, by definition, a zero-sum game; if one person wins, the other loses. So if someone like René starts to excel, the others will do their best to bring her down. Because we all know the cost of being at the bottom, and to keep our places we have to do battle with those who rise, we have to do battle with each other.

SW: Early in your writing life—before that decade-long hiatus, if I have your timeline correct—you had the opportunity to work closely with Toni Morrison. In what ways is her thumbprint on this novel, and on you as a writer?

PS: I can only hope that Toni Morrison's thumbprint is on me as a writer! Though I fear it's too much to ask.

But I do want to say that it has been a great blessing of my life to get to work with her. Her generosity—in looking at and responding with candor and encouragement to the writing I've given her over the years—has really been the source of my ability to get back to writing after such a long time. As with all my teachers—Helen Griffiths, Kelly Brown, Douglas Unger, Tobias Wolff—I thank her from the bottom of my heart.

SW: Does writing a novel set in South Dakota change how you feel about the place? Does your fictional imagination still wander there, or has it moved to other locales?

PS: I love South Dakota. I always have. I've spent a lot of my life both yearning for it and trying to get away from it. So yes—my imagination still goes there.

I need to be writing about other places too now, places that are also important to me, like New York City and what it might mean for a South Dakota girl to find herself living in that oh-so-foreign place—on that foreign planet?—at a very young age.

But South Dakota is in my heart. South Dakota will always be my home.

Finding a Way Back

PAULA SAUNDERS

This essay was first published on Powells.com.

I hadn't been writing or even reading fiction for a long time. Maybe ten years. Instead, I'd started a lovely journey into the study and practice of Tibetan Buddhism, which was giving me the necessary time and the tools to reflect on things, to develop some greater understanding and appreciation of my life, and I didn't see any reason for coming back to reading and writing fiction, or any route that might allow it.

Then came an article in *The New York Times Book Review* about a mysterious Italian author, Elena Ferrante. The article was intriguing and made the writer sound unmissable. A good friend of mine—a fellow Buddhist practitioner for whom I hold something beyond tremendous admiration—had also read the article, and we were both curious. We decided that we'd each get one of Elena Ferrante's books, read, then trade, so we could each read both.

I devoured mine, in awe. I felt I'd never read anything quite like it: such striking, direct prose; such a gnawing, bone-crunching, grinding look at daily life, inner life, trauma. It all felt so close, so real to me.

My friend, on the other hand, read the first few chapters of her book and couldn't go on. It was too dark, too disturbing, she said. She didn't want it back, and she didn't want the one I'd just read.

What joy—I got to keep both books!

This friend and I had been tutoring together for the past few years—teaching very special young Tibetan Buddhist children from Tibet, Nepal, and India, by way of Queens, how to read and write in English. I'd taught a very young boy—a perfect, terribly bright, but naughty little sweetheart—the basics. We'd got through the alphabet, consonants and vowels, word formation, early readers, all the way to E. B. White's children's novels, and he was an ace.

By the time my friend and I read *The New York Times* article and got ahold of our Elena Ferrante books, I had moved on to teaching a group of four lovely young girls, maybe twelve to thirteen years old. We'd been reading and discussing Laura Ingalls Wilder's *Little House on the Prairie* series together, and, as I was a writer (in what, by this time, felt like a past life) and was from South Dakota myself, Wilder's landscapes and the hardships she describes made sense to me. I hadn't read any of her books since I was a child, but teaching them to the girls, and seeing the simplicity and directness of Wilder's prose and the way she recounts what happened to her family in their efforts to settle on the Great Plains, made me think (more than once): *Hey, I could do that!*

Then came the Elena Ferrante article.

I read *The Lost Daughter* first and was enthralled. I read *Troubling Love* and was overwhelmed, dazzled, awestruck. I found myself walking around with my mind suddenly bent toward the stories

I'd always wanted to tell—the dizzying stories of my own family life. I read Ferrante's Neopolitan novels next. They were gritty and dark, following without apology the quotidian flow of daily life and troubled relationships, and suddenly I understood that maybe, just maybe, I could write my stories, too. The everyday ups and downs, the frustrations, fulfillments, and deceptions of close, difficult relationships—all that was acceptable ground, worthy of indulgence and exploration.

So I started writing again. After so many years, after raising two children, after a decade of reading only Buddhist texts, I started writing fiction again. And I started where everyone starts: with a blank page.

Around this same time, as I was driving over the hill in our small, upstate New York town, likely to the grocery store, I happened to hear a very old friend of mine, Claire Shipman (with whom, sadly, I'd long ago lost touch), speaking on NPR. She and her writing partner, Katty Kay, had written an article that appeared in *The Atlantic*. It was titled "The Confidence Gap" and was about how, often, men who do not have the skills for a particular job are hired over women who do, because men are willing to claim skills they don't already have, confident that they can acquire them as needed. Men have the confidence to believe that what they don't already know they will learn, while women tend to think they need to know something perfectly before they can claim it, before they can even get started. So women end up, most often, underrepresenting themselves, saying they don't have skills they actually do possess, and robbing themselves of the chance to advance.

At one point Shipman told the interviewer that women needed to constantly "overcorrect for confidence." It was a shocking phrase, turning everything like modesty and self-effacement on its head, and it stayed with me. It seemed to be just what I needed to hear, just when I needed to hear it. It was exactly what I had to do to meet the task I'd set in front of myself.

From then on, every day, I went into my study and faced the blank page with that phrase in mind. And every day, when I'd finished whatever writing I was able to do, I concluded the same way, reminding myself again and again, "Overcorrect for confidence." No matter what I'd written, no matter what it was like—engaging or boring, funny or sad, elegant or unruly—my only job was to adjust my mind, to realign my attitude, to see the good in what I'd accomplished so far. Whatever needed fixing could be fixed tomorrow. Today, I was just going to get the words down on paper and pat myself on the back for doing it. I was going to do the work and *overcorrect* for confidence.

And so I began putting down the first pages of *The Distance Home*. (None of which turned out to be the first pages, and few of which even ended up in the book! Ha!)

But writing again, reading fiction again, was like a fresh new world opening up for me, even richer than when I'd closed the door on it those many years ago. It felt as if somehow I'd planted seeds in a garden behind a tall gate, then locked the door, turned my back, and gone away. And while I was gone, it had so happened that the sun and the rain had been doing their work. Because when I turned back around, when I unlocked the gate and ventured back into the garden—expecting to find only the wilted stems of unblossomed flowers and thorny overgrown weeds—to my great surprise, the whole place, the whole world, it seemed, was filled up with flowers.

I did the work, I wrote the pages I'd wanted to write for so long, and even though time had passed and I knew I was getting a late start, I was happy and grateful to have followed the clues set in front of me and found my way back to something I loved, something I'd wanted to share so much for so long.